When the Leaves Stop Falling

Kelly Moran

Cover design by Kelly Moran.
Photos courtesy of DollarPhotoClub
ISBN-13: 978-1542941792
ISBN-10: 1542941792
Createspace Edition
Published in the U.S.A.

Praise for Kelly Moran's Books:

"Breathes life into an appealing story."
Publishers Weekly

"Readers will fall in love."
Romantic Times

"Great escape reading."
Library Journal

"Touching & gratifying."
Kirkus Reviews

"Sexy, heart-tugging fun."
USA Today HEA

"Emotional & totally engaging."
Carla Neggers

"A gem of a writer."
Sharon Sala

"I read in one sitting."
Carly Phillips

"Compelling characters."
Roxanne St. Claire

"A sexy, emotional romance."
Kim Karr

Chapter One

*A*s discontent as she was to see the dreary, frigid rain that seemed to never end this week, Edith Meyers was damn proud of herself. She was opening her diner tomorrow, and there was much satisfaction in that. Months of building, and planning, and designing were finally at a close. Sneering, she willed the carpenters to a hell dimension for all the headache.

Her only and secret wish was that her beloved late husband could still be around to see it. She rarely let her emotions to the surface, and that was just how she wanted it. Few people were privy to the softer side, the side she often saw as a weakness. Oh, how she missed him, though. If he were here, he wouldn't have let her drive fifty miles out of their small town in the driving rain to pick out a jukebox no one would use. He would make some of his famous hot chocolate, wrap a blanket around her shoulders, and read to her from his little green book of poetry.

But Zebb Meyers was laid in the ground six months ago, with his little green book and tears from the whole town for a good man lost. He left his faithful wife of twenty-five years more money than either of them thought they had when he passed. And so, she built her diner, complete with a bell on the door and a picture of him by the register.

Edith glanced at the dashboard of her aging truck when it blinked a check engine light again for the third time this week. Ignoring the mild annoyance and rolling her eyes, she pushed in the cigarette lighter with a click and snagged a Salem 100 from her bag next to her. Pulling over onto the shoulder, she decided to wait the torrent out. What good would all her hard work do if she was dead in the ground?

The wipers on full speed were issuing a rhythmic sound and scarcely clearing away the sheets of water pounding the truck and highway before her. Droplets bounced off the asphalt and clay as if running from the earth. She couldn't recall the last time Arizona had ever seen a downpour like this, outside of the wet season. The fog made visibility near nothing, as she carefully lit her cigarette.

That's when she noticed something...odd. Blowing out a puff of smoke, she squinted her eyes through the windshield and rain.

By all appearances, it looked like a wounded animal, lying on the side of the highway. Grunting to herself, not knowing who to be angrier with, the stupid animal for bolting into the road, or the insensitive humans for running the poor creature down. Unsure why, she was drawn to it. Not usually one to give into curiosity, she watched the lump with interest. What the hell else was there to do? Fleetingly, she shifted her eyes around to check for signs of disturbance and found none.

So, she sat there, on the side of the road, in her old truck, for what felt like hours before she even blinked. Hell. It was just road kill, right? But it lay forty feet or less from her bumper, sending chills of a not so good variety up her spine the longer she stared. Her grip on the steering wheel tightened, turning her pudgy knuckles white.

Then it moved.

A gasp caught in her throat. Smoke filled her lungs, choking her while her heart pounded inside her chest in rapid succession. Road kill doesn't move. If she was positive of anything it was that. Of course, this one barely had. Squinting her eyes again as if her sight would improve doing so, she wondered if it was a coyote or dog.

It moved again.

Without a second thought, Edith jumped from her truck into the bitter downpour, leaving her cigarette to sizzle and die on the wet pavement. Pulling her well worn flannel higher around her neck, she bent down next to the body on shaking knees.

A...person lay crumpled on their side, involuntarily trembling. There was no bag near them, just a pair of tattered jeans and a white t-shirt covering their thin body, now soaked from the torrent. Waist length stringy blonde hair was matted against a pale face in disarray.

Edith, her hands usually steady and sure, gently rolled them on their back with little effort, pushing away the hair to get a better look.

"Oh, dear Lord!"

A girl. She was young, too young to be lying in a ditch in the middle of nowhere. Bruises covered her arms and what could be seen of her chest. A series of tiny cuts lacerated her face with small amounts of blood seeping from them and disappearing from the rain. Her lips, slightly opened, were puckered and blue tinted. Dark, deep shadows bruised under long pale lashes.

Edith stood and glanced around, gravel crunching under her boots. There was nothing for miles but desert. They were between small towns that seemed to plague this part of the country. No one to help. She bent down and hazardly placed her hands on the girl, checking for other signs of injury, panic setting in. The girl didn't wince or flinch when Edith dragged her hands over her arms and legs.

How long had she been out here? What had happened? Hell. Didn't matter. Something had to be done now. The girl's breathing was shallow and Edith knew, with uncertain dread, that there wasn't much time. The girl was freezing, probably starving, and possibly injured worse than Edith could assess.

The youngster quickly opened her eyes, only once, and Edith found stark blue glaring back at her with confusion. The color of a storm when its clouds roll in. Blue battling with gray. Edith held the girl's face in her frozen hands, mesmerized by those young, frightened eyes. A flash of sensation, too powerful to name, shifted the atmosphere, pushing the breath from Edith's lungs. It was as if the girl was seeing right inside Edith's head, dissecting thoughts and stroking emotion. Before Edith could say anything, the girl closed her eyes and went limp.

Not knowing what else to do, except she had to get the girl out of here, Edith ran to the passenger's side of the truck, pushing away empty cans and paper bags to grab a blanket.

Racing back, she carefully wrapped the girl in the blanket and, without much effort, carried her to the truck. She didn't stir at all. Not even a moan. There wasn't a hospital within sixty miles. Edith was soaked to the bone. She could only imagine how logged the girl was. Cranking the heat, she drove like a bat out of hell, heading for home. She'd call their town doc, Richard, and have him get a look at the girl.

Then they'd decide what to do.

TEN YEARS LATER

Zebb's Diner, off of I-40, near the Arizona border, reeked of grease and stale coffee. It was the kind of place drifters came to only when passing through on their way out of town, or if they were unfortunate enough to exist in the small town it centered. It was supported by men who ate too much fried food. Men who would sit for endless hours playing poker or checkers and arguing about the weather to pass time. Seemed as if the place was stuck in a continuous time loop of absence.

Courtney Morgan glanced around at the pale green walls stained with time. The pink and white tiled floor needed mopping again. She'd do that in awhile. The coffee maker was gurgling, indicating the brew was almost finished. She smiled weakly. Somehow this existence was her heaven.

She glared yet again at the group of men near the window she'd been serving everyday since she'd come here, broke and in need of a place to crash. She tried not to think about how it wasn't much different than where she ran away from, other than the people. But then again, people were all the same no matter where one went.

She flinched when one of the men slammed his fist down, making the booth they'd squeezed into squeak a little more. Old habits died hard. One day she'd quit being afraid of her own shadow.

Knowing their blood pressure didn't need any more caffeine, Courtney filled their coffee cups silently. One of them muttered a, "thanks darlin'," hardly noticing her, and continued to growl at his companions as one laid out a winning hand of Five Card Stud.

She returned to her corner of the diner, waiting to fill the cups again. Did they ever pay attention that their mugs were always full, or would they ever acknowledge who filled them?

She didn't know whether it was a blessing or a curse no one ever seemed to notice her, except the few people who'd helped her so long ago. Where she'd come from, she'd tried hard to go unnoticed or there were consequences. Consequences that left permanent scars on her arms and various other hidden places.

She couldn't help but wish for something to make her heart flutter or snag her interest. In that far off place in the corner of her mind, a place she rarely acknowledged even existed, she hoped for...more.

Shaking her head, Courtney willed the past from her brain. It did no good dredging it up. She was here now. Mrs. Meyers, she thought fondly, found her wandering almost ten years ago and now she was safe.

Courtney turned her head and smiled as the old woman balled out, without glancing up from one of her hopelessly romantic novels, "Max, you smack my booth one more time and I'll smack you."

"Yeah, yeah," the guy muttered and downed his coffee.

Mrs. Meyers owned Zebb's Diner and seemingly never left. She was a round-faced noble woman, who had a knack for telling things how it was. She could yell at customers, serve up breakfast, and take an order all at once. Her dark brown hair was receding to gray, and was kept in a tidy bun, more for convenience sake than beauty.

Courtney didn't ever call Edith Meyers by her first name, and thought with a smirk, that no one else seemed to either. Townsfolk called her Mrs. Meyers, as if she was an old schoolmarm demanding respect.

"And what, my dear, are you smiling at?" Edith's voice came out harsh and ragged, the consequence from years of smoking.

Courtney sighed gently. "Nothing." She dropped her chin in her palm and leaned against the ivory colored, coffee stained counter. Before this town found her she had no idea how to talk to people or behave. She'd learned, in those long first sixteen years of her life, to be who her father expected her to be and nothing more. Never anything more.

And somehow it was never enough.

She didn't have to watch what she said or how she said it anymore. There was no one to yell at how unkempt the house was, though she may have spent all day cleaning it. No one to scream vulgarities at how ugly or scrawny she was. There was no one to curse her for seeing things, calling her *witch* for the events that weren't there or had yet to happen. And no one to beat her down, when she had not an ounce of strength left in her to shield the blows.

Some wounds took too long to heal. It took almost ten years to breathe easily again and, most importantly, not to have to look over her shoulder.

For years after she ran away, she'd checked the street before leaving the house in case the smell of gin was there, followed by her staggering father. She thought she saw him everywhere she went. Between the shelves in the library he'd be there, his dark greasy hair, eyes that bored into her, sinister with anger. In the diner, she would see him open the door, as her breath caught in her throat, and he'd raise his cane. Even the ghost of him followed her.

Mrs. Meyers closed her book with a snap, as if knowing what Courtney was thinking, and replaced her glasses on top of her head. The worry lines on her forehead more prominent, she asked, "Why don't you take the day off and go find yourself a man?"

Courtney forced a smile, bowing her head to hide her irritation. The endless argument of *a hero for Courtney*. Heroes were as fictional as Mrs. Meyers' romance novels. She might have felt honored to be worried about, if not that everyone seemed to think she needed a man in her life. "Like who? I think old man Finley's son is getting his third divorce. Maybe he's available."

"Okay, smart mouth." Mrs. Meyers pointed. "Go home anyway." She ignored the Courtney's protests and shooed her toward the door. "You won't meet a man sitting around here."

"You know I'm only going to go home and do nothing."

Edith grunted as her self-proclaimed cold black heart twisted in her chest. "You're twenty-seven years old, Courtney. You need to be married and chasing rug rats."

Courtney had no argument for that. "Fine, I'll go home. But there's no man there that I'm aware of."

"Always a smart mouth."

Courtney thought long and hard about what Mrs. Meyers' had said back in the diner, as she usually did when the woman spoke. She had a way of making even the devil grovel, but Courtney had no idea why this time *the man* discussion drew heavy on her thoughts. It was an everyday occurrence. *How was your day? Have you found yourself a man?*

But for the first time in almost ten years, she *felt* lonely. She was usually satisfied amusing herself and mustering through every day alone. Today, however, every commercial on the television had families or couples gallivanting around being happy. Even her fish looked joyfully blissful sitting in his bowl.

Rubbing her face and laughing at the sheer absurd thought, she got up and paced around her kitchen. There wasn't anything wrong with being alone. Plenty of people were unmarried and went on to live fulfilling lives. She would certainly be one of them. Of course, those people had friends to fill the void.

Courtney didn't have friends.

While walking down Grant Street earlier, she'd been up close and personal with the town's couples. The younger ones would hold hands and laugh at some private joke between just the two of them. How she wished she knew what it was. The older couples, like the Wrayburns, who had been married forty-three years, strolled with her arm through his as if no time had gone by at all. She would lay her head on his shoulder and sigh, a smile on her wrinkled face, and he would go on telling her of his day and days past.

And all the while Courtney walked with her own thoughts for company. No one had noticed when she'd brushed by them. No one looked up when she'd passed and smiled. No one said *hello*, or *how are you*. They just walked right by, lost in themselves. No one saw her at all.

And today that bothered her.

She peeked around her small apartment Mrs. Meyers had helped her find all those years ago. The couch was second-hand, like most of her furniture. It had been given to her by the previous tenant who'd no longer needed it. The television used to belong to Dr. Maynard, no longer wanted. Her bed in the other room was found on the curb, waiting to be thrown out. She used TV trays as tables, and saved up all her money to buy plants and food and the rugs hiding the stained carpet.

She'd fought hard to get out of where she'd grown up, and maybe didn't deserve all the support the town had given her, but she'd accepted it, as she accepted everything else. Guilt shifted in her belly for not appreciating all she had. For even being alive. Something she wouldn't be if not for Mrs. Meyers.

11

She just needed a pet that wasn't in water. A dog or cat to come home to, who would be happy to greet her when she arrived home from the diner. Who would cuddle with her at night. Maybe then her footsteps wouldn't echo and the bed wouldn't be so cold at night. She'd have more than a blanket to keep her warm.

Growling in frustration, Courtney decided she needed to get out of the apartment right now or she'd go insane. Sitting around feeling sorry for herself did no good. She'd spent nearly half her life doing that. Half afraid, hiding in shadow. Half in a state of auto-pilot, going through the motions.

She pulled back a lace curtain and peered out at the dark street. It was only ten-thirty, after all. She could go back to Zebb's and see what interesting people came in from the highway. There wasn't much else to do after hours in this place except Jerry's Tavern. But the run down bar at the edge of town would be full of married men who wanted a night away from the missus or someone to bitch to about their day. Not exactly what she needed, especially the stench of liquor, which had her stomach rolling just thinking about it.

She often went to the diner at night to casually talk with Doc, or listen to Mrs. Meyers rave, or to watch the highway people drift in. Nothing out of the norm there. Urgency clawed at her belly to go, like ants dancing under her skin, the longer she stood by the window contemplating. Why it was important for her to go now? Demand and necessity wrapped around her, calling her to...something.

Odd.

She let the curtain fall back in place. Rarely did she ignore what the feelings told her anymore, now that it was safe to do so. Making the decision right there on the spot, Courtney grabbed her denim jacket and ran out the door.

Serena Edwards picked up her cup of highly sugared green tea from the cup holder and drank deeply. Her brother's words played over and over in her head as she watched the highway and yellow dotted lines before her.

"You need to come home."

Home. She hadn't been back home since Christmas three years ago.

She adored her small loft in beautiful San Diego with its view of the beach and all that permanently sun tanned skin. Families, like the one she'd never have, playing and enjoying themselves. Despite the envy, she'd built a life for herself there, away from home and all on her own. It hadn't been easy. She'd had the inheritance, but money couldn't buy people to recognize her art, couldn't buy friends. When she'd left Georgia in search of a different life, different memories from the ones back home, she never thought she'd be coming back...for good.

Part of her couldn't even remember now why it was she'd left. She recalled setting out to see the world and gauging how far away from home she could go before forgetting who she was. She supposed that was the whole of it, to forget. Forget all the badgering of friends asking how she was and people trained to give her a hand as if she couldn't lift one herself. Trivial reasons at this point.

She thought for certain she would regret leaving California and most of her belongings behind as she passed the "Welcome to Arizona" sign. She had chosen California, above all other states, for mystical reasons. She'd read that California was a Spanish name given about an imaginary island from a poem. She had no idea if it were true, but the romance of that had sold her. She always was too much of a romantic.

Of course, now she was going back. The sorrow didn't come as she imagined it would. She loved Georgia, its southern charm and friendly people. Too friendly, some of them. But most of all, and more than anything, she longed to be back in Grandmother's arms. Grams would hold her and tell her not to be afraid, that it was going to be okay. And she desperately needed that now.

When her and Austin's parents had died in a car accident, they'd only been five at the time. Both hardly remembered them. But Grams had kept them alive with her scrapbooks and stories on the front porch swing. Suddenly, Serena craved the smell of a warm summer breeze lofting in the estate windows from the garden and the sound of the old porch swing creaking.

She didn't have much time left. Of course, the doctors had told her parents that when she was born. And yet, here she was, twenty-eight years later. Her twin brother had been born with a healthy heart. But that was just physical nonsense. Doctors couldn't explain how she made it this long. They weren't sympathetic to the feelings behind life. It was all science and tests and lab results.

They had known she may need a transplant one day, had been warned about it from her birth. But what her twin brother Austin didn't know was that when she'd left for California three years ago, the condition had been worse. Deteriorating. It had been the main reason she'd fled, her last chance to...live. She'd been on the national heart transplant list since then, but with a rare blood type of AB negative, it made it that much harder to find a donor. Now, in what the horrid doctors called "end stage heart failure," her body may possibly be too weak to receive one if the call ever came.

She felt fine. So she got short of breath easily and could never do as much as everyone else. In the anger phase, the doctors were liars and she'd refused to believe them. She missed the denial and anger phase of the five stages. Then, once grief was past, acceptance hit her like a blow. Though she felt healthy now, in a couple months she wouldn't be able to do much of anything. The pneumonia she'd struggled to fight off a couple weeks ago had taken its toll. The hospital had told her she should make arrangements, that they would make her as comfortable as possible.

Comfortable. As if they cared at all. She could only be comfortable in one place.

The hardest thing she ever had to do was to call her brother last night and tell him. Being twins, they always had a connection. They were close in everything they did, sometimes even feeling each other's moods. Both having dark hair and eyes, both being incredibly stubborn. The pain of what could never be sliced through her. Tore at her chest.

Austin hadn't said much of anything, she knew he wouldn't. He simply pleaded for her to come home. She felt a pang of regret that he was going to have to tell Grandmother soon, before she arrived.

Dragging herself into the present, and knowing she'd need to eat soon to take her pills, Serena checked the highway signs for a place to stop. She recognized the gas pump and the little fork and spoon next to it.

Two miles.

She craned against the steering wheel of her Mustang to fleetingly stare at a perfect clear night through her windshield. Arizona, being the first state she had to drive through to get home, was known for its beautiful springs and clear nights. There were stars too many for the counting, unhidden by the city lights and smog.

She sighed and, leaning back in her seat, got off at the next exit.

Austin Edwards paced his office in the upstairs apartment above his bookstore for the third hour in a row. He hadn't been able to look at the pile of paperwork on his desk since his sister Serena had called last night. His whole life he'd been prepared for "the" call, hoping technology would mean it would never come.

But it did. He felt the panicked tremor almost before the phone rang out a piercing scream next to his bed, waking him from a reoccurring dream he'd had since childhood. Closing his eyes, he retrieved the dream image from memory, as it always calmed him.

The small, delicate hands of a young woman brushed over the top of a headstone next to his mother's in the cemetery. Blonde-- almost white--hair caught in the breeze as she dropped her head in mourning. Her slim figure was wrapped in a short black dress, neither seductive nor plain, and every time Austin dreamed of her, he felt some unknown emotion that couldn't be put to words. She never spoke in the dream, never moved, except the brushing of her hand along the cold stone in front of her. He'd always wake before she could turn her head, leaving him grasping at air and desperate to see her face.

Austin always thought of this dream woman as an angel, something his mind conjured to help him through the loss of his parents at a young age. Especially because the image of her was always graveside. Like a relapse of film, the dream never morphed or changed. Not once.

Except last night. In his dream last night, she'd spoken. "I'm coming," she'd whispered, her voice riddled with grief and lofting on an echo.

He didn't know if she'd been talking to the grave or to him, but a fullness consumed his chest until his eyes welled. He used to stay up all night, praying God would make him sick instead of Serena. Child-like tears gone to waste.

Perhaps the woman *was* an angel, the one who'd lead his parents to Heaven, and was now waiting on Serena.

The guilt came, as it always did, rising in his gut and spreading. He was healthy enough to survive his sister twice, and she wouldn't live to see thirty. He had a forever kind of vision in his mind of Serena, lying in the cool long grass, laughing, watching him play as a kid. Her wild brown curls would spill around her head like a halo. That's how he always saw her, young and happy. Most times, Jake had been with them, climbing trees or swinging the baseball bat.

Jake had to know she was sick, had to be told. Jake and Serena may have broken up when she'd left for sunny California, but she was a part of him still. Her and Jake been friends since the beginning, as kids, and soul mates since they were old enough to understand attraction. Austin had seen the inevitability of them coming together even before they had. Between the long stares and the smug grins, they hadn't hidden their mutual attraction well. How moot it was now that at first he didn't care for his sister falling for his best friend.

Last night she'd made him promise not to tell Jake, that she would do it. Austin didn't like it, not one bit, but he would respect her wishes. He always did. He could never tell Serena no.

But Grams? That was another story. He was telling her tomorrow night. He thought there was something very wrong with informing your grandmother, over cornbread and fried chicken, that the baby she'd raised was dying.

Austin paced to the window to glance out at the night, at people wandering the main street in town, as he tried to ignore the phone that had been demanding his attention all afternoon and evening. He didn't want to deal with anyone.

Beginning to focus his weary mind back to work on the shipments for his store, to stay sane, he picked up the phone and forced a pleasant greeting.

"I've been trying to call you all day." Jake's slightly angry tone had Austin flinching.

"Sorry, I've been doing paperwork."

"I finished the tables you wanted and the rocking chair."

16

Jake had been doing some new furniture pieces for the renovations of his book store. Jake was good at building things. "Great. When can you bring them by?"

"Tomorrow, if you want."

"Make it before four. Grams is making dinner."

"Okay. How's the remodeling going?"

Grateful to be thinking of something else, Austin leaned back in his chair and rubbed a large hand over his short dark hair. "Good. The shelves are up in the sitting area. They just need to be stained. I bought new books for them. The damn shipment on the cappuccino machines isn't here yet, but the divider wall is finally in place for the gift shop."

"Sounds like it's going okay, then. Want help staining this weekend?"

"Yeah, that would be good."

He knew it would get done faster and done right if Jake did it anyway. He made a mental note to tell the contractor he was no longer needed.

"How's Grams doing?"

Austin was glad Jake wasn't in front of him to see his grim expression. "Good. You know her. She loves the summer for her gardens. She never stops." Austin thought she wouldn't be good for long after his news, and immediately felt the remorse for having to keep it from his best friend.

"How's Serena?"

He always asked. Austin used to wonder if it was out of politeness or genuine concern when Jake asked about his sister. After awhile, Austin knew better. Jake still loved her. He always had and always would, making it ten times harder to support Serena's request. Jake never got over her leaving.

"She's coming home," was all he could think of to say.

There was a long pause on the other end of the line. The silence saying way more than words ever could. Before Austin could fill the void, Jake cut in with a solemn question, more rhetorical than anything.

"Is she now?"

Austin shuffled the papers on his large mahogany desk Jake had built for him, uncomfortable with the silence. In all their years as friends, they've never had an uncomfortable silence. He prayed his

17

lifelong friend wouldn't ask why. Why the silence and why Serena was coming home.

"For how long?"

Austin rubbed his eyes, red from tears last night and fatigue. He eyed the picture on the corner of his desk. The one of the three of them in the old field behind the house, arms around each other, laughing. It almost make him smell the lilacs now.

"For good."

Chapter Two

Courtney sat with Dr. Maynard at the counter in the diner and giggled as quietly to herself as possible when Mrs. Meyers let out another string of curses. Doing her monthly totals always put the woman in a sour mood.

There hadn't been much excitement tonight. A few truckers were brooding over their steaming coffee while their rigs were gassing up next door. None of them paid any attention to the three of them at the counter, so long as their coffee was kept hot. She figured the townsfolk were out enjoying the warm quiet night or were tucked safely in their houses among their loved ones. Courtney plopped her chin in her palm and fought off the stray thoughts running through her crazy brain tonight.

Mrs. Meyers glared at her hyenas with a scowl. "Richard, why don't you start bringing your boy around here, instead of laughing at me, so Courtney can begin wooing him."

Richard chuckled, slowly shaking his head at Courtney's dropped jaw. "He's only fifteen."

"Never too young to start," she mumbled without looking up from her work again.

He rubbed his eyes with a fond smile and turned once more to Courtney. "So, how has it been going?"

Keeping her chin on her fist, she shrugged. "Okay, I guess. You?"

He expertly ignored the question and asked another, as he was prone to do. "Has the side been causing you any discomfort?"

She remembered the ache from her broken ribs ten years before, which hardly bothered her at all anymore. Arthritic shadow pain, Doc had called it. "Only when it rains, so I'm good, considering we're in the desert." She gave a fleeting look as a trucker wandered in from the highway for a break. "Besides, Doc, it was years ago."

"I still see you holding it sometimes."

Courtney reached over and grabbed the coffee carafe from the burner. "I'm okay." She nodded to Mrs. Meyers before she could ask Courtney to take the trucker's order.

When they thought she was out of earshot, Mrs. Meyers said, "You see, Richard? There's nothing for her to do here. She comes in the diner, on her night off, for fun."

"You know how long it took her to trust us. Where do you expect her to go?"

"Somewhere other than here. She's wasting away."

Doc belted a laugh. "Hardly. She's doing well now."

Courtney sighed, shaking her head, and walked to the table as if she hadn't heard. Once finished, she returned at sat on a stool. "He just wants coffee."

"Courtney, have you ever thought about moving on, trying out a new city?" Doc asked. When she frowned and Mrs. Meyers raised her eyebrows, he quickly added, "I mean, well...You're young, and smart. You could take a vacation or...Why don't--"

"You two are going to give me a complex. You sound like you don't want me here."

Edith smacked her hand on the counter, making Courtney jump in response. "Damn it, girl! You know we love you. It's not about us not wanting you here. You've been stuck too long, and you're healthy, so there's no excuse not to travel, see the world." She grunted and gentled her tone. Courtney had been yelled at enough in her lifetime, God knew. "We want more for you than this. There are other people to meet, places to go."

"I have no one but you guys, where else should I be?"

The familiar jingle on the door saved Courtney from the conversation, but her body went on instant alert. She sensed the woman even before seeing her. A twinge pierced her chest she couldn't quite explain, causing a whoosh of air to escape her lungs as if she'd been struck.

The newcomer nodded at them, causing her curly, shoulder length dark hair to fall around her face.

Courtney's grip tightened on the countertop edge as she struggled to pull air into her lungs. She closed her eyes, breathing through the pounding in her chest. Damn, it had been a long time since her Spidey sense had gone into hyperactive.

When settled, she walked to the booth the woman had slid into. "Coffee?" she offered.

The newcomer looked up and, with a polite smile, waved her petite hand. "No, thanks. I never drink the stuff. Do you have tea?"

Courtney felt an urgent need to rub tension from her chest. She'd never had chest pain before, but then again, this wasn't a pain really. More of an...ache. Before she could brood over it, she lost her focus in the woman's deep, golden brown eyes framed by lashes she would kill for. Not an attraction. Nothing so innate as sexual, but a connection of sorts. A tether of a bond slithered in the space between them and knotted.

Courtney shook her head to clear it. "Um, hot or iced tea?" she asked awkwardly.

"Hot please."

Courtney nodded slowly and, without thought on her task, went behind the counter to start boiling water. She leaned close to Dr. Maynard, who had been watching her closely. "I just got this strange feeling in my chest."

Doc's usual pliant smile dialed to concern. His dark brown gaze skimmed over her, forcing his worry lines to stand out. "Are you dizzy at all? Short of breath?" He placed a hand on her wrist as if to take a pulse.

She immediately backed away from his touch. This wasn't medical, but how to explain it? "No, it's not me." His concern faded to confusion. "I mean, the woman, who just came in...I think she's...Never mind."

It was difficult to explain the strange sensations she got from people. It wasn't everyone, and it didn't occur at all hours, but some people's emotions could slam her into a wall. Whoever this woman was, her soul was the loudest Courtney had experienced to date. It left her more than a tad shaken.

Mrs. Meyers and Dr. Maynard looked at her with apprehension. They'd picked up, almost from the start, that she had this way about her. Like she wasn't like everyone else, even though she hadn't discussed it with them. Ever. She'd chalked it up to her defenses being down when they first took care of her after finding her in a ditch.

When the tea kettle screeched, Courtney turned and transferred the water into a cup, grateful to have a distraction. She ignored the hairs on the back of her neck, a sure sign they were still staring at her. She grabbed a tea bag and walked back to the booth.

"There you go. Can I get you anything else?"

The woman's golden gaze dipped to Courtney's clothes. "You don't have a uniform on."

Courtney looked down at her jeans, faded from use, and her white blouse. "Oh." She smiled. "I'm not working. I'm just helping out for a minute. It's my night off."

"Would you be able to join me then?"

What an odd request. Hundreds of patrons traveled through the diner every day, all people who would barely glance at her, nevertheless ask her to join them. She found herself drawn to the golden brown eyes again searching back at her for an answer. "Sure."

The woman's smile turned into a full grin as Courtney slid into the booth. "Thanks. I've been traveling awhile, going back home. Gets lonely, I could use some chatter."

Courtney grinned back, surprised at her immediate comfort with the wanderer. It typically took her too long to get used to people. "Where you headed then?"

"Georgia, back to Grandma's house." She gingerly she sipped from her tea.

Courtney noticed the slight southern accent then, the one she tried to mask, putting it in place. "Over the river and through the woods."

Her companion laughed in a deep-throated, almost sexual way, and nodded her head. "Yes, something like that."

The woman pulled a bottle from her purse and poured a small white pill into her hand. She tossed it back, swallowing it dry, then picked up her tea and sipped. She looked pale. It didn't seem to be her normal complexion, but rather from exhaustion. She had just a slight shadow under her eyes, almost hidden by beautiful high cheek bones and long dark lashes.

She was petite and carried herself with confidence. She moved with a grace rarely seen in these parts, as if ingrained propriety ran deep. Courtney thought it unusual she chose to wear a black turtle neck in this climate, but then again, she was traveling.

The flesh between Courtney's breasts burned, sizzling a long path to her naval. She had a brief flash of a scar swim before her eyes and was gone.

"You'll need something to eat with that pill." Courtney rose, not knowing how the wanderer's hidden scar made its way from her chest to Courtney's vision. "I'll just get you a bowl of soup. Be right back."

Courtney ladled chicken and wild rice soup, trying not to focus on that little white pill, or the sensation rooted behind her ribs. The woman was her age, no more than maybe two years older or younger. How could scar that size mar her chest? It hit her then, as it always did, fast and not at all pleasant. A hospital. Antiseptic filling her nose. A pitying pat on the hand with sympathetic eyes from a man in a white coat. The beep of a monitor irritating her ears.

Her visions were always right. There was no justice in them, and at times like this, she wished she could shut them off. The woman she was about to serve was dying. And soon.

She pulled in a shuddering breath and snatched a package of crackers. Setting the bowl back down on the table in front of the woman, she slid back into the booth.

Her companion looked up with a smile not quite reaching her eyes. "Thanks. How did you know I needed to eat?"

Courtney thought it best not to say the truth. People didn't understand, and tended to fear anything out of the scope of normal. She could almost hear the drunken slur from her father's mouth. *Witch.* "You came into a diner." She shrugged. "And most medications you need to take with food."

A moment passed between them. Not the awkwardness she'd expect from a stranger, but intense in its joining power. As shocking as lightning or an earthquake, a seal seemed to vibrate between them. Words couldn't describe the enormity of the moment, but for an instant, Courtney had known the woman before her all her life.

The smile faded from the other woman's oval face, making the shadows under her eyes more prominent as, seemingly, she felt it too. As a distraction, she blew gently on her spoon, and then tasted the soup. Her thin, arched eyebrows rose. "This is great."

23

Courtney cleared her throat. "Mrs. Meyers will be glad to hear it."

"Did I hear my name?" As if on cue, Mrs. Meyers walked over and slapped her chubby hand down on the back of the booth with a look that said she was up to something.

"She said the soup was good," Courtney replied, not surprised in the least that Mrs. Meyers had been listening in.

She belted a dry laugh, holding her round belly. "Isn't it always?"

Courtney twisted her lips and explained to the woman, "Mrs. Meyers isn't modest."

Her companion's mouth quirked as if unsure whether to smile.

"No, modest I ain't." She focused on the woman again. "So, where you headed to all by your lonesome?" With that as an invitation, she nudged Courtney over and sat next to her.

"Georgia. A small community just outside Athens." Her manner was polite, but her expression indicated she wanted to know why she was being asked.

"Well now, Courtney, you've never been there." She slapped her on the arm affectionately, not even trying to be subtle.

Mortified, she rubbed her eyes and sighed. "No, I haven't."

Mrs. Meyers had a dark gleam in her eye. "I was always sayin' my girl should travel more."

Courtney groaned. "Leave the girl alone, Mrs. Meyers. She's had a long trip, and a long way to go yet."

The dark-haired wanderer chimed in, much to her surprise, as if she was being pulled by strings. "You should go sometime. It's beautiful there." She smirked behind her cup.

"A nice young girl like you," Mrs. Meyers pointed at the stranger, "should not be traveling alone." The woman only laughed, giving her an open invitation to continue. "You should take this one here with you. She has tons of vacation time she's never used."

"Mrs. Meyers!" Courtney turned back to the woman, imploring apology, as embarrassment heated her cheeks. "I'm sorry. She doesn't have a tact gene, but she means well."

The woman shrugged, amusement lighting the previous shadows in her eyes. "It's quite alright." She looked into her cup with a sly twitch of her mouth. "I wouldn't mind the company, actually."

Courtney felt the color draining out of her cheeks and grew dizzy. "You just met me." She rubbed her forehead. "It's a ridiculous idea."

Mrs. Meyers patted her hand, gaze softening. "You can't stay here forever. Take this chance, Courtney. You'd know if something was amiss and if this wasn't right." She turned her gaze to the newcomer. "She has no criminal record and she'd give a stranger the shirt off her back. You could do worse for a friend."

Courtney looked from her companion to Mrs. Meyers and back again. This was the most absurd thing she'd ever heard. She hadn't even known this woman all of five minutes, and she wanted her to just get in the car and go. The worst of it was they both seemed to like the notion. This stranger had no qualms about letting someone she'd just met into her life, take her home.

The woman darted her eyes between the both of them, seemingly in hopes for a resolve. Not a sliver of apprehension hit her expression.

For a brief second, Courtney thought about this town that took her in so long ago, when she had more scars than dreams and not even a change of clothes. She wouldn't even be alive if not for the large pain in the ass woman next to her, who was now telling her to flee for the second time in her life. Her only plan when she'd run from that horrid place all those years ago was to get out. Well, she'd done that.

But leaving now? What would be the goal? She had a place of her own and a job. There was no reason to go. Except... She reflected on her lonely apartment waiting for her return and all that Mrs. Meyers had done for her. She wanted to grant this one request, something to pay her back for all the love so feely given. But in all the time Mrs. Meyers had been encouraging her to venture out, the truth was Courtney never had.

Because she was scared. Scared of what was out there, all she didn't know.

"It's a lovely place," the newcomer said, breaking into her thoughts. Her golden eyes were kind, and not unaffected by the strange connection almost from the second she'd walked in the diner. "I don't know you, nor do you know me, but for the first time in a long time, I'm...at ease." She shook her head and laughed rather unsteadily. "I know this sounds crazy, but I feel like I've been waiting to meet you."

Courtney drew her brows together, surprised that she'd had the same thought. She wasn't sure why it felt right--cosmically so--to have two complete strangers run away into the night. An innate awareness told her this woman was the friend she never had. No harm would come to her as long as she was smart, followed her gut.

If she was one thing, it was smart. Not book intelligent, but street wise. Back then, she'd known when to speak up and when to stay quiet, hiding in the shadows. She had become a master at blending into her surroundings as to not be seen. In those few minutes after her father had fallen asleep, with a bottle of gin tucked under his arm, she identified it was her time to run. Just as she knew, with nervousness in her belly, that it was her time to run again.

Courtney knew things about the woman sitting across from her, things she shouldn't, and one thing she didn't. "I don't know your name."

Her companion laughed, which ended on a sigh as if thankful Courtney agreed to accompany her. She smiled, a little sad and a whole lot relieved. "Serena. My name is Serena."

Courtney awakened slowly from the dream, the smell of gin still in her nose and fear fading from where it had been lodged in her throat. She shoved away visions of dark hair and the thin mouth twisted wryly in disgust. She attempted to stretch, but there was nowhere for her legs to go. It took her too long to comprehend she was still in the car with Serena.

Opening her eyes and straightening, she found it was daylight. It had been near midnight when they'd left the diner.

A wave of uncertainty filled Courtney about this trip, and not for the first time. After running from home years before, she'd learned to trust her instincts, so she tried to push down the doubts. Her sense thought this was the right move.

"Morning," Serena chirped from next to her. "Are you hungry?" Her eyes were as kind as her voice.

Taking stock, she nodded. "You drove all night."

Serena flicked her a glance and returned it to the road. "I don't sleep much lately, though I do need to start sticking to a schedule."

"I never did sleep well, either." She immediately regretted the slip. No one wanted to know of her childish sleeping problems. "You probably want to stop and rest." She skimmed her gaze around. "Where are we, anyway?"

"Um, we're coming up to Las Cruces." Serena must've detected Courtney had no idea where that was. She smiled warmly at her again. "New Mexico."

As Serena drove a little while longer, looking for places to stop, she suddenly remembered something Mrs. Meyers had said about Courtney not ever traveling. It wouldn't hurt to take in some sights while they were on the road, show her around since she'd never been anywhere. She knew it would also be her only time to do this, as her time was running out. She'd never really stopped to look herself at anything along the way. She'd been in such a hurry to reach California that she hadn't taken the time to see all there was to this world. They could both take it in for the first time.

"Hey, I was thinking we could do some sight-seeing along the way." Serena briefly turned to her and back to the road. Those blue eyes lit up and she grinned from ear to ear like a child.

"Really?"

That smile was contagious. Serena found herself grinning as well for the first time in a long time. "Sure. Las Cruces has these wonderful caves. I've never been, but I hear they're marvelous."

"I've never seen a cave," Courtney murmured in response, thinking what a stupid thing to say. Her cheeks heated in embarrassment.

Serena noted the blush, and wondered why Courtney felt she could never say anything right. It was is if the moment they hit the city limits with nothing but open highway before them, Courtney had clammed up and crawled into herself. She was also a little socially awkward, making Serena wonder if she never had friends.

Maybe if she just reassured her new friend that she could speak freely? "I've never seen a cave either."

"You haven't?"

"No. My family didn't vacation much." Because she was always sick and Grams was getting up there in age, even when her and Austin were young.

Courtney wanted to ask why, and better yet, wanted to know the reason they were going to Grandma's house instead of Mom and Dad's. But instead she nodded her head and turned back to search out her window. The land was pretty flat, seasoned with oranges and browns against a cobalt sky. The contrast was striking and her fingers itched for her camera. Boulders dotted the landscape, as if to throw a wrench into the picture to be contrary. A few scrub bushes and cactus spanned out, creating long, irregular shadows on the packed, dry earth.

Serena cleared her throat. "Let's get a hotel room, eat, then we can go see the Carlsbad Caverns. We'll stay the night here. Does that sound good?"

"Sure." It sounded wonderful, but she tried not to seem too enthusiastic, lest Serena didn't like playing tourist after their first stop.

Carlsbad Caverns was nothing like Courtney thought it would be. She had almost lost the tour group twice by gawking in sheer amazement.

Rocks jutted out of the earth and surrounded themselves with this beautiful cavern, so deep, so wide, so tall, that Courtney questioned if anyone had ever really seen it all. Formations hung down from the top that looked like icicles she'd only seen in Utah. She knew they couldn't be, for the tour guide had said something about stalactites and stalagmites, but she wished she could reach that high to touch for herself. Running her hands along the walls as she walked, the cold and damp seeped into her--smooth and just a little wet.

The tour guide walked backwards to face the group, and her voice echoed off the cave walls. "...subterranean chambers. There are 300,000 Mexican free-tail bats that stay here from early spring through to October."

Courtney had no idea how many pictures she took with the camera Dr. Maynard had given her last year, but she was glad at that moment he thought enough of her to bestow the present. She fought him tooth and nail about it then, saying it was too expensive and she had no initiative to use one.

He'd merely sighed in his patient way and said, "You have a gift of sight. This will help you use it." He'd demonstrated how to load the film, focus, the right lighting, and some other things he'd picked up along the way while enjoying his hobby he'd shared with her. He would chuckle every time she got the film back from developing, saying she was far better at it in ten minutes than he'd been in ten years.

She couldn't wait to send him copies of her trip. Giddy at the thought, she imagined him now, huddled around the counter. Mrs. Meyers would be cooing that she was right to send her away. Dr. Maynard would chuckle, as he always did, and rub his beard.

The thin tunnel opened up into a labyrinth of rock formations, low into the ground, with a wide open, almost cathedral-like ceiling. Light poked in from the top, cascading in through streams, and resting down below.

She waited behind the others as they descended stairs cut into the rock, and into the cavern below. She aimed the lens of her camera up, and after adjusting for focus, took the shot of a beam of sunlight jutting through the rock wall ceiling. It was almost heavenly, the way it was so serene and mystical--as if God Himself had directed the rays of light toward her.

Something pulled inside her chest, a feeling she'd never be able to explain to anyone with ears. An utter calm and peace shifted through her, starting with her core and spreading out. Filling crevices and sealing dark with light. In her entire life, she'd never had a single moment of pure...euphoria. She rocked on her heels, unsteady. Her eyes grew wet, her throat tight.

Camera paused midair to her face, she searched below for Serena. Finding her almost immediately, their gazes locked. Understanding dawned in Serena's eyes, as if Courtney's bliss had been passed to her. Stormy blue eyes met a pair of golden brown, and held. As if Serena was right next to her, instead of forty feet away, Courtney reveling in the heat and warmth of the moment.

The extended rope of budding friendship Courtney sensed from first meeting Serena strengthened into a knot. Tied together, no matter what.

29

Courtney pressed her lips together to keep tears at bay and nodded her head, looking away. There were no words needed to acknowledge her friend felt it too. Courtney held that tranquility, a stillness Serena so desperately needed, if only for a brief minute.

Clearing her throat, and after a second to compose herself, Courtney took a couple more shots and headed down.

While seated on a quilted bedspread with her back to the bathroom door, Serena rolled her eyes at the phone. Luckily Courtney was still in the shower. "Austin, you're not listening--"

"I heard you just fine!"

She gave up and laid down with the receiver to her ear, giving in to the exhaustion. The bed in the motel they'd found off the highway was so comfortable she thought she would sink into the mattress. Sighing at her brother's impatient tone, she uttered again, "I feel fine."

"Oh yeah, you sound fine." Serena rolled her eyes again at his sarcasm. "You go tooling around in some cave, in the desert no less, with some person you never met, who will probably kill you in your sleep."

She chuckled, despite better efforts not to, thinking Courtney couldn't even hurt herself if she wanted to. She propped her arm over her face.

He'd been so protective of her their entire lives. That was part of her reason for escaping three years ago. She loved her little bit of family left, more than she could ever bring herself to admit. But she couldn't take the pity stares and the "are you okay's" anymore.

Sitting up, she let the sound of water from Courtney's shower drift into her to calm. "Austin, this woman couldn't hurt anyone." Contemplating how to say the next part, she sighed, noting he was listening now. "She has this scar on her arm, and she's so...hesitant. I think someone, well...I think someone from her past hurt her."

Austin paused. "What do you mean?"

"She's never traveled before, as in at all, and acts as if everything she sees is a new wonder. Which is so strange because she has this world-weary way about her. Like she's seen too much. And her eyes, Austin! I swear she can see right into my head. But she refrains from touching of any kind and doesn't know how to take a compliment."

"Where did you pick her up again?"

"In some small town just inside the Arizona border, but I don't think it was the people there hurting her." She envisioned the round faced diner owner who pushed her way into the booth, who cleverly pushed them both so expertly into this adventure neither had time to stop and think. "The woman who owns the place she waitressed at isn't family. I don't think she has any. But she was kind. Courtney made a brief reference that she took her in years ago."

"I see."

Austin could never turn his back on someone who needed it. She smiled, remembering all the stray animals he took in when they were kids, driving Grams nuts. He would bend over backwards to help anyone, even if he didn't know them. She got that part of her heart from him, the only good part.

The water shut off behind her so she took her bottle of pills from the nightstand and shoved them into the bag by her feet. "I gotta go soon."

"All right, but you need to call me three times a day until you get back."

"Okay."

"I mean it, Serena. And you are to take it easy."

"Okay! We should be there by Saturday."

Steam poured into the room. Turning, Serena watched silently as Courtney, with a small white towel draped across her midsection, fumbled through her bag on the bed. She pulled on a dark blue pair of pajama pants, and with her back to Serena, shed the towel. When she reached for her top on the dresser, Serena's gaze landed on a large white scar, running diagonal the entire length of Courtney's back, almost hidden by her creamy white skin.

"Oh, my God." Serena was off the bed before even finishing the sentence.

Franticly, Courtney covered the mark with a light blue shirt and whirled around, backing away from where Serena had moved closer. "No questions, please." Her eyes were pleading, eyebrows drawn together as if the scar still hurt.

31

Serena stayed where she was, not wanting to alarm her. They knew nothing about each other, not even a shred of history. She had no idea what was going on, what had happened to her new friend, but somehow determined fate interfered for a reason. Tears clogged the back of her throat, hot and heavy as she tried to swallow them down. She pressed her lips together and covered them with a shaking hand.

"I'm sorry." Sorry someone had hurt her, more than she sorry she'd pointed it out..

"Don't cry," Courtney said helplessly, at a loss. No one had ever cried for her, not in all her years, and she had no idea how to handle it. She went against instinct and took Serena's shaking hands in hers. Warmth and something dark shot up her arm from the contact. Anger, not with her, but for her. Empathy? Courtney dropped her hands and took a step back in retreat. The silence was worse than the pity in Serena's eyes. "I cleaned out the tub, if you want to go take a bath and relax."

After a couple moments, Serena lowered her eyes and nodded. "I'll be out in a little bit." Serena seized her bag and headed toward the bathroom. "The food should be here soon. They're delivering."

When the bathroom door closed, Courtney sat on the bed. Though it was only four o'clock in the afternoon, she had no energy left. Had she really gotten in a car with a stranger? She thought about calling the diner. Talking to Mrs. Meyers would remind her why she'd made this hasty move.

Instead, she glanced around the motel room. The dark burgundy interior was shut off to the outside world by heavy floral printed drapes which hung all the way down to the dark green carpet. They opted to get a single bed, since it was forty dollars cheaper. The headboard was attached to the wall, and above it were little light fixtures that dimly glowed.

She couldn't believe she'd let Serena see the scar. She was usually more cautious than that, but she'd let her guard down. Should she explain to Serena how she got the scar? Since she'd never spoken about her father to anyone, words fumbled in her head. Excuses. He had just tried to raise her right, with morals and values. If she was a better daughter, he wouldn't have had to hurt her. He used to press his Bible to her chest, hoping to bless the demons out of her that caused the visions. It hadn't worked, so he'd used other recourses.

It never worked. No matter how hard she prayed, they still came, along with the strange feelings. She couldn't even make her father happy, how was she supposed to do anything right for Serena? She would tire of her as well, and that strangely made her unbearably miserable. When she ran from her childhood home, she didn't do it to escape the hate that festered there. She left because she let him down, and didn't know what to do, or even what she did to make him stop.

A thought, one she'd had often, shoved its way into her mind before she could fight it off. Something she contemplated often since she'd been rescued by Mrs. Meyers. Maybe it would've been best if Mrs. Meyers had left her on the side of that highway ten years ago. The rain would have washed away Courtney's sins, and maybe, just maybe, God would have heard her then.

"I don't know how to use chopsticks."

Serena smiled and placed her hands over Courtney's. Nudging her pointer finger between the sticks, she guided her in how to open and close them. Dipping into the paper carton, Serena helped her pick up some shrimp fried rice, and with her hands still on hers, brought it to her mouth. "There you go. It just takes practice."

The dry heat of the day had begun to fade while the sun dipped west. It brought a beautiful arrangement of oranges and reds over the horizon and, sitting back, Serena inhaled deeply.

The balcony outside their room was just large enough to hold two plastic lawn chairs. The slight breeze cooled her warm skin and shuffled her hair. She had on a yellow spaghetti strap tank top and shorts the color of the sunset, which she feared may not be warm enough. Plus, she hadn't planned on having another passenger, so the night shirt did nothing to hide her surgical scar. It didn't bother her, as it usually does, since Courtney had scars of her own. Her companion hadn't asked about it either, just glanced at it briefly, as if not surprised, and then turned away.

Curiosity was getting the better of her. Plucking out some white rice from her own carton, she debated how to go about starting a conversation in a way that wouldn't upset Courtney. "I'll tell you about my scar if you tell me about yours."

Courtney stilled. Carefully, she placed her chopsticks in the carton and set it on the floor, appetite gone. She swallowed hard, thought about not answering, but the lure of the sunset was one unlike she'd ever seen, and Serena's kind golden eyes were holding her gaze. She sensed talking about her past with Serena would be okay. The hollow void Courtney had been living with was gone with Serena around.

"I already know about yours."

Serena's brow furrowed in confusion. "My what? My scar?"

Courtney nodded and lowered her gaze. Any moment now the judgment and skepticism would come.

"How do you know?"

Here goes. "I feel it." She patted her chest and then her temple. "When you first walked into the diner, my heart shuddered. Like it missed a few beats, and then this tingling went through me."

The confusion faded from Serena's face and was replaced by a blank expression Courtney couldn't read. Was she disgusted? Scared? "It's been happening with some people since as far back as I can remember. Sometimes it's with a touch, sometimes I just need to be in the same room. Their thoughts run over mine, and I feel what they're feeling, see what they're seeing."

Serena had no idea how to respond. She had certainly heard of psychic ability, but had never really given it much thought. People used to say it was the sight between her and Austin. Being twins they often finished each other's sentences and were extremely in tune with each other's moods. But not in the way Courtney described.

"I understand if you don't want me to continue to Georgia with you. I can hitch a ride back."

"No!" Serena drew in a breath and softened her tone. "I'm sorry." She took Courtney's hands, finding apprehension in her eyes and in the twist of her mouth. Did she think Serena would hate her? "It doesn't scare me, if that's what concerns you. You have a gift, Courtney."

"It's not a gift. It's the devil." Said deadpan, as if that was the only truth she'd known.

34

Serena's already fragile heart broke. "What? Who told you that?"

Courtney's face held little emotion when she tucked a stray piece of blonde hair behind her ear. "Tell me about your scar. I feel the presence, but don't know the history."

Courtney was avoiding her question, but Serena wanted her trust. "I was born with a heart defect. It didn't pump right and was weaker than it should have been. They put a pacemaker in when I was a girl, but after time it wasn't doing what they hoped it would, and not as well. I'm on a transplant list, but my blood type is too rare."

Courtney wondered whether Serena knew her voice became bored and robotic when she talked about her condition, as if she'd done it so often her life had become an uneventful story.

Serena looked out over the horizon. The sun was almost set, leaving it dark around them. "That's when I left Georgia and went to California. I didn't tell Grams or Austin about my condition getting worse, but I think Austin knew. My whole had been sheltered. 'Don't eat this.' 'Don't take on too much.' 'Don't do this, don't do that.' I was so sick of it. I needed out. Needed to...live before I died."

Serena rubbed her eyes and laid her head against the chair. "There's another surgery they said they could do. It's new. Something called a left ventricular reconstruction, or whatever." She waved her hand absently. "It's supposed to increase function by remodeling the heart, making it contract correctly. But I caught a cold bug, which led to pneumonia a couple weeks back, and I'm too weak for it."

Those golden brown eyes spilled over and tears clung to her long dark lashes. Serena's pain washed out all other thoughts in Courtney's head. It wasn't just the sickness, but fear for her brother and grandmother that tore at Serena. Courtney sensed someone else there in her friend's mind, someone who hadn't been brought up before in their short time together.

"That's what the pills are for. My kidneys started acting up, and I retain fluid if I don't watch my salt intake and how much I drink." She swept a tear from her cheek and sniffled. "I don't think it'll be much more than a few months, which is what the doctors said."

"When the leaves stop falling," Courtney mumbled. Immediately kicking herself, she swore under her breath and dropped Serena's hand as visions of red and orange leaves fell before her mind. Standing, she paced the two steps to the balcony rail and held tight.

The sky was dark as she focused up at the stars and breathed deep. A child from one of the other rooms was crying in a fit of rage, but Courtney barely heard it. Another person's anger, a long ago memory, was filling her head. "He grabbed me once, my father. Not an unusual occurrence, but that time I knew in my gut it would be different."

Serena edged forward in her chair, ignoring the comment about the leaves and straining to hear. Courtney spoke too softly, her head back, as if talking to the stars and not Serena. Her blonde hair danced at the gesture.

Courtney sighed, the sound drifting into the night. "The phone rang, or at least I thought it had. I told Dad I would get it, so he wouldn't have to get up from his chair. He had this recliner he sat in when he came home from work, gin in the crook of his arm. I went to answer the phone, it kept ringing, but he grabbed my hair from behind and threw me down."

She spoke rapidly now, a defense mechanism Serena had noticed a few times in the car, but Serena didn't move or reach out to touch her for fear she would stop talking.

"I didn't know what I did wrong. I thought I was helping, so he wouldn't have to get up. I remember thinking when he went to work the next day I should try to wash the stain out of the carpet. I kept looking at the stain while he shrieked at me and called me a witch. 'I will beat the devil out of you!' I knew then that the phone hadn't rung, not yet. I just knew it was going to. I heard it in my head." She smacked her hand against her temple, and it shook when she set it back on the rail.

Serena wanted to hug her, hold her close and soothe the hurt, take it away somehow. But Courtney didn't seem to like touch and worse, Serena feared she'd never had someone to hold her through rough times.

"The belt cracked." Courtney shuddered. "He always snapped it three times first. That's how I knew a strike was coming. He never let me look at him, face him. I was too ugly, too much a disappointment, which made him more irate. I tensed and bit my tongue until it bled. The blows didn't hurt so much then. But that time it did. This warm liquid spilled over my back. I thought he'd dumped coffee on me at first. Then my back burned. Throbbed. It was so hot."

As if the memory snapped her back, Courtney turned around, gaze sweeping over the tears slipping from Serena's eyes. Serena didn't blink, or wipe them away, just let them fall from her chin and into her lap, a silent show of understanding for Courtney.

"He only hit me once that time, that's all it took. He slit my skin open with the force of the leather, and it bled such a long time. He was mad about that too, but afterwards, he looked…ashamed almost. Like he was sorry he did it." She leaned against the railing. "Keeping the wound dressed was hard. I couldn't reach my back. I think that's why it scarred so bad."

Falling silent, Courtney took in Serena's trembling hands, her pale face marred with tears, and immediately regretted the decision to tell her. She never spoke about her past. It shamed her to know what her father had done, what she'd made him do to her for being the way she was. She hadn't meant to say so much, but once she started, it all came pouring out.

Serena wouldn't be as nice to her now that she knew the truth. Courtney was a freak, had always known that. They wouldn't be friends or have late night chats or anything else normal people did. Serena would detach, and regret taking Courtney along. The pain of it shot through her, and left her bereft.

Might as well put the nail in the coffin. "I can still smell the gin on his breath and my blood on his hands. He didn't hit me again for a long time after that, but eventually, he started again. Again and again." Because she deserved it.

Courtney ran her hands up and down her exposed arms, wondering if Serena would ditch her at first light. A shudder tore through her. When did it get so cold? When did the fear of losing someone, especially a stranger, make her so unbearably frigid?

Serena hadn't moved, still composed with a stick straight spine and tears running down her thin face.

Giving her time and a chance to bolt, Courtney slid the glass door on its rails and stepped inside, leaving it open for Serena to follow.

It was almost sunrise when she did.

Chapter Three

Grams had dismissed herself politely from dinner, and for the first time in Austin's memory, left him the dishes to clean up. From there she had gone quietly into her room down the long hall upstairs, and made not another sound. Worry ate at his gut. Grams was far from frail, had seen her share of grief and lived on, but health was temporary, and so he worried.

She had handled the news well. Too well. He'd fumbled for the right words since Serena had called him, going over and over again what he would say to Grams. She merely nodded her head. Her thin mouth, which was rarely without a smile, had been set firm. Her only sign of weakness had been when she'd stood and placed a shaking hand on the dining table she insisted they use, even when it was just the two of them.

Austin rubbed a hand over his bare chest and headed toward the large kitchen, the cuffs of his low-riding jeans scuffing along the floorboards. Doing the dishes would be a welcomed distraction, and then he just might head to Jake's and drink himself into a stupor.

Jake. The memories he and his sister collected through the years were fond and too many for the counting. They would spend hours, days even, behind Grams' house, doing whatever children do in their youth. The three acres she had left after selling most of it to Jake was virtually untouched, except for her gardens stretched through the center of the estate.

He meticulously washed each dish and rinsed it off. Maybe he'd clean the house tonight, needing the distraction from his sister and whoever this woman was traveling with her.

Serena thought someone had hurt this Courtney person before, said she was real jumpy. He wondered if the woman's husband was after her, if it was a spousal abuse situation. The guilt in his stomach spread as he remembered how selfish he'd acted when she'd called. He didn't even listen to her, just yelled at her for picking up some stranger that they would have to baby-sit.

It wasn't like Serena to turn her back on someone who needed it, and he would do anything to make his beloved sister happy in these last months. If Serena didn't think this stranger was dangerous, then he would take her word for it and trust her. Serena had a big heart. It was good she'd found someone, a friend. Conceivably, this woman could help Serena to not take on so much at once. Even just being there, being a crutch, would be welcome.

Drying his hands, he shuffled toward the library to do some dusting. He made a point to walk through the sitting room to make sure the fire had been put out in the fireplace. Grams loved to have a fire going almost every night, whether it was summer or the dead of winter. "It makes the house more welcome," she'd say.

It was Serena's favorite room. She was sitting on the floor now, in his memory. She had her paints scattered out in front of her, creating whatever masterpiece was in her head. The fire had been blazing, making the little bit of auburn in her dark tresses come out.

Heaving a sigh, he backtracked and pushed through the double doors down the front hall. This was getting insane. It was becoming harder and harder to think of her as she was now, a grown woman. His mind would regress back to how she'd been as a child, when they were both children, and he needed to stop. Growling, he slammed the door of his sanctuary behind him and leaned against it.

The library was his pride and joy. A few years ago, he and Jake restored all the old cherry wood and had new shelves put in from wall to wall. The dark burgundy room held little furnishings except for a large leather back chair of chocolate brown in the heart of the room, with an end table in the very wood as the shelves. His desk, which he rarely used out of principle, was against the far corner and faced the door. The chandelier was lead crystal, hung in the center of the twenty foot ceiling. A solitary window faced the back of the house, on the main floor, and right into Gram's gardens. If he pulled open the floor length drapes, twenty acres would span out in panoramic glory. He would see the three of them running around the plantation as kids, so he kept them closed.

He decided he needed to stay busy or when he stopped he would break down and lose it. Serena and Grams needed him to be strong.

With more concentration than necessary, he removed every book and wiped down each shelf. He sorted through the papers on his desk, and with much disappointment, found everything was in order at home. It would have been a welcomed distraction if there were bills to concentrate on or tax forms to go over.

After three hours, at last he felt the exhaustion and welcomed it. Shutting off the lamp on his desk, he turned to retreat upstairs and bumped directly into Grams. Biting back an oath, as he never swore around her out of respect, he detained her shoulders at arms length to hold her steady.

"What are you doing up?"

The smile didn't reach her eyes as she looked up at him, the top of her head not quite kissing his shoulders. "I couldn't sleep, as I imagine you couldn't either."

He blew out a breath and rubbed his hands up and down her arms. He placed a kiss to the top of her head and left his cheek to rest there as he held her close. Her hair was salt and pepper, which Austin assumed had never been cut. If she let it out of the loose knot she usually kept it in, the length would sweep long past the center of her back in a smooth, soft wave. She smelled of fresh soap, and it comforted him to know some things never changed.

"I'll make us some tea."

She didn't argue at being pampered, and Austin figured she was too tired. He assisted her into one of the kitchen chairs at the small table and turned to find the kettle. "Green or black tea, Grams?"

"Green, dear. Thanks."

He kept his back to her and nodded, filling the pot. Before turning around he took effort to erase the worry lines from his forehead. Skimming a hand across his chest, he wondered how to politely tell her to go to bed and not fret anymore, knowing he wasn't able to manage that task either. Women were better suited at managing emotions, and he was man enough to admit it.

"You do that when you're thinking about her, or feel guilty."

"Do what?" The tea kettle screeched and he shifted to the stove. He poured the hot water into cups for them while reaching above him in the cabinet for the tea bags.

"Stroke your chest." She waited a few beats and adjusted her peach colored satin nightgown. "It's not your fault, you know."

Sighing, he walked to the small table and set down the cups. "I know."

"Do you?" She peered at him with such concentration he squirmed under her gaze and closed his eyes. "I wonder sometimes."

"I know it's not my fault she's sick, Grams, but I can't help but wonder why it wasn't me. We shared the same womb, the same birthday. Why her?"

"God has His reasons, dear. Sometimes it's hard to understand. Besides, asking "why me" implies it should be happening to someone else." She patted his hand in her old comforting way, warmth and love seeping from the embrace. She never had much to say, but when she did it was as if she had been rehearsing it for hours. Every word of advice or comment was teaming with her years of experience. He couldn't help but obey and understand.

Sighing again, he wiped his eyes. "You know, Jake used to tell her that her heart was just too big. That's why she had problems with it."

She smiled wistfully into her cup. For the first time since he'd told her about Serena returning, it reached her hazel eyes. "That's a nice way to put it." She sipped her tea and glanced around her domain.

The great plantation's kitchen cabinets were built around the appliances, and made out of oak. Some so worn through the years that Austin itched to replace them, but Grams would never have it. He could update and fix the rest of the beautiful estate, but the kitchen was hers. The black and white checkered tile floor was original, and looked almost new. Grams took care with what was hers. The large room was full of windows so she could gaze out at her gardens to see what needed to be done. To let all the light in.

"When Great Grandpa built this house, he put in an extra room we never did find."

She had that melancholy tone back in her voice and Austin sat back to listen. He recalled fondly sitting for hours clinging to her stories about their parents, or anything at all. She had a voice filled with knowledge and the memory of ten people.

"When I was a child we looked for it, imagining treasures or anything else we might find." She chuckled quietly to herself. "I told that sister of yours once about that." She shook her head, causing the knot of hair to tumble loose. She tucked a gray strand behind her ear as if she didn't notice. "She and Jake went top to bottom looking for secret passageways and hidden levers."

Austin grinned at the memory, grazing a hand over his short hair. "She had Jake believing they'd be rich and swimming in gold coins."

"That boy would follow her anywhere." Grams breathed deep and bowed her head.

"He still would." Austin felt the tension creep slowly back into the room. Cautiously, he took a sip of tea and found it cold.

When Grams looked at him, her hazel eyes held all her emotion and brought it to the surface. "He doesn't know, does he?"

He couldn't look at her, so instead he stared into his cold cup as if it were the most important thing in the room. "No, he doesn't. Serena said she would tell him when she got here. Said it should come from her."

Grams nodded, solemn. "She's right about that, though it won't make it any better to hear."

She stood and gave a fleeting look around her kitchen. The pale yellow wallpaper had once been bright with color. Her daughter, now laid in the ground too young, would climb on the stools under the island built to separate the table from cooking area. The granddaughter she raised as her own would soon be lying next to her mother and father. She questioned if it would ever be her time to go. All these people she had raised, had watched grow and loved, had to lay to rest. And here she was, watching her kitchen walls fade year after year.

"I'm going up." She patted his hand when he didn't look up. He had demons too. "You should try getting some sleep. Staying up all night won't help her."

"I know, and I will soon." He lifted her hand, warm and wrinkled with time. He kissed her knuckles and rested his cheek against her palm. "Goodnight."

He didn't hear her feet pad away. Grams floated in and out of rooms, people never knowing she was there half the time.

She may have a way with words, but their little midnight talk over tea didn't sit right, nor ease his mind any. He peeked out the window at all the acres and Grams' garden, and decided to take a late night stroll down memory lane.

On the other side of their three acres, just past Gram's garden, Jake was probably in his bed sleeping, and completely unaware that his long time childhood love was coming home for different reasons than he expected.

Austin closed the door behind him and headed toward the children's laughter he somehow knew would forever be etched into the breeze over the yard.

Jake trekked Austin strolling across the field in his long, lazy stride long before he reached him at his barn behind the house. His only horse, Brown Eyes, had been ignored lately due to his workload, and he wanted to spend some time with her. She was the only frivolous purchase in his whole life, and he never spent a moment regretting it.

He wasn't expecting anyone else in the county to be up. He ran the brush along the painted mare's side one more time, smoothing down and patting her soft brown hair, then set the brush down on the bench. She nuzzled her nose against his neck in appreciation and whinnied softly.

"No shoes, no shirt, no service, my friend."

Austin chuckled under his breath as he looked down at his lack of attire. "Shut up and give me a beer." He leaned against the doorway of Jake's barn and folded his arms.

Jake scratched the back of his head and grinned. "I was just headin' in anyway. Come on."

Austin followed him inside and sat down at the table in the small kitchen. Jake's house was significantly smaller than his and Grams', but was always cared for just the same. When Jake's parents had moved five years ago to head further south, Jake had torn apart the whole place to make it his. He'd restored the old woodwork, replaced cabinets, built new furniture, and added a porch out back.

Jake slid him a long neck bottle across the table and sat opposite him. "What brings you out so late?"

"Couldn't sleep." He shrugged. "Started walking and ended up here."

44

Jake nodded, knowing there was more to it than that, and wondered what was going on. "That's not like you. You sleep like the dead."

Austin shrugged again and took a long pull from his bottle.

Jake sighed and rubbed his neck. His shoulder-length light brown hair needed a cut. It was almost to his collar. "How's Grams?"

The crease in Austin's forehead deepened and Jake's gut sank. They'd always been able to talk to each other about anything. But something had been holding Austin back for going on a week.

"Grams is good." He paused. "Serena will be back on Saturday." Austin's tone was too casual for Jake's liking. "She said she'd like you to come over for lunch on Sunday. Wants to talk with you. I told her I'd mention it."

Now he knew something was up. "She's been home, what, once since she took off for the west coast? And not one word from her, as if I was nothing to her all these years."

Austin's gaze changed. His already dark eyes grew darker and torment edged their depths.

Jake regretted his tone and lowered it. "What's she want with me after all this time?"

"You were always something to her, you know that."

No, he didn't know, because she'd just up and left. And if he was "something" to her, she was his *everything*. But that hardly mattered now. There was weariness in his friend's voice, and Jake decided to leave it alone for tonight.

Nodding his head as the anger subsided, he said, "All right. I'll talk with her on Sunday then." It would be here soon enough.

Austin grunted in response. He stared into his bottle.

"You had the dream again, didn't you?" At first, Jake thought this reoccurring dream his friend had about the mystery angel woman was amusing. But lately, Austin had been having it more and more, and instead of calming Austin like it used to, it seemed to disturb him.

Austin shrugged, but the weight in his eyes didn't mirror the casual gesture and he ignored the question. "Serena's bringing someone home with her."

Jealousy crept up to close around his throat and he fought to control it. So that's what this "talk" was about. She'd met

45

someone. Jake wondered when the day would come he'd hear she got engaged or married. That was supposed to be them, sharing a life together and growing old. Pain knifed his chest.

Austin cleared his throat. "Some woman she met in Arizona. They're traveling together."

What? A woman? "Huh?"

"Yeah. Serena ran into her in some small town, and after girl chat, decided to bring her back home. By the sound of it, they both were maneuvered."

"Okay," he drawled slowly. "Just like that? She brings home a stranger."

"So it seems." He shrugged. "She said she thought someone had hurt this woman before, but it wasn't anyone from where she was staying when Serena met her." He sighed. "You know Serena, always has to help."

Jake chuckled and drank his beer. The knot in his chest finally started to loosen. "Yeah, and I know just where she got it from too."

Austin smiled, but it didn't hit anywhere near the vicinity of his eyes. "Well, we'll find out all we need to know soon enough." Standing, he rubbed his hands over his dark hair and then looked around as if confused. He tossed his bottle in the trash. "I'll see you at the store day after tomorrow?"

"Sure. We'll finish the bookshelves and start the coffee counter."

Nodding, Austin headed for the door.

"Hey," Jake called before he could step out, and waited for his best friend to turn around. "You know I'm here if you need anything, right?"

Austin nodded, his expression fixed to torment.

Jake watched the screen door close behind him and thought that Sunday maybe too long to wait for answers after all.

Courtney reflected on their stop through Dallas long after they were back on the road. Old City Park was this historical village they'd visited, and she'd taken so many pictures she didn't know how she'd send them all back to Mrs. Meyers to tell her about the trip.

She laid her head back on the seat and eyed the highway before them. Trees whirled by, their leaves a bright summer green and cheerful. She smiled, recalling a snapshot she took of Serena standing by an old knotted oak when her friend hadn't been paying attention. Serena's head was crooked down, her body off to the side, and her eyes had this far off distant look. Stunning, dark shoulder-length curls were tucked behind her ears, a slight smile curving her lips, as if recovering something fond from the recesses of her mind. A yellow ankle-length skirt danced in the wind behind her.

Courtney knew Serena had been thinking about a man, the one she had yet to speak about. Fragments of him drifted to Courtney's mind when Serena was deep in thought. He was on her mind a lot, more than Serena probably even knew.

She turned her head to watch Serena as she drove. Even now, she was thinking of him and that longing was on her face. Every once and awhile she'd raise her thin brows, wrinkling her beautiful face in a memory not so happy. A pain that hurt more than sickness.

"Will you tell me about him?"

Courtney had been astonished and confused the morning after their talk in New Mexico. She'd expected to wake up alone in the hotel room. Instead, Serena had smiled sweetly, grabbed their bags, and headed to the car. She hadn't backed away from her with disgust, or said callous words, or batted an eyelash after learning about her abilities or what her father had done to her. Courtney sensed no cruelty or anger from her at all.

She darted a glance at Courtney and back to the road. "His name is Jake Warner. He grew up in the house next door to Grams' estate. He's actually Austin's best friend, but when we were little, they let me tag along all the time." She smiled and tucked a stray curl behind her ear. "They didn't care that I couldn't run as fast or do as many things. They'd just wait for me to catch up."

Courtney sensed hesitation. "If you don't wanna tell me, it's okay."

"No." She shook her head. "It's all right." She checked her rearview mirror and changed lanes to let a car pass before continuing. "The summer I turned sixteen was also the summer I was in the hospital on and off for complications. I had just had my

47

surgery to put in the pacemaker and he came in my room with a handful of tulips." Her laugh came out as smooth as smoke. She rubbed her forehead as if to dispel a headache. "He asked me out!"

Courtney looked back at her, caught up in her tale, just as surprised as Serena must have been at the time. She grinned fully, nudging her to continue.

"I couldn't believe it! I mean, sure I looked, but I wasn't kidding anyone. Jake has these piercing green eyes, the color of emeralds in the sunlight. Austin teases him about his hair all the time." She gestured with her hand the length. "It's about this long, to his collar, and is a light brown. But his smile is what got me every time."

She had that pained look in her eyes again, and her voice held no amusement now as she continued. "We'd been an item since then, you could say. I used to wonder what he was doing with me, this sick girl who couldn't do most of what the other girls could do. Oh, they came around." The chuckle under her breath was unconvincing and dry. "But he never looked at them. Only me. God, I miss him still."

Courtney, for the first time in her life, understood the sentiment of what love was. She had never experienced it herself. No one had ever touched her or looked at her like that. She'd never even been kissed before, but she felt it, at least what Serena felt, for that brief lapse when she'd talked. It was the first instance where Courtney ever regretting not experiencing romance. Which was foolish. She was invisible, had made herself that way on purpose. That's why no one talked to her, or asked her out, or brought her flowers.

It was easier somehow to not know. You couldn't miss or crave what you never had.

"Hey." Serena patted her leg. "What are you thinking about?"

Shoving away her thoughts, she forced a smile. "How wonderful it must have been, to have someone care for you that much."

"There was always love at Grams' house. Austin, Jake, and I spent every waking moment together. But then I left, and I don't think Jake ever forgave me."

"He will." She turned her head to look out the window.

Serena ignored the comment, not wanting to believe it as much as she hoped it was true. It had been three years since her and Jake

48

had seen one another, and he hadn't only been angry at her leaving. He'd been leveled.

She checked her gas gauge, realizing it was getting low. "Hey, we're coming up to Shreveport and need to fill up. It'll be dark soon. We should stay here tonight."

"Okay."

Serena wanted to ask why Courtney's mood had shifted so drastically, but before she could comment Courtney asked, "Can we stop and get the film developed? I want to send Mrs. Meyers some pictures."

"Sure, we'll do a one hour so they're ready to go out tonight."

"Thanks."

Serena smiled, noting their exit was coming up. "Let's go to the bars tonight. Louisiana has great taverns and we can play some pool, get dressed up."

Courtney suppressed the queasiness in her stomach and smiled. "I don't have anything appropriate to wear, and I don't drink."

"Well," Serena responded with a dry tone, "I can't drink either. But we can flirt and have some fun."

"I don't know how to flirt," she said so matter-of-factly that Serena threw her head back and laughed.

"Oh, honey, every woman can flirt. You'll have the boys chasing your baby blues before you know it."

Nodding, because it was just easier than arguing, Courtney sat back and dreaded the next stop for the first time since they'd left Arizona. But if Serena needed to get out and have fun, then she would oblige. After all, she had done so many things for her already, she could bar hop to return the favor. No one would be looking at her with Serena around anyway.

"Do this with your lips." Serena puckered hers to illustrate. When Courtney imitated the gesture, Serena applied some lipstick the shade of pale pink rose petals and sat back. "Done."

Courtney walked into the small motel bathroom and studied herself in the mirror. "I've never worn make-up before."

"Really?"

"Yeah." She angled her face to get a better look. She didn't even recognize herself. She wore a black dress, one of Serena's that was too low in the chest for comfort and too high on the leg. It fit tight around her waist as she fidgeted.

Serena dug around in one of her bags she'd brought from the trunk and held out a pair of strappy sandals. "Here, these go with the dress."

Courtney took them and continued to stare at the stranger looking back at her. Serena came up behind her and laid her chin on her shoulder. There was love and understanding emanating from Serena. Friendly. Emotion swam in her brown eyes. It threw Courtney off. No one ever cared this much or even put up the effort to pretend to, and they'd just met. She'd question the validity if she wasn't certain Serena was genuine.

"You look great," Serena said with a smile. "I never filled out that dress right. It looks good on you." She reached in her purse and grabbed some gloss, applying it. "Tomorrow, before we leave, we'll stop at that drug store again to get you some more film and some makeup. Something that suits you, easy to apply." She smacked her lips and turned to Courtney. "You ready to go?"

Courtney skimmed her eyes up and down Serena's outfit. Her red dress clung to her small waist and down to her ankles. It was high-collared to hide her scar, and her massive amount of dark tresses fell to her shoulders in what appeared to be sexy, organized chaos. "No, but let's go anyway."

"What's the matter?"

She knew it sounded stupid even as she said it. "I don't know how to act in front of men."

Serena lifted her brows and pouted her lips in thought. "You never had a boyfriend?"

"No." She put her arms out helplessly and sighed. "Look at me."

"I am," she said with more pity than understanding. "You look damn good." She must've read the disbelief on her face because Serena took her hands and squeezed. "Courtney, you are beautiful. It doesn't matter if you have experience or not, it doesn't change the fact that you are. You just haven't been exposed to a lot before, and that's okay. I'll be right there the whole time, and we'll leave if you get real uncomfortable."

"Okay." Sincerity poured from Serena in waves, so Courtney nodded. All she could find looking back at herself was a scrawny girl with scars, hidden behind makeup, hairspray, and a nice dress. But Serena seemed sure otherwise.

As if knowing what she was thinking, Serena said very quietly, with such sadness it took Courtney by surprise, "No one's ever told you that before, have they? That you were beautiful?" She turned her by the shoulders and looked her square in the eyes. "You are beautiful. I don't care what anyone else has told you. You are." Nodding her head, Serena stepped back. "Let's go have fun."

The bar was directly next door to their motel, cloaked in cheap perfume and cigars. Smoke clung to the air and swirled around the people dancing near the back wall. The lights were low, with a red tint, and the music was ear-splitting. The front door was propped wide open, letting in little relief to the summer heat and humidity. People were packed in, laughing at private jokes and drinking without amble.

Courtney followed Serena to the bar along the right wall and sat on one of the only available stools. She tugged down her short dress, only to have it crawl back up her bare thighs. She eyed the bartender, a short, balding man of about forty, as he walked over to them with a hitch to his step. An ache shot up her leg as a visual bombarded her. His limp was the result of a motorcycle accident five years ago.

She closed her eyes and drew a slow breath until the foreign images of his wreck erased in her mind. She focused on the here and now to keep from drawing attention to herself.

His blue shirt was buttoned down almost to his waistline and he had sweat marks under his stocky arms. He impatiently pushed up his sleeves and cocked a grin out of one side of his mouth. "Welcome to Cajun South, ladies. What can I getcha?"

Serena leaned over the bar and yelled over the music. "Two Cokes. Thanks." She held up two fingers as if to demonstrate. She planted herself on the stool next to Courtney and smiled. "Not so bad, huh?"

Actually, it wasn't. A little loud and hot, but not as scary as she'd figured. Amused, she watched the people from across the room lean into each other and flirt, wondering if she'd be able to pull it off. "No, it's not bad." She grinned at Serena to prove it.

"Here you go," the bartender said, sliding over their drinks.

Serena slipped him two bills and swiveled her stool around to face the room. "Don't look now, but the guy at the end of the bar in the white T-shirt has been staring at you since we got here."

Serena caught the flutter of panic round Courtney's eyes and quickly patted her hand. "It's okay. It just means he's attracted to you. In a second, casually glance over there, pretend you didn't notice him looking at you before, and smile."

Courtney took a sip of her drink without really tasting it and set it on the bar. She did just what Serena said, and a young red haired man with wide shoulders smiled back. Her stomach flip-flopped. He grinned wider when heat infused her cheeks. He hopped off his stool with a bottle of beer in his hand. When she realized he was heading her way she gripped Serena's hand tighter.

"Okay, he'll probably ask you to dance, or just talk. Don't tell him your last name, but be friendly. Smile and just pretend he's someone you're comfortable with."

"Hey." The guy held out a rather large hand with a class ring on his third finger. "I'm Trevor."

Courtney smiled, hopefully not awkwardly, back at him and, after only a moment's hesitation, took his hand and shook it. "Um, I'm Courtney."

He nodded as if extremely satisfied with this knowledge. "Cute name. It suits you." He glanced over at Serena and held out his hand for her. "Another beautiful name," he commented when she told him hers. He focused back on Courtney and leaned close to her ear. "Wanna dance?"

She strained to keep a calm expression on her face when her stomach revolted. He smelled like beer and too much aftershave. "Sure." She slid from her stool. He took her hand and led her to the far back wall where others were crowded around dancing.

Serena kept an eye on Courtney from her stool until a sweaty hand touched her back. She looked up to find a tall man with dark hair and a hopeless smile.

"Can I sit here?"

She glanced at Courtney and back to him, infusing a polite smile of her own. "Sure."

He sat down and raised his hand to call the bartender. After ordering a club soda he focused her. "I'm Tom."

"Serena. Nice to meet you."

"Not from here, huh?"

Caution rang alarm bells in her head. "No. Why do you ask?"

His hands came up in a friendly gesture of surrender. "It's just your accent. It's not Louisiana type of southern."

"Oh." She sighed. "No, I'm from Georgia. We're heading back there now."

"Ah, okay then." She could still feel his eyes on her while she kept hers on Courtney. "You're watching her like a mom."

Serena offered an apologetic look. "Sorry. My friend doesn't get out much."

He dipped his head, causing a dark strand to fall over his forehead. "Can I give you some advice, then?"

"Sure."

He pointed to Courtney with his glass. "That guy your friend is with? He's a bar slut and is four beers in already. Keep an eye on him."

"Really?" She studied the dance floor where Trevor had his arm around Courtney's waist and was spinning her around. "Want to dance with me? So I can keep an eye on her?"

He set down his drink as the band set up a slow country song. "Never could turn down a pretty woman."

Courtney caught Serena approaching the dance floor and breathed a sigh of relief. When her companion kept his arm around her waist during the music change, she didn't fight it.

"You're cute," Trevor said, blowing the stench of sour beer into her face. "Wanna head next door with me? We can do some other kinds of dancing."

He hauled her closer before she realized his intent and held her in a vise. The pressure of his erection rubbed her abdomen and she thrashed to get away. Fear and dread crept up her skin when he didn't relax his hold. Damp sweat coated his shirt and the nausea rolled up from her stomach to her throat.

He planted his wet sloppy mouth against hers. Hard. His teeth gnashed her lower lip. It happened so fast she froze at first, until the metallic taste of blood coated her tongue. He took lack of response as an invitation and kissed harder.

She couldn't breathe. She attempted to pull away, but he had her arms trapped between their bodies. With everything spinning, she tried to yell no. He used that as leverage and forced his tongue between her lips and swirled it around.

Bile rose in her throat when she heard someone yell, "Get off her." And then she and Trevor were pulled apart. She fought to bring air into her lungs and grabbed her chest. There was shouting in the background, but she couldn't place what was being said.

Courtney sensed Serena there, even before she had her arms around her and talking to her in a calm voice. Someone questioned if she was all right. It was all so fast. Then a guy bent down in front of her, the man Serena was dancing with, and asked again, "Are you okay?" All she could do was nod her head.

Before she knew what was happening, she was weaving in and out of people and being guided to the parking lot. The humidity hadn't lessened from earlier, but it was significantly cooler outside than the bar.

She inhaled deeply and found Serena looking at her with concern. Guilt shifted in her belly. She'd ruined the evening. "I'm sorry."

Serena's head reared back. "What are you sorry for?" When she didn't answer she slipped her arm around Courtney's shoulders. "It's okay. It's not your fault."

"I didn't know what was going on. We were dancing and then…"

"Shh," she said in a soothing voice and patting her hair. "It's all right now."

Serena sat on the motel bed with the phone between her ear and shoulder, watching Courtney sort through the pictures she'd taken. Austin relayed the message that Jake would meet her at Grams' for lunch on Sunday. Her stomach rolled over in nervousness. It had been so long since she'd seen him and their reunion would be steeped in bad news. How exactly was she supposed to tell her first love that she was dying?

She closed her eyes. "Thanks, Austin."

"Just make sure you tell him."

She laughed without any humor at all. "Don't you think he'd find out anyway? Yes, I'll tell him."

"That's not funny." He paused, conceding the argument. "Where are you two at anyway?"

"Shreveport, Louisiana."

"You should be home before Saturday then."

She picked up one of Courtney's pictures from the bed and found herself in the photograph. "Probably not. We've been stopping to do some sight-seeing and I need to quit driving by late afternoon."

"All right." His voice was tight with concern. "Where did you go tonight?"

She frowned. "To this bar next door. One of the assholes there trapped Courtney and tried to assault her."

Austin bit back a string of curses and instead asked, "Is she all right?"

"Yeah. This really nice guy helped us out." She laughed. "He punched the guy right in the jaw. Probably broke his hand doing it too."

"Is she there now?"

"Yeah, we're looking through some pictures she took. I was going to take a bath anyway. You want to talk with her?"

He rubbed his neck. "Uh, I guess so."

Serena mumbled something away from the phone, and then a peculiar, very feminine voice came on the line. "Hello?"

"Hey, it's Austin, Serena's brother. She told me what happened tonight. Are you all right?"

She didn't answer at first, and he imagined a faceless woman winding hair around her finger in nervousness. Her voice was hesitant when she finally spoke. "I'm okay, thanks."

"Good." There was an awkward pause. He tried to think of anything at all to say, but she cut him off before he could.

"We shouldn't have been in there anyway. There was too much smoke for her."

"I like you already." Besides the fact that she seemed to be looking out for his sister's interests, her voice was like a wet dream. Sultry, quiet, and smooth. A pang nailed him right between the legs and he bit back a curse. She was just a woman. One he'd never seen. No matter how long it had been since he'd been with someone, a voice shouldn't get him this excited.

Unlike a moment ago, her voice became shaky and hesitant. "Really? Why?"

"It's good to know someone is looking out for her. Serena is very fond of you."

That earned him a nervous laugh. "The feeling is mutual." She breathed into the phone and the hair on his arms rose as if she was right there against his ear. "She's letting me do some sight-seeing. I know it's not as much for her as it is for me, but it's been fun. When we stopped in Las Cruces we went into this amazing cave. I got great pictures."

She was chatting a mile a minute and Austin couldn't help but laugh. She was just as Serena described--innocent without being incompetent. She sounded as if she really cared for his sister's company, and he was glad for it. He couldn't wait to meet her and put a face with her angel-like voice. Without realizing it, he said so, cutting off her rambling about their sight-seeing.

"Oh, I'm sorry. I'm probably boring you."

Anything but. "No, not at all. I'm very sorry I interrupted you. It's just that I'm intrigued to meet this person who won over my sister in twenty minutes." She didn't say anything, Austin didn't even hear her breathing. "Don't stop talking. Please, you have a great voice."

"Um, okay."

"Tell me about your photos," he prompted. He had no idea what this sudden urge was to keep her on the phone, but for that instant, he needed to hear her voice like he needed his next breath.

They were still at it when Serena stepped out of the shower and stood in the doorway of the bathroom, unnoticed, long enough to overhear Courtney tell her brother about every picture she'd snapped so far. Serena couldn't move. Courtney was not only opening up, but appeared comfortable doing it. Warmth spread around her heart that two people she cared about greatly had felt a connection with each other. It might make Courtney more relaxed when they got back home.

Not wanting to disturb them, she padded to her bag where she pulled out her pajamas.

As if just noticing her there, Courtney put down the phone. "Oh, Serena. Do you want to talk with him again before we hang up?"

Her smile lit up the whole room, completely reaching her eyes and making them a livelier blue.

"No, that's okay. Tell him goodnight for me. I'm just gonna rest."

Courtney said goodbye to Austin in a tone of voice that took Serena days to get out of her. And look at that. Her grin was contagious.

58

Chapter Four

Dear Mrs. Meyers,

I hate to say this and inflate your already large ego, but I'm having such a great time! Thank you for making me go. That was clever of you to persuade us both before we thought it through. I might not have come then.

I feel this abnormal and new comfort with Serena. She's such a wonderful person with a giving heart. I just wished it worked better. Remember that strange feeling in my chest when she walked into the diner? Well, it's because she's sick. Her doctors say she doesn't have much time left. I look at her sometimes and try to will some of my strength into her. I know that sounds silly.

I talked to her brother Austin on the phone tonight and he's real nice. It's so strange to me how close they are, and all the love they share. But I'm learning. You should hear the way she talks about Grams' house. I can't wait to see it.

We've seen such great things on the way. I sent copies of the pictures I took. There's a lot, but I couldn't help it. Share them with Dr. Maynard, please. Tell him hello for me.

Do you think there's such a thing as angels? I know this sounds odd, but when we were in this cave in Las Cruces there was this sunlight coming down from the ceiling. There's a picture of it in your package I sent you. I felt as if it was heaven. I often wonder if Serena is an angel. But then why would she be sent to me?

I hope all is well there. I don't know how long I'll stay with the Edwards', but I'll let you know. We should be in Georgia by Saturday.

Love and miss you,
Courtney

Edith carefully slipped the note back into the envelope and fought back tears. She did do the right thing after all. The girl needed to get out, see other things, and meet new people. She had a whole other life waiting for her somewhere, she just needed to find it. She would have to say a prayer for Serena, and hope she gets well. And if not, at least find peace.

So Serena had a brother, huh? Well, well, things were sounding better already. Edith cackled and then peered at the door when Richard strolled in. She slammed her fist down on the counter. "Ha. I was right!"

Richard sat on one of the stools by the counter and chuckled. He rubbed his beard. "And what were you right about this time?"

By midday, Austin and Jake had the shelves for Austin's coffee-slash-bookstore stained and the coffee counter installed. Austin was pleased to discover he'd probably be ready to reopen by the end of next week. When he decided to close the store completely, he had to assure his regulars that he wouldn't be closed longer than a month. It looked as if he would be able to deliver that promise. Willowsby, though close to bigger cities, was a small community without a library. His was also the only bookstore.

He looked around with satisfaction and pride, plopping next to Jake on the hardwood floor. "It looks good, huh."

Jake tipped back his beer and nodded. "That it does, my friend."

"They assured me the cappuccino machine will be here today. Other than that, I think it's just painting that's left to do."

Jake leaned back on his elbows and stretched out his long jean-clad legs before him. "What color did you decide on?"

"This section for the bookstore will be dark blue, the gift shop yellow, and the cafe in olive green with the mural Serena is doing." If she was well enough to paint.

"What about these divider things?" Jake asked, referring to the half-walls they crafted in the large space to make it seem as if it were three separate rooms.

"A heavy cream color. Too distracting otherwise." He chuckled. "Or so Grams says."

Jake nodded and straightened. "I always said she was a wise woman." He took another swig of beer. "Serena still getting in tomorrow?"

Austin sighed, wanting her home more every minute. "Yeah." He rubbed his eyes and dropped his hands to his knees. "I hope all this traveling hasn't worn her out." He said the comment before he could take it back. The ease he felt with Jake through the years was being compromised by his loyalty to a promise to let Serena tell Jake she was...sick. A promise that was getting harder to keep.

"Well, she's made the drive before. I'm sure she'll be all right." Jake wasn't certain he was ready to see her again. For the first few months after she left three years ago, he'd spent the lonely nights awake, hoping for her fragrance to stop lingering. He would spend hours away from Brown Eyes. The hurt of being with his beloved horse, named after her, was too much. Even the field, the acres he bought from Grams, couldn't be strolled through in early evening. His favorite time of day.

She was everywhere and nowhere. Still.

Jake never saw Serena again. Not since she'd walked away from him, tears streaming down her face as if she was actually sorry. Three years. He'd asked Austin how she was doing occasionally, and his friend told him about art shows she'd attended, or a painting she'd sold, but never anything personal. Once that line crossed, there'd be no going back. No moving on. And that's exactly what he had tried to do. After three years, he almost had himself fooled that he was over Serena. Almost.

And now she was coming back, dramatic laugh and all. He missed her laugh most of all. And coming back for good, Austin had said. Jake didn't know why, but he had a sinking suspicion it wasn't because she missed home. Something was wrong. Knowing she wanted to talk with him on Sunday offered no help for his crazed imagination.

Brooding over the hurt and the bruise to his ego when she'd left had done no good after the anger subsided. He could never stay mad at her. She was like a disease with no cure. With miles of symptoms.

"I talked last night with that woman Serena's bringing home."

Austin's voice was a welcomed distraction from his thoughts. "Oh, yeah? What's she like?"

Austin laughed and shook his head. "Like innocence and a fantasy all at once." He stood up to pace, flinging his arm out in a rare helpless gesture. "It's irritating as hell. I talked with her for like five minutes, and I heard her voice in my sleep."

Jake scratched the back of his head and tried not to grin. He stuck his tongue in his cheek instead. "Interesting."

"Shut-up," he said in a half-hearted scold. "Anyway, I think it's because Serena's become so close to her. Our twin connection is in overdrive."

Jake smiled, meaning it. "That's good. We could always stand more good friends." He rose to gather his tool belt. "Besides, you said this woman may have been hurt before, so it sounds as if she needs a friend too." He left out the part where he thought it was impossible not to love Serena.

"Yeah, you're right." Austin helped to gather the rest of the equipment and took a last look around until he would be able to come back on Monday. "Well." He sighed. "Let's be off, then."

The small air conditioner inside the hotel room did very little to chase away the humidity of Alabama in June. They'd stopped in Montgomery for the night, which was the last major city before Willowsby. Courtney sat in a chair with her bare feet crossed in front of the air unit, trying to hear Austin on the phone over its noise. She had no clue how Serena was willing to take a hot bath in this weather. Courtney was only wearing her pajama top with underwear and she was still sweating.

"…so we just finished it today," Austin said, referring to his shop.

She smiled, half guilty she'd only heard part of what he said. "It sounds lovely. I can't wait to see it."

"Serena is doing a mural for me on one of the walls. I have no idea what she's painting, but I suppose I should trust her." His tone was cute when he was self-depreciating.

Courtney stifled a yawn as she pulled the heavy drape aside to peer out into the night. "I didn't know she was an artist. What kind of stuff does she do?"

"I don't know much about art, but she called it surrealism, or something." He laughed into the phone. "I asked her once what that meant and she said she paints her own little world. Real life, with something thrown in to make it her own version. She's very good."

"I believe it. She--" A thud from behind the bathroom door made her shift in her seat, her heart rate leaping. Something was wrong. The hairs on her arms rose and a sudden wave of dizziness swamped her. Not her own. Serena's. She waited to hear another sound, but nothing came.

"Courtney? Hello?"

Austin all but forgotten, she dropped the phone and ran the few feet to the bathroom door. "Serena? Are you all right?" When no answer came, she pounded on the door while viciously pulling on the knob and fought back the panic in her chest. "Answer me! Are you okay? Serena!"

She ran back to the bed and picked up the phone. "I... I heard a thump and she's not answering me. The bathroom door's locked. What do I do?"

"Can you kick down the door?" With no other solution to her fast ramble, his heart pumped hard in his chest. Wondering how long it would take to drive to where they were, he heard her put down the phone and yell for his sister again.

"Serena? Can you hear me?" Courtney pushed the tears away and sniffled. She stroked away the pressure in her chest and called to her again. "If you can hear me, Serena, move away from the door. I'm going to try to break in."

Courtney rattled the doorknob again with no luck and took two steps back. She raised her foot high and stomped with the flat of her foot as hard as she could. The cheap wood splintered and caved a little at the pressure. She backed up again and, with a rush of adrenaline, kicked it again. After two more attempts, the door finally gave way and Courtney pushed her shoulder against it to pry it open.

She found Serena on the floor, leaning against the outside of the tub, paler than a person had a right to be, and her eyes slanted open. The steam billowed out of the room as Courtney knelt beside her, out of breath. Her heart hammered against her rib cage at the sight of her friend, naked, and looking very much…

"Serena?" She took Serena's face in her hands, which shook so much it took her two attempts. Serena was warm. Dead bodies weren't warm, right? "Oh, God! Answer me!" She shook her a little until Serena laid a limp hand over Courtney's against her cheek.

"I…just…got dizzy, is all." Her voice was weak, and Courtney had to strain to hear her. Serena was taking in shallow breaths. Her scar appeared to be protruding from her skin. For a split second, Courtney thought it had a life of its own as it slowly moved with her short pants.

Courtney stood and took a towel from the rack behind the door. After wrapping Serena in it, which was as white as she was, she ran to the bed and pulled down the sheets. She went back to where Serena was slouched against the tub, noting she was getting some of her olive tone back. Thanking God silently, she assisted Serena to her feet with strength she didn't know she had, and helped her slump on bed. Courtney snatched the pills from Serena's bag that she had directed to give her if she got weak.

"Take this," she said to her quietly, as she placed the small blue pill on her tongue.

Serena swallowed it dry and took a sip of water from the cup she held at her mouth. She swallowed again and smiled as she tipped her head back.

Courtney set the cup down on the nightstand. "You scared the crap out of me. No more hot baths in ninety degree weather."

Serena smiled, her eyes still closed and, after only a moment, drifted off to sleep. Since her breathing seemed fine and her color was back, Courtney rose and tucked the sheet up around her friend, placing a kiss to her damp forehead. Reality had slammed its way into the room, giving her a reminder of what was to come. Courtney didn't like it, the pain or the fear. Tears burned her eyes. "You rest. I'll call Austin and--"

She had completely forgotten he was on the phone. Before she could even run to pick the up the receiver, she heard him screaming for her.

"Courtney!"

"It's okay, it's okay." She pushed calm into her voice. "She just got dizzy with all the steam and the heat. I gave her the pills she told me to and she's in bed now."

His sigh of relief seemed to penetrate through the phone line and into her. "Thank God."

"I'm so sorry. I should never have let her--"

"It's not your fault. God, if you weren't there…" He had no idea what would have happened. Better yet, he didn't want to think

64

about it. He ran his hand through his hair, fisting the strands, and sagged in his chair. This stranger with the voice of an angel may very well be one after all. "Are you okay?"

Tears rose in the back of her throat. They slipped from her eyes, her body shaking with adrenaline crash. She slipped back into the chair by the air unit before she fell. "I... I was so scared. I didn't know what to do." Her voice broke as her chest felt like it had cracked wide open.

It was as if Austin could feel her tears on his cheeks, no matter the distance between them, no matter how irrational. His hands clenched as he fought the helplessness, the urge to pull her into his arms and rock her until the tears passed. Maybe the emotional connection was because of Serena, their twin bond, or maybe Courtney had just scratched her way past his reservations all on her own, but he stopped fighting whatever was at play. She was hurting, and damn it, because she was he hurt too.

He let her sob for a few moments, knowing she probably needed a good cry after her shock. Austin understood. He and scared were interwoven bedmates. Fear for what Serena's end would be like. Hoping she would go quickly, so there wasn't pain. Praying she doesn't die at all so he could be with her always. Relentlessly thinking about what it would be like without her here at all anymore. The fear wraps itself around you, until you can't breathe anymore. Until you can't think of anything else.

Courtney sniffled and gave one of her many apologies. She was always apologizing.

"You have no reason whatsoever to be sorry. You deserve a thank you. For the millionth time since you met my sister, I'm real glad you're with her."

She said nothing in response. If not for her light breathing he would have sworn she'd hung up. Need and interest pulled at him, and he tried to push it away to the back of his mind. It was not possible to feel so much from and for someone he hadn't even seen. It was as if he craved her voice-- in his sleep, waking hours. Constantly.

"Tell me about your parents," she said finally after the long silence.

It was a request, not a demand, but it was something he hadn't expected her to ask. He sat back in his leather chair in the library and thought about all of Grams' stories on the front porch swing. "My mom was a music teacher. She taught piano. She used to play Fur Elise until you could hear every note in your sleep." He smiled as if he could still hear the melody. "My dad owned the shop I have now. He worshiped books, like I do. I bought the store back a few years ago and restored it, but you know that." He rubbed his jaw. "They were on their way back from one of my mom's concerts for her students when they lost control of the car around a curve."

He hadn't thought about this in such a long time. Grams should be the one telling her, since she was the master of story telling. He often wondered which memories were his own and which ones were what Grams' told him, to keep them alive for him and Serena. "We went to live with Grams after that. We were five, almost six."

Her sigh ran silkily up his spine. The very same way it had the other night. "I've never lost anyone that close to me," she said. "But then again, I've never had anyone that close either. I wonder which one of us is worse off."

Talk about struck stupid. He couldn't think of a reasonable response. The sheer simplicity of her statement left him speechless. It dawned on him that Serena was not only right about Courtney being hurt before, but that she had never been cared for either. Pain shot an arrow straight into a place he thought dormant. The need to comfort and hold her was so strong he struggled to get a hold of himself before he said something really asinine.

"Good night, Austin."

He closed his mouth with a snap and resisted the urge to keep her on the line for no apparent reason. "I'll see you tomorrow."

"Yes, tomorrow," she said, and then hung up with a quiet click.

He cursed that click, but tomorrow? He'd finally meet her.

She had tried to sleep. Courtney would often go on only a few hours of sleep at night if she was lucky. But she hadn't had any tonight. She had paced the small motel room for most of the night, whirling and running to Serena's side every time she made a sound.

Serena never stirred, not once. She slept peacefully, curled inside the blankets, her chest a rhythmic rise and fall. All the while Courtney guarded her like a hawk.

She'd called the motel manager earlier and explained about the bathroom door. He'd said, with restrained irritation, not to worry about it, it was an emergency after all. She'd hung up when he muttered something about insurance rates.

After that, she'd kept herself busy with disposing of the splintered wood fragments that had been left behind. She couldn't believe she'd done that. Kicked down a door! She couldn't remember her heart ever beating so fast, or ever having that much strength, nevertheless kicking down a door. She supposed all those action movies her father watched had paid off somewhat.

Her conversation with Austin shot to mind. She'd been itching to ask Serena about her parents, wondered what it was like to have people love you. Austin had told her right away when she'd asked, and his response only made the hollow void in her chest grow.

Laying down and trying to sleep, she thought about Serena and Austin, only five years old, and losing their parents. How hard it must have been, how close they seemed to be. She was starting to grasp the concept of a normal family from listening to Austin and Serena speak about theirs. Serena said that there was always love at Grams' house.

There was never love at the Morgan house. There was anger, and fear, and hate...but never love. She was starting to wish she had had just a piece of what her friend had growing up. To know you were loved so unconditionally like they were.

Courtney understood there had been something wrong with her father, because there was never anything she'd deliberately done to make him mad. He would go off on tirades and she didn't even have to be in the room. He was sick and needed help. She had been an innocent child. Her head, at least, understood that much. But the rest of her had to question what was so wrong with her that even her father couldn't love her. Wasn't that ingrained?

Her gift, as Serena called it, had been the devil's work to her father. But Serena had said her visions helped people. If Serena was right, how could something so evil make others feel good? Was it evil at all? She'd never realized how frightened she was of using her visions until she'd run away from her father. Living in

67

terror so long that it was hard to tell if he was lying or telling the truth.

Serena was telling the truth. Even when she was angry or frustrated, Courtney sensed honesty and consideration.

So many new changes, it was no wonder her head was spinning. Plus, if she allowed herself to admit this much, she couldn't ever remember being treated like a person. Like a human being with feelings and needs. Even Mrs. Meyers, bless her, was more of an overbearing mother going through the motions. Almost from the moment of her rescue, Courtney had begun doing things just because Mrs. Meyers had wanted her to. Because it was easier than arguing. And she was grateful for everything the woman had done.

A new panic crept up her spine and spread. They would be back to Serena's home in Willowsby tomorrow. She would get to meet Grams, with all her stories and gentle laugh. She would meet Jake, emerald eyes and addictive smile.

And Austin. Face to face with the voice that remained in her head long after they'd hung up the phone. She couldn't ever remember being so at ease with a man, except Dr. Maynard, and that took a long time. Maybe because Austin was a another half of Serena. Any part of her, even a miniscule part, had to be good. But there was something different about him. The way he always asked if she was okay. The manner in which he laughed. How he listened when she spoke, as if what she said was important to him. Or how effortless it was for her to talk to him. He never poked fun at her, or made her feel stupid.

The logical part of her brain battled with the fear forever there. She believed the good things, the compliments, Serena told her, understood that she believed them. But there were truths that couldn't be glossed over.

This curiosity Austin had with her would surely end tomorrow. She would accept it as she had everything else in life… as a fact. But in the mean time, she had Serena's friendship for as long as she had left, and hopefully, in time, Austin's too.

After the leaves stopped falling, when Serena was at peace, Courtney would go back to her corner of the diner in Arizona and wait for the bell on the door to ring. That was her place in life. That's where she belonged. She had her photos to remember these few months, and a friend who showed her how to love.

Walking back to the bed, she slipped between the sheets. Still asleep, Serena turned on her side and sighed. Courtney brushed a curl away from her friend's face and was surprised to find Serena was dreaming about her. Images fluttered and drifted. For a split second, Courtney saw herself through Serena's eyes, and for the third time that night, had to wipe away tears.

"I love you, too, my friend."

Chapter Five

Willowsby, Georgia, was lined with small independent shops in the center of town and had beautiful white pillared plantation homes on the outskirts with more acres of grass than Courtney had ever anticipated possible. Mimosa, cypress, and river birch trees bordered the yards, hanging with Spanish moss, giving the elongated driveways some privacy from the road. Weeping willow braches drooped low in a way that seemed to shield their patrons from harm, protecting their loved ones. Porches wrapped around the homes, processions of flowers in boxes adding splashes of color.

Serena had the top down on the Mustang, and Courtney breathed in the aromas. Cut grass. Damp, rain-scented air. Someone was grilling off in the distance. Children were running about in a way she was never allowed. Their laughter hung in the air, playing a sweet song in her ears. A gentle breeze cooled the humidity that clung and teased her skin in a soft caress.

There was so much to look at, so many feelings inside her she never underwent, that she could barely hold back tears. Everything was so idyllic, like a postcard. "Is this Heaven?" she mumbled.

Serena smiled, her tone wistful. "God, I hope so." She swerved the yellow car to the right and pulled into a long driveway that looked very much like all the others.

Once they rounded a curve, a house came into view. House was too meager a description. The place reminded her of an old plantation from *Gone With the Wind*. Black shutters were a stark contrast to the white siding, pillars positioned proudly near the open entryway. Mature trees wove through the property, providing shade.

Serena turned off the engine and briefly glanced to her left, where a smaller brick house was partially hidden and tucked back among the estate. It, too, had a porch, but the house was a ranch as opposed to the mansion in front of them.

Serena took a deep breath and, with much effort, tore her gaze away to smile at Courtney. "We're home."

"Yeah." She gaped at the towering fortress before her. "It's so beautiful. I've never seen anything like it."

The front screen door slammed, jerking her attention to an older woman in a long jean dress jumper with a white shirt and bare feet. She leaned against the pillar, a slight stoop to her gait, and smiled, making her observant hazel eyes light up. A piece of her long gray hair tumbled loose from its knot and danced gaily in the breeze. Grams.

A man with dark hair and wide shoulders bounded past her and toward their car. Serena jumped out and wrapped her arms around him. The biceps under his white T-shirt bunched as he drew her flush to his chest.

Courtney watched from her seat, unable to move for all the adoration that poured through them. His eyes were just like Serena's, golden brown and kind. He was taller than Serena by a head, but had the same high cheekbones and wide grin. It was his voice though, the rough southern drawl, that brought Courtney's memory back from all the conversations they had that week on the phone.

Austin. Her heart flipped.

"God, I missed you!" He held her at arms length and ran an assessing gaze down the length of her. Before long he pulled her to him again and held tight, kissing the top of her curls. Her arms barely went around the wide expanse of his back.

Courtney stepped out of the car, not wanting to intrude on their reunion, and reached into the backseat for their overnight bags. She stood with the car between them, not knowing what to do next. Her nervousness held a ball in her stomach and caused her hands to shake. When Serena rounded the car holding Austin's hand, Courtney's grip tightened on the bags she held as a shield between their bodies and hers.

Her against the world. Always.

"Austin, this is Courtney." Serena held out her free hand to take the bags from her. With nothing else to do with them now, Courtney wrung her hands together in front of her and stopped breathing when Austin's gaze collided with hers..

Austin lost all train of thought. All he saw was blue. Infinite eyes that looked back at him warily and unblinking. Like looking into a storm-tossed sea. There was a scar on her right eyebrow, drawing little attention. Her nose was pointed, making her features seem slightly off balance. Her skin was the color of butter cream, without a flaw to mar it. And her hair was silk. Silk. Golden and straight, framing an oval face and a small pink mouth.

He couldn't look away. He had conversed with her over the phone lines, her voice clinging to his mind every night for a week, but had never in his wildest imagination depicted her looking this... this...

"Austin?" Serena nudged him with her elbow. "What's wrong with you?"

"Hmm," he said, and with great regret, looked away to find out what Serena wanted. "Sorry," he replied, holding out his hand for the angel. "I'm Austin. It's a damn great pleasure to meet you." Silence stretched. He stared at his protruding hand she'd yet to take, rubbing away the knot forming in his gut and waiting for her to catch up.

"Hi," she murmured in that smoky, meek voice that ran chills up his arm. And finally, blessedly, she took his hand. It looked so small and fragile inside his. A pale contrast with his olive skin.

Courtney sucked in a harsh breath at the contact and skeptically glared into his golden eyes, wondering about the shocking current. But his eyes were Serena's eyes. They were as kind and just as open. Honest. His touch was warm, so invitingly warm where his hand held hers, and relief flooded through her system so quickly she had no time to prepare. Austin's personality poured out, not in flashes, but as a wave. Generosity and trust. Charm and wit. And something else, an emotion completely new to her. The heat caused her insides to swell and her heart to race and her knees to falter.

Serena rushed forward. "It's okay, Courtney. He's--"

"I know," she whispered, without taking her eyes off Austin's. "He's just like you." Then she smiled, her shoulders sagging in relief, and she turned to Serena. "He's just like you."

"Yes." She nodded. "Nothing will hurt you here."

Serena turned when the woman on the porch appeared by her side and wrapped her arms around Serena. "Grams!"

She seized Serena's face in her wrinkled hands. "It's good to have you home."

"It's good to be home." Serena noted the confusion on her brother's face as he continued to stare at Courtney in a way she'd never seen him look at another person before. "Courtney, why don't you go up to the house with Grams. She'll show you where to put your stuff while I have a chat with Austin."

"Come on, dear." Grams held out her hand for Courtney. "I'll pour us some sun tea and we can get acquainted."

Once the screen door snapped behind them, Austin tore his gaze away from those long shapely legs in the khaki shorts and turned to his sister. "What was that about?"

Serena heaved a weary sigh and walked to the porch steps to plop down, giving Austin no choice but to follow. She leaned on her elbows and stretched her legs in front of her. "Remember I told you that it seemed as if Courtney can see right inside my head?" He nodded his head, urging her to continue. "She can. She's psychic."

"What?" His tone was so flat it didn't even sound like a question.

"I'm serious. You have to hear her explain it. She didn't even know what it was, Austin. I don't think she knows its full power or its limitations yet. She was never allowed to explore it." She sat forward and ran a hand down her face. "Her father had her convinced that her gift was the devil, or some crap like that."

Austin mulled that over, remembering the way Courtney looked at him when she took his hand--the short intake of breath and the sudden alarm in her eyes, laced with fear. He'd never given much thought to the credence of psychics. His only experience had been the whack jobs on TV. There were a lot of unexplained things in the world, but he wasn't sure he believed in...that. Regardless, the latter part of Serena's statement registered, and his spine stiffened.

"Did he hurt her? Her father?"

Serena's mouth trembled open and tears filled her eyes. "He beat her bad, Austin." She sniffled and impatiently wiped away the tears. "She's got this scar on her back from where he broke skin when he hit her with a leather belt."

"Jesus!" He closed his eyes and bit down another string of curses. Delicate, soft-spoken Courtney. Broken. Bleeding. His hands fisted, his temples throbbed, and he sucked in a lungful of air before his head exploded.

"She's got other scars on her arms that I don't even know about. The worst of it is the head game he played. I just now got her convinced this ability is a gift. She freely talks with me now, but that took awhile too. Austin." She gripped his hand. Hard. "We have to be careful with her until she gets used to all this. I think...I think she believes she deserves what he did."

Rage was making a comeback. "That's crazy--"

"I know," she said, her tone distracted.

It was inconceivable how anyone could lay a brash hand on anything that looked like Courtney. Such...innocence. He'd known her a week by phone and five minutes by face, but she didn't seem to have a mean or belligerent bone in her body. Serena said they'd met in a diner. How long ago had Courtney broken free from the man?

Her eyes. Christ, those eyes. When her gaze had locked with his, there hadn't been an emotion on the spectrum that warred in all that blue. He had the strangest feeling he could spend hours looking into those eyes and lose--or find--himself.

"That's exactly how I felt."

He must've said his thoughts aloud. He shook his head, regressing back to where Serena had met Courtney. "Who was this diner lady? How long has she been working there?"

"Mrs. Meyers. After Courtney ran away from home, she gave Courtney the only home she ever knew. Other than keeping her safe, I don't think the situation helped her much." She sighed and stood to stretch. "When we were in that bar in Shreveport, this guy was all over her. I could tell, before we got him off of her, that she'd never even been kissed before. I don't even think she knows she's pretty."

No way in hell a woman as beautiful as Courtney didn't have experience, past lovers. "What? Women who look like that *know* they look like that."

"She doesn't." Serena glared at him, her tone a warning. "If you keep looking at her the way I just saw you doing, you'd better be prepared to take it slow." Her voice softened, losing the edge. "I know you'd never hurt anyone, Austin, but you could hurt her and never even know you did."

Too much shit shoved around in his skull. "I wasn't--"

"Yes, you were."

75

He lowered his head, rubbing the grit from his eyes.

She knelt down on the bottom stair between his knees and kissed his cheek. "One more hurt could put her back in that shell. She's not like everyone else."

He looked at his sister, into eyes that mirrored his own. He loved her so hard his bones hurt. "I'm not interested in dating right now. You come first."

She kissed his forehead. "You're interested." She pulled back with a knowing look similar to Grams'. "You should be. Courtney's a great person. I'm sick, Austin. There's nothing we can do about it. We knew this could happen someday. You have to put yourself first sometime."

Pain punched his chest. He wasn't ready to do this, not yet, so he rose and brushed imaginary dirt off the seat of his jeans. Denial, his friend. "Let's go in." He placed a smile on his face with great effort. "Grams has probably told that poor woman our life story by now."

Serena breathed out a laugh and followed him.

Courtney fell in love with Grams on the spot. They were seated together at her dining room table and sipping iced tea. The house was enormous, what little of it she'd seen. Sitting rooms and even a ball room. A spiral staircase. High ceilings and crown molding. Hardwood floors gleamed and polished. The style was a nice blend of old and new.

Courtney told her about every stop in each city along the way to Georgia, all the while, Grams sat with her chin in her hand and a warm smile on her face. Her hazel eyes would light up every now and then with something Courtney had said, and then she'd throw her head back and laugh.

That's where Serena got it from. That laugh.

Grams spoke about her grandbabies with pride, told her several stories of the things they did as children. Grams asked very few personal questions, but Courtney had a strange feeling she knew plenty without Courtney revealing anything.

Grams finished the last of her tea and set the glass down, staring at it as if in thought or measuring her words. "You have the sight, don't you?"

A tingle shot up her neck. "The sight?"

She smiled reassuringly. "The sight. Knowing things others don't. Seeing things others can't. Feeling things that aren't your feelings."

Courtney squirmed in her chair. "I...well, yes. But I wasn't trying to--"

"Oh no, dear. That's not what I meant." Grams' smile never faltered, calming the bit of trepidation. She placed her hands over Courtney's and studied her a moment, sadness seeping into her smile. "I see it in you. Your eyes show everything." Grams traced a finger around the scar on Courtney's forearm. She fought the urge to pull her arm away. "Someone hurt you before."

Courtney dropped her polite smile and replaced with a blank expression she had mastered over the years. "He did."

"He won't anymore. You start new now. Things will scare you, as they do, but nothing will hurt you like that again."

Courtney believed her. She had never met anyone that understood her feelings before, especially not in a positive light. She glanced at the small gold cross hanging from Grams' neck, and wondered if her father had been wrong about her visions, what else had he wrong about?

Before she had time to voice her doubts, Serena and Austin came in, the screen door snapping shut behind them. Austin smiled out of one corner of his mouth, all lazy southern charm, making her heart pound against her ribs.

He scrubbed a hand over his dark brown hair. "Did Grams talk your ear off?" He grinned fully when Serena smacked his arm. "What? What'd I say?"

Grams stood. "Oh, hush up. He's trouble," she said to Courtney with evident pride. "Me and my granddaughter are going to start dinner. Austin, why don't you show this dear where her room is, and around the rest of the estate, since we never got to that."

Austin leaned over Courtney's chair, his grin never wavering. He smelled like fresh grass and sunshine. "What do you say? Want a tour?"

There was no rational reason why her knees were weak, and how she managed to stand was a conundrum, but her smile came easily. He wasn't so intimidating after all. "Sure."

Courtney followed him out of the dining room and through the sitting room. Austin explained it was Serena's favorite room, and how she used to paint in there. The chairs were massive, and ranged in color from dark blues and greens, to creams and yellows. There was a deep sapphire rug covering the hardwood floor and made the room look all the more comforting.

She trailed him through the rest of the house, noticing the family portraits and open doorways. It was really beautiful. The windows were large and there were plenty of them. Natural light bathed each room. Grams had beautiful heavy drapes, in all colors and patterns, to frame them. Every room seemed to have its own theme, its own story. She listened intently to Austin's words, clinging to his southern accent, which drawled thick when he laid on the sarcasm. Courtney discovered, with great confusion, that she could sit for hours and listen to him talk. He had a way, without even knowing it, of easing every nerve out of her body. It was poetry.

He showed her the library, informing her that if she couldn't find him, he was probably in there. It was incredible. Her mouth gaped open as she stared at shelves and shelves of books. Floor to ceiling was covered with them. There was ivy in the little space left between the top of the shelves and ceiling, and the rest of the space was dark burgundy in color. The drapes were closed, masking another massive window. A lone leather chair and table with a small green lamp in the center of the space gave the illusion of privacy. The desk in the corner was littered with papers. A light on the computer monitor blinked rhythmically.

She slid her hand over the desk. Strength and determination pressed into her hand, remnants of old feelings from the craftsman.

"Jake made that for me a few years ago. Jake's... an old friend."

She nodded, already knowing that, and tucked a piece of hair behind her ear. His gaze followed the movement and then dropped to her mouth, making her self-conscious. "He does good work. It's lovely."

He didn't respond. Just stared at her mouth. Elongated seconds ticked by on a grandfather clock. She cleared her throat, and wondered what on earth he was looking at.

"Have you actually read all these books?"

That seemed to snap him out of his thoughts and he studied the room, as if avoiding her all together. "No, but most of them."

When they slipped from the room and mounted the winding staircase, he continued to talk as if nothing had happened, so she was almost able to put it in the back of her mind. Until she looked up and found his backside right in front of her.

She lost track of what he said then. His jeans were worn and low on his hips. The white T-shirt he wore tugged at his back muscles and biceps as they flexed with his movement. The shirt was coming out from where he had it tucked in to the waistband of his jeans, exposing a thin patch of tanned skin. She swallowed hard, hoping her face wasn't as red as it felt.

"So which do you prefer?" He whirled around.

When did they reach the top of the stairs? "Um, what?"

He chuckled. "That's okay. I'll put you in the room next to mine. It has the better view. All the rooms on the west side have balconies."

She didn't think the house had a bad view. She trailed him through the doorway of the fourth door on the left, into what she presumed was her room, and stopped short, dropping her jaw.

It was huge, like out of a magazine. The walls were a butternut cream, as were the bedding and drapes. Large plush pillows covered the queen-sized bed, with sheers hanging down from the canopy. The balcony had French glass doors, which he opened.

She drifted over the beige carpet and around the bed to stand behind him. He took the breath out of her lungs when he turned, bumping solidly into her. He gripped her shoulders to stop her from falling and her skin heated where they touched. Her gaze caught on the light shadow of a beard working his jaw. A strong jaw. Wide. She wondered if the whiskers would be rough or soft. His scent wrapped around her once more. Sunlight and lazy fields. He obviously spent a lot of time outdoors. She swayed closer, drawn by the safety and pull of...desire he transmitted.

"Sorry," he said, his voice rough and low. He cleared his throat.

Her gaze whipped to his. The golden brown of his irises was nearly swallowed by his pupils.

He dropped his hands and, as if unsure what to do with them, swiftly put them in his pockets. He was doing it again, looking at her mouth. Her heart punched fast in her chest and she found it hard to breathe. She couldn't get a good read on him. Just sparks here and there. Like the transmission was being intercepted.

He transferred his weight to his other leg and rubbed his neck. "Are you okay?"

"Hmm." She smiled, wanting his to return as well. Specifically the grin he'd given her downstairs earlier--the one that made the dimple poke out on his left cheek. "You ask me that a lot."

He laughed and snaked a hand through his hair, disrupting the strands. "I do, don't I?" He looked around the room, apparently searching for something else to say. And there came a smile, like he'd just remembered he should. Nervous and boyishly adorable. "Well, we should probably go back downstairs. I'm sure dinner is almost ready."

At dinner that evening, Serena found herself eating baked chicken with rice and steamed veggies, feeling like no time had gone by at all. It was as if she had never left. She sat next to Grams, who chatted away about her garden, and watched Courtney relax little by little as the conversation went on. Every once and awhile Austin would lean over and mumble something to her friend, causing Courtney to beam a girly grin as if she'd known him her whole life.

Broken as it may be, it did her heart good to see them together.

Grams' house even smelled the same, like aged paper and lemon dusting spray. The oak dining table in the heart of the large dining room was polished and well cared for. The crystal chandelier above them was without a scrap of dust, which always amazed her. Light fragments speckled over the cream colored wall paper from the window. In the corner, a china cabinet, carefully arranged, held all of Grams' stunning pieces she'd insisted on using for tonight. She couldn't see it just now, but on the other side of the wall, she knew their family portrait hung in the same spot it always had. Her mother and father with an effortless smile, holding her and her brother in their lap when they were four. Time took the opportunity away to have another portrait done.

"Enough of that," Grams said firmly, as if knowing Serena's thoughts. "We need to discuss your birthday next week." She folded her napkin next to her plate and linked her fingers together in front of her.

This would be her last birthday. The realization slammed into her hard. She wouldn't live to have another birthday. She and Austin rarely liked fussing over the day, but neither had the heart or strength to complain this time as a distressing look passed between the two of them.

"I didn't know you had a birthday coming up." Courtney set her fork down. "How old will you both be?"

"Twenty-nine," her and Austin said simultaneously and laughed. Serena looked at Courtney. "On the eighteenth."

"That's Saturday, isn't it?"

"Yes, it is," Grams avowed, matter-of-fact. "And, my new dear, we will plan a party for them."

Serena and Austin groaned at Grams' declaration, causing Courtney to smile fully. "Now, you know this is no surprise party, because I'm telling you about it. Courtney and I will arrange something nice." She wrung her hands together at the thought of a new project and looked at Courtney expectantly.

"Okay, Grams." Courtney sighed, completely comfortable with the kind old woman. "But I've never planned a party before, so I will not be responsible for any disasters that arise."

Austin met her gaze. "I somehow doubt anything you have a part in could be a disaster."

Her smile dimmed. "Thank you."

"You're welcome."

Serena pressed her lips together. Not interested huh? Yeah, right. "When's your birthday, Courtney?"

All amusement left her friend's face and was replaced by a closed expression. Her small hands began to fidget with a napkin. "I don't really celebrate my birthday, so…"

Before Serena could stop him, Austin was pushing for an answer. "You must tell us. We'll just do a quiet dinner or something."

"Austin, its okay." Serena said at the same time that Courtney muttered "I don't have one."

The shocked silence stretched so long that Serena couldn't take it. "He never told you what day you were born?" How could a father not acknowledge his daughter's birthday?

"No." Courtney sighed, as if irritated by the conversation. "We never celebrated my birthday. Mrs. Meyers would bake me a cake on the anniversary of when she found me, but…" She shrugged as if it didn't matter to her.

Austin clasped his hand over hers. "We'll pick a day to use as your birthday then." He glared at his sister with disbelief, still gripping Courtney's hand. He had no idea how to respond, what to say, so he searched his sister's face for an answer. She just looked back at him with sadness and shook her head. Courtney attempted to pull her hand from his, so he squeezed it gently and let go.

Grams stood to clear the table. "Well, my dear, most people don't get to choose what day their birthday falls on. You pick whatever day has significance for you. That day will never go uncelebrated in this house."

Courtney was humbled. "Thank you."

Serena rose to help Grams clear the table.

Austin couldn't move. He wracked his brain for a solution, a way to fix what damage her father had done, realizing it was far worse than Serena had thought. There were so many things Courtney must've locked away, atrocities he feared were only the tip of the iceberg and went beyond physical abuse.

An idea began to emerge. He waited for his sister and grandmother to leave the room and then turned to her. "What city were you born in?"

She offered him a side-glance laced with confusion and a trace of fear. "I didn't mean to ruin dinner."

"Hell, Courtney." She was killing him. He scooted his chair closer. "You didn't ruin dinner."

She turned her face away from him so he couldn't see her expression.

He got the distinctive impression she didn't believe him, so he went back to his plan. Actions spoke louder than words. "Do you know what city and state you were born in?"

She sighed as if giving up. "Ogden, Utah."

He nodded his head, putting that in his memory for later. "And how old are you now?"

"Twenty- seven," she said, without a hint of emotion.

He resisted the urge to seize her hand again, but the wedge of pain in his throat kept him still. Weariness and pain filled her eyes.

"I just have one last question." She nodded her head, still not looking at him. "What's your last name?"

She smiled then, not quite reaching her beautiful blue eyes, and looked right into his, trapping him to her for a fleeting moment. "Morgan."

She stood to clear her dishes.

He itched to touch her.

Grams returned through the doorway and ordered her to sit down. "Guests in my house don't clean." She took Courtney's plate from her and made a shooing gesture with her hand. She swept back into the kitchen and out of sight.

Courtney, later that night, rapped lightly on Serena's bedroom door across the hall. She poked her head into the soft pink room and found Serena on the bed with a pile of tissues. Her eyes were red and her nose pink.

Courtney closed the door behind her and sat next to her friend on the crimson and white quilted spread. "What's going on?"

Serena shook her head violently, causing her dark curls to bounce and tears to spill into her lap. "I was just worrying about what to say to Jake tomorrow." She wiped her nose. "Before we even started dating all those years ago, he was my friend. It broke his heart when I left and now I'm back, only to tell him…"

Courtney let her words hang as she traced the swirl pattern of Serena's quilt with her finger. "I would just tell him the truth."

Serena smiled half-heartedly as she reached for a tissue on the nightstand. "I know, but it's hard trying to figure out his reaction to me coming home and to this. He never understood why I left. He blamed himself. It wasn't him at all, and I could never make him get that. We haven't spoken in like three years."

A late summer breeze blew Serena's white sheer curtains from their spot against the window seat. A row of porcelain dolls watched over them from a shelf. There were no sounds but the crickets chirping and Serena's breathing.

But the voices, the memories, in Courtney's head, were loud. "He'll forgive you." She looked back at Serena to find her expression blank. "He has no choice, and he'll be upset, but not for the reasons you think. He'll forgive you."

"God, I hope you're right." Serena searched Courtney's face for untruth, knowing she wouldn't find any. Sadly, she didn't think Courtney even knew how to lie. "Did you need something?"

"I'm sorry. I didn't mean to interrupt." Courtney stilled her hands and bit her lip. "It's just, well, we're going to church tomorrow and I've never been to church. I don't know what to wear."

"God doesn't care what you look like." The troubled expression didn't leave her friend's face, though. "I usually wear a light sundress." She rose and moved toward the closet. "I'll find one in here for you. Monday, before we go to Austin's store, we'll go shopping for some clothes for you. You hardly have anything. A woman should have a plethora of clothes." She chuckled as she fished through her closet.

"I don't have much money..."

"Oh, don't worry about that." She dismissed that with a wave of her hand. "Hey, what will I need it for, anyway?"

Serena twisted around. A haze of tears swam in Courtney's eyes. Crap. "I'm sorry, that was...bad humor. Austin and I both have a lot of money from the insurance after Mom and Dad's accident. Neither of us knows what to do with it." But Serena didn't think Courtney would be any more comfortable with a handout than she was around strangers. "We'll talk with Austin tomorrow," she amended. "He could probably use help at his store if you're concerned about money."

"Okay."

"When I'm done with that mural, probably by next weekend, he'll reopen. You could waitress at the coffee counter or work the register in the gift shop."

"Okay," Courtney replied again, appearing to feel better.

Serena resumed fishing through the closet. "Ah, here we go. This will fit you." She held up a light blue sundress with white daisies. "It goes with your complexion too. You can keep it. I never wear it."

Courtney started to say thank you when Serena whirled around to the closet again. "You'll need shoes. Let's see." She rummaged through a shelf. "Here we go. My white sandals should work. I had many compliments about my legs while wearing these babies."

Courtney chuckled. "That was you, though. I'll just look like... like me."

Serena raised her brows as she shut her closet door. "Woman, I've told you, you are beautiful." Serena read disbelief on her face, so she added, "Haven't you noticed the way Austin looks at you?"

"No," she mumbled, with apparent confusion.

Serena fixed a slight smile on her face. "You will." No sense in frightening her more, so Serena let the topic drop. She plopped down on her bed and crossed her legs. "After church, we'll come back here and have lunch. I'll tell Jake...what's going on. Austin said he'd walk you through Grams' garden while I talk with him."

Courtney nodded and, acting as if she'd been dismissed, paced to the door, eyeing her new dress. After pausing with her hand on the knob for a few moments, she turned. "It really will be okay. With Jake, I mean."

Courtney lay on her bed, thinking about this church they would be going to and how many ways she could embarrass herself. Her body had grown used to her sleeping schedule years ago, but tonight she was craving the solace of dreaming. She groaned and looked at her clock again on the nightstand. How could it only be two in the morning? She rolled onto her back and draped her arm over her face.

Frustrated, she listened to the sounds of the crickets quietly chirping and tried to make her body relax. Wind chimes tinkled off in the distance and...laughter? Was that...children laughing? She rose and adjusted the ankle-length white nightgown Serena had given her while her clothes were being washed and made her way to the double French doors. She had left them open, enjoying the smells of summer.

Barefoot, she stepped out onto the balcony and gazed over the back of Gram's estate. Weeping willows lined the horizon, and running through the center of the yard was a path, surrounded by flowers and bushes that danced when the breeze picked up again, taking the hem of her nightgown with it. Water fountains and other statues lay peacefully in the night, guarding the beauty. A porch light was on by the brick house off to the left, where oaks encased the property. Beyond them, she could barely make out a red barn.

There it was again, that laughter.

Her eyes scanned the yard, squinting through the dark shadows to figure out where the laughter was coming from. It was so faint, like it clung to the breeze and lived off it. She glanced to her right to see if Austin's doors were ajar, to see if he heard it too, but his doors weren't open, and his light was off. She hadn't heard him come up from the library while she laid awake, so she determined he was still locked away in there downstairs.

She eyed the gardens again. Curiosity getting the better of her, she edged away from the balcony and headed out of her room.

Jake strolled out of the barn sometime after two A.M., his body physically exhausted but his mind in overdrive. All he'd do if he tried to crash was lie awake and think of Serena, tucked in her bed just across the way, so he decided on a walk to clear her from his mind. Not that it would work.

There was never an escape in his mind. Only her.

Hadn't he stood on his porch not two hours ago, watching her bedroom window until she turned out the light? Having her home only resurfaced all the pain he'd struggled to ease these past three years. It was killing him. And damn it, he wanted to go over there and kiss all sense out of her like he used to do, when things were normal. When his world was right.

Only an acre away and it seemed like miles. He pictured her in her room, the shades she never closed, those eerie dolls that always seemed to be staring at him, the pale pink child-like walls she refused to paint. And that bed, the one with her in it.

He was an idiot to let her get to him after all this time.

His boots made no sound in the grass while he walked. They used to take a walk together in the evenings like this, hand in hand. Her laugh would erupt from that full, lush mouth at something he'd said. She would throw her head back with the gesture, exposing her long neck and smooth olive skin.

He could always make her laugh.

He didn't know why she was back in Willowsby, but he knew it wasn't for him. And that was just fine. He didn't miss her scent of vanilla, or that damn laugh of hers, and especially not those golden brown eyes that clouded over…

He halted as movement to his right caught his attention.

Now he knew he was seeing things. An angel. A ghost?

No. Not possible.

A woman floated--no, not floated, walked--across the field not twenty yards in front of him, golden blonde hair shielding her face. A long white nightgown touched the tops of her bare feet and flowed with her movement. The thin straps exposed creamy white skin, and the gown was fitted enough to hint at curves underneath.

He shook his head, rubbing the back of his neck. Austin's dream woman must be confused, as she was appearing for Jake now. While he was awake, no less. He looked away, knowing for sure when he turned back that the sleep-deprived hallucination would be gone.

She wasn't.

And why couldn't he move?

Her face tilted toward the stars, bathed in moonlight, and then turned to him, as if calling him. Blue eyes wavered a moment, appearing startled to find him there.

His feet moved closer, her gaze trekking his progress. "Am I dead?"

She smiled, an endearing, comforting lift of her lips. She responded in a voice so calm it ran bumps along his skin. "I don't think so, seeing as you're standing there, talking to me."

He didn't answer, because now his mouth didn't work. He just stood there like a moron, trying to figure out where she came from and who exactly she was.

"You're Jake?" she questioned, almost with certainty, as if she didn't even need to ask.

He nodded. "How do you know me?"

"Serena said you have eyes the color of emeralds in the sunlight."

He jerked at her name, bringing him back to reality with whiplash.

"She was right about your eyes."

Gradually, his brain began working again and he took a couple steps in her direction, sealing the distance but a foot between them. "You're her friend? The one who traveled home with her?"

She nodded.

Austin had said she was innocence and fantasy wrapped together. Jake grinned and looked down the length of her. Yep, that would be the right description for her. He felt no pang of longing, no greedy lust, but he could appreciate beauty when he encountered it. She was quite lovely standing there, looking like a heaven sent.

He held out his hand. "Jake, as you know. Nice to meet you."

She took a moment's hesitation, then slipped her small pale hand in his. "Courtney. It's good to meet you too."

"So what brings you out so late?"

"I heard children laughing." She turned her head to glance out at the estate.

Goosebumps skittered up his arms and the hairs on his neck stood erect. She stood there, staring at him with those eyes, and he realized she was serious. "Austin says he can hear laughter sometimes too. I never could. He thinks it's..."

"The three of you as children," she finished for him, causing him to take a step back in shock.

"Um…yeah." Who exactly was this woman? He swore she climbed inside his head and started digging around. "I couldn't sleep either," he said stupidly.

"You're a nice man." By the vex of her brows this came as a surprise to her. She tilted her head, like she was rummaging in his brain again. "Serena also said that your grin got her every time. Now I know what she meant."

His "grin" slipped as his heart twisted behind his ribs. "She said that?" He paused, unsure what to make of the knowledge. "Does she talk about me often?"

She pressed her lips together in thought. "She thinks about you more than she speaks of you. It hurts her too much."

What did that mean? He stared numbly at her, getting the distinct impression she *could* read minds, and wondering why he was inclined to believe her. He swallowed hard, backtracking. Wait. Serena was hurting? She's the one who left him.

"She'll tell you why."

His gaze whipped to hers. This entire encounter would be creepy if she wasn't so...ethereal. Hell. Maybe he was dreaming.

"She'll tell you." As if she knew what he was fighting inside himself, had been fighting for years, she smiled with a trace of sadness. "Goodnight."

She walked to Grams' house, leaving him to stand there and gawk for long after she had disappeared inside.

Sleep was overrated anyway.

Chapter Six

Saint Gabriel's Church looked just like an old farmhouse on the outside, except for the tall steeple and bell that chimed every hour. People were crammed by the truckload inside, so there was no escape from the humidity and took all available air. Yet the congregation sang loudly and said phrases in unison. Hands were raised in praise. Some fanned themselves, while others just pulled on their collars with little relief.

Most of all, Courtney hadn't gone up in flames when she'd walked through the door. After her childhood, part of her expected that.

From her seat in between Austin and Grams, she followed suit as everyone rose again. In the thirty minutes she'd been there, she had stood up, sat down, and knelt at least three times each. She didn't understand it, but she mirrored those around her so she didn't draw attention.

The priest said, "Go in peace," and then music played again. People followed after him and gathered just outside the door.

She stayed close to Austin, no longer having the sense of contentment once outside. It was odd, the immediate comfort she had the second she'd entered the church. It had an old and unique scent, like something from another time. The place gave her the feeling that warm caring arms were wrapped tight around her, protecting her from the outside world. Though she understood none of it, she welcomed it openly.

Austin walked over to where Serena was talking to the priest. Courtney followed.

"Well, Miss Serena Edwards, it's good to see you back in Willowsby. How have you been?" Father Mike was a short man, with a thick head of short auburn curls and a robust voice that carried.

Serena glanced briefly at her brother and back to the priest. "I was wondering if I could set up a time with you next week to talk over some things?"

"Sure, sure," he responded without missing a beat. "Anything wrong?"

Courtney silently watched as Serena played over things in her head, warring with herself on an honest tactic. Jake was on her other side listening intently to every word and she hadn't told him the truth yet.

"Just want to talk."

The priest smiled politely and shook hands with an older couple as they passed by. "Sure. Friday good for you?"

"That's fine. Early afternoon?" She nodded when he agreed. "I'll see you then."

"And who is this?" Father Mike turned to Austin.

Austin smiled to reassure Courtney and drew her close to his side. "This is Courtney Morgan. She and Serena are close friends."

"Well, okay!" Enthusiasm boomed his voice. "How did you like the service?"

When she couldn't find her voice, Austin chimed in for her. "This was her first time to church. I'm afraid she was just a bit nervous."

The priest's lips twisted, skeptical. "No need to be nervous with God. Come by the rectory with Serena on Friday. We can chat and get to know each other a bit."

Courtney sensed sincerity and understanding from him, and slowly slipped out from underneath Austin's arm. Even though she liked it there and they seemed to fit like an interlocking puzzle, she wanted to stand on her own. "I will, thank you."

Jake winked at her. She fought a grin. He was anxious himself about talking with Serena again, but took the time that morning to make goofy faces at her or wink to put her more at ease.

She meandered over to him when Grams and Serena started walking to the car. "Still think I'm a ghost?"

He laughed and rubbed his hand over the top of her head to muss her hair. "And how would you know I thought that, darlin'?" His green eyes lit up and brightened at their inside joke from last night.

She shrugged her shoulders teasingly. "Maybe because you asked if you were dead."

Austin watched the two of them flirt back and forth and tried to hide his annoyance. They'd only met an hour ago and already she was smiling as if she'd known him forever.

Jealousy reared its ugly head.

No. Not jealousy. He didn't get jealous. Did he? He never had before. And Christ. This was Jake, for the love of grits. "Can anyone join this conversation?"

Courtney pulled on the hem of her knee-length daisy dress, and it took all his willpower not to stare at her shapely legs. When she bent over to adjust her sandal, he caught a glance at the top of two creamy white breasts before she stood completely upright again. He pinched his eyes closed as if he could unsee the beautiful image. The muscles in his jaw twitched.

Jake cleared his throat. "Innocent or fantasy this time?" He slid his gaze sideways to Courtney as if Austin had no idea to what he referred.

Austin shot him a lethal look. "Shut-up." Then he smiled at the joke, despite himself, and raked a hand through his hair.

"It's her," Jake whispered. "Dream woman. It's her."

Austin sucked in a breath and looked at Courtney with new purpose. Could it be? Her shape was familiar, though in his reoccurring dream, he'd only seen her from behind. The hair was definitely close, long loose strands of wheat colored tresses.

No. No, things like that were fiction, like the books lining his shelves. Woman didn't leap from dreams he'd had his whole life and into reality.

Courtney stood between them, confusion wrinkling her forehead.

Austin resisted the urge to kiss her there and shook his head. "Jake here is just being a dumbass."

"Me? Never."

The tension erased from her face and they began to tread back to the car again when Austin remembered the start of Jake and Courtney's conversation. "What were you two talking about before anyway? Ghosts and stuff?"

Courtney's amused eyes met Jake's. He grinned at her in turn and they laughed, leaving Austin out of the joke.

Serena clenched her cup of tea while she sat on the davenport in the formal living room. Jake looked at her intently. She would have to spit it out sometime, but the words just wouldn't come. One cannot start a sentence by saying, *Hey, it's good to see you after so long. By the way, I'm dying.*

Damn those gorgeous green eyes of his.

"You used to be courageous. What happened? California make you soft?"

"I'm sorry, Jake."

The heartbreak in her tone shut him up. He reclined in the spot across from her, draping his arm over the back of the sofa, and lifted his brows.

She stared into her cup and sighed. "I'm sorry I left the way I did. And that we haven't talked since." She swallowed with difficulty. This was harder than she thought. She was living on borrowed time, and if she was going to spill all, she may as well start with the part where she'd stomped on his heart, and any plans he'd made for them.

He had no expression now as he meticulously set down his cup, his spine rigid. "You came home to tell me that? Three years too late, don't you think, princess?"

God, she hated when he called her that. Worse in that rehearsed voice so unlike her Jake. Her hands wouldn't quit shaking, so she set down her cup before it dropped. Jake was the most laid back person she had ever known. He'd only taken that tone with her once before and she shook that memory away. "I'm even sorrier I made you a cynic."

He rose. "You didn't make me anything but a fool."

This was going nowhere. She needed to tell him. Stop beating around the bush and just do it. The same as she had with Austin over the phone. So when Jake turned his back on her, she stood and rounded him. She gripped his hands, rough and calloused from years of working with them, and stared at their linked fingers. She pressed her lips together and looked at those emerald eyes to bolster her courage.

"Don't do this to me again, Serena. I couldn't take it a second time."

Every ounce of will drained out of her. His eyes, so earnest and loving, pleaded. She fought for control of her emotions. "We can't ever be together that way, and I won't promise to never leave again, but I will always be your friend. We have been since the beginning."

Raw pain cut his gaze. He abandoned her hands to step back, leaving hers cold. It had to be this way. They couldn't be more than friends again. Not ever. Her leaving was final this time. But when he looked at her like that, like it had just been yesterday they'd made love, it made her want and crave all over again.

"I'm sorry, Jake. For everything."

"You don't want me anymore?" He kept his back to her, his voice hollow.

She lied. It made her stomach burn and ripped the breath from her lungs, but she had to. She had to lie to keep his heart safe. "No."

He put his head down in uncharacteristic surrender. "And you came back to tell me that." He whirled on her. "I kinda figured out you didn't want me when you moved across the country. I didn't wait for you, Serena. It's been three years, and you come home with an 'I'm sorry,' and expect everything to be as it was?"

"No," she said, with definition. With finality. "I don't want us as we were. I want you to forgive me. And I want my friend back."

He tore away again and began to prowl, the way he always did when his nervous energy was left unresolved. She watched his stick-straight spine, and then watched it dissolve. It nearly broke her.

Then, out of nowhere, he picked up a photo from the coffee table, running his finger along the glass. His gaze grew distant as if lost in the past. She knew which picture it was--the three of them in the field at the edge of the yard, smiling with their arms around each other in front of Grams' lilac bushes when they were eleven years old.

"This is what you want?" He turned the photo for her to see, holding it like an accusation. "Five short years later you were in my arms in my parents' barn." He made an unrecognizable sound in his throat and shook his head. "But you want this?" The photo shook in his hand.

She paused a moment, wondering where her once loving friend and passionate lover had gone, hoping her gaze was as steady as she willed it to be. Three years could do a lot of damage. "Yes."

95

Jake carefully set down the picture and faced her. The change in him was so drastic she froze. He'd shut himself off. Completely. "Fine. Welcome home."

"**A**nd this is where Jake fell and broke his arm." Austin motioned to a large oak with a grin. He followed it up with a joke, though damn if he could remember which one.

The tour he was giving Courtney took both their minds off of what was going on inside the house. He remembered the panic, the pain, the sorrow deep inside when he heard Serena over the phone that night. Had it really been only a week ago? And Jake was going through it all now.

Courtney's laughter brought his head around. He never thought he heard a sound so sweet in his whole life. Her eyes were a brighter blue. Her small pink lips quivered.

"I can actually picture it in my head."

He froze, grin widening. "It was a sight."

And so was she.

Her mouth. Damn, he could watch that mouth for all eternity and never tire of it. Whether she was biting down on her lip in nervousness or when they were spread wide in laughter, it...gutted him. Stirred a pining so long forgotten he thought himself incapable. He'd had women before. Several, in fact. A few he'd even been a little serious about. But no one, not a one, had him enthralled like Courtney. She was a breath of fresh air and a punch to the gut.

She started drifting back to the house, so he followed in tow.

"Do you think we gave them enough time?" Courtney stopped at the back door.

"I hope so." He must have scared her, judging by the panicked look on her face, so he squeezed her shoulder. "It'll be okay, promise."

They found Serena and Jake in the living room, hands on their hips, heads down. Tension crackled the air.

"How are you doing?" Austin asked Jake. Serena would always come first, and telling Jake would've been hard on her, but she'd had some time to come to grips with the scenario. Jake, on the other hand, had to feel like he'd been clocked by a chair. Three

96

years may have passed, but Austin knew he'd never gotten over her.

Courtney went to stand by Serena and took her hand for support.

Jake shrugged. He wasn't crying, yelling, or leaving. If Jake Warner had one weakness in this world, Serena was it. He should be a smoldering pile of ash right now. Hell, Austin had known for a week and he still battled not to lose his shit. The fact Jake was breathing at all meant his sister hadn't delivered the news.

"Austin," Serena warned.

"You didn't tell him?"

"Whoa, wait a minute." Jake raised his hands at Austin's tone. "She apologized. There's no need to get upset with her. We're talking things out."

"You didn't tell him?" he bellowed again, ignoring Jake. "You knew it was unfair for me to keep this from him."

Serena's eyes fluttered closed as she drew a breath. "I--"

"Tell me what?" Jake ordered, growing more confused and angry by the minute. He positioned his hands on his hips and looked between the two of them, finding no answers. Cold fear crept up his spine.

Serena, eyes wet, tore her gaze away from the two men she cared for most in this world and froze when she spotted Courtney. She sat on the floor between the davenport and the coffee table, stiff as a board, white as a sheet. Her vacant eyes indicated she wasn't even in the same room.

"Courtney?"

Austin followed Serena's gaze and did a double take. He darted across the room and huddled down next to Courtney. She was trembling so badly he thought she'd break, her hair a curtain around her face. What in the hell happened? She looked...Hell. She looked catatonic.

"Are you okay?" She didn't answer, not even to blink. "Jesus." He looked up at the other two in the room, one looking very confused and the other very concerned.

Remaining where he was, he kept his tone cool and low. "Serena, take Jake for a walk and tell him what's going on."

"But, Austin--"

"Now," he clenched through his teeth. Panic clawed at his chest. "I'm taking her upstairs."

Austin waited until he heard the door close and then tentatively placed his hand on her back. She flinched. He briskly rubbed his face with hands not so steady and looked at her again.

"It's Austin, Courtney." She gave him no response, other than a blink, but that was a start. Had she gotten like this because he'd yelled? Was she in sensory overload from her gift?

He reached up to pull her hair back from her face, but hastily drew his hand back again. Sighing in frustration, he leaned back on his heels and wished he knew what the hell to do.

Going on instinct, he scooped her up into his arms, and headed through the room, toward the stairs. Her head fell limply on his shoulder, cocked down so he had yet to see her face. Her dress had hiked high up her legs, and he focused on a jagged white scar on her inner thigh. He tore his gaze away, berating himself for feeling that pull of longing for wanting her, and holding down fury for the mark he found in the process.

He set her down on the guestroom bed, curled on her side, and went to grab a blanket from the chair in the corner. She wasn't quaking when he placed it over her, so he sat down carefully next to her. Drawing the hair away from her face, he found tears drying on her cheeks.

His chest squeezed. "Please don't cry."

When fresh tears came in their place, he clenched his fists. How was it women could bring men down to sniveling cavemen with tears?

She sniffled and wiped her cheeks as if irritated. "I'm sorry." She sat up with her back against the headboard, quickly shying away from him or any comfort he offered. "I'm so embarrassed. The emotions were too much. Too many. I couldn't switch them off."

If this was a gift, she should return it. Regardless, gift or not, after seeing her today, he wouldn't wish that nightmare on anyone. "I shouldn't have yelled like that, especially to her. That probably didn't help."

"You were upset about keeping Serena's secret from Jake. It's understandable." He'd give his right arm to hear her laugh again, to remove the haunted torment from her voice. "And it wasn't

98

really the yelling. Well, maybe a little. It was the pain. In my head. My chest. So crushing. It was coming off of all three of you, rebounding."

If her psychic connection was this strong, how had she coped before? He wanted to ask her about her scars too. Instead, he froze because she finally looked at him.

He forgot his own name for a second when the vast blue of her eyes searched his, tears clinging to her pale lashes. Small smudges of mascara left tiny black marks under her eyes.

Their hips brushed when he lifted a tissue to wipe at the smudges. Only the tissue didn't make it. His hand halted mere centimeters from her face. Such a beautiful face. Her eyes widened, aware. He brushed a knuckle down her cheek, the need to touch her so bad it hurt.

At her sharp intake of breath, his gaze fell to her mouth. It was his undoing. He'd been watching those lips since her first words to him, wanting to know what they tasted like. Waiting to see if they were as soft and giving as they appeared.

He inched closer, closing his eyes and stopping just before his lips touched hers. "I've wanted to kiss you since I first laid eyes on you." Before really. Since their first phone conversation, if he was being honest. Meeting her in the flesh only sealed the deal.

"You have?" Her warm breath feathered his jaw.

It was torture, being this close, and yet he held back. For a thousand and one reasons, he held back. "Yes."

Her nose brushed his. "I've never…"

"I know," he muttered, and cut her off when he took her mouth in surrender. A man could only withstand so much.

She was softer than he expected. Her lips were closed in a sweet and almost awkward brush, and he knew he should've left it that way. Given her time to adjust. Because that innocence he'd read from her? It was a tangible fact. But he had to taste, coveting her, he had to taste. Gently, he nudged her lips with his tongue, running it along the seam, and she willingly opened.

It was as if there was nothing under him. The bottom dropped out. His hands went into her hair and cradled the back of her head. She tasted like saline and heartache. She smelled like soap and virtue.

She was so supple and giving, tentatively touching her tongue to his in a languid glide, he couldn't take it. He tore away. A mistake, for he was already craving her again. He pressed his forehead to hers, not knowing how to apologize for doing what felt too good to apologize for.

Before he could say anything, she brushed her lips across his cheek. "I'm not sorry, so don't be." Then she humbled him completely by kissing his forehead and looking into his eyes. "Was it that bad?"

"What?" Her gaze was... lost. As if she really had no idea she just pulled the floor out from underneath him. He pressed both his palms to her cheeks. "No. That kiss was many things, bad not being one of them." Understanding flowed back to her expression. "As a matter of fact, I better get out of here before it happens again and I can't stop."

Her lips curved, still a little unsure, and his heart rolled over. She had so many different varieties of smiles that he didn't think he'd seen the same one twice. He could spend the rest of his life trying to pull one from her. That lone thought stole every breath from his lungs, trying to remember the last time, if ever, he felt this way.

"Why are you still here then?" she asked coyly, as if trying to be playful and not understanding how. Effing adorable.

"My legs don't work just now."

She breathed a laugh. "You could stay in here while I take a nap? I'm tired all of a sudden."

Before he could respond, she lied down and curled up with her head in his lap. In moments she slipped into sleep, long pale lashes fanning her cheeks, her clean scent enveloping him, and he wondered how long she'd stay like that.

Austin was kinda hoping for forever.

"First, you're going to tell me what's wrong with Courtney, and then you're going to explain what that outburst with Austin was about."

Serena sat on a bench at the far end of the garden and dropped her hands in her lap. Sunlight bathed her olive skin, brought out the natural highlights in her dark hair. Regal, she glanced ahead as if fortifying herself.

Jake ignored how tired and scared she looked and concentrated on his anger instead.

She brushed a strand behind her ear. "There's a lot about Courtney we don't know, that I don't yet know." She paused, as if weighing her words. "She was severely abused by her father up until the age of seventeen when she then got the courage to run away. She ended up in this small town where she remained until we met." Her head dropped in her hands, causing her dark curls to mask her face. "While on the road with her I discovered she has some sort of psychic ability. She's afraid of it because she was ridiculed for having it, but she's getting better. I just hope what happened in there didn't regress everything."

He swallowed hard, images of a pale, trembling Courtney on the floor shoving to mind. No one deserved abuse, least of all a child by her own parent's hand. Anger subsided as fresh pain and empathy took its place. He'd known the woman under twenty-four hours, but she was a genuine oracle. If her facial expressions didn't give away her every emotion, her gentle demeanor said aplenty. Heart on her sleeve, that woman. No one was that good an actor.

He didn't try to understand the psychic thing, didn't want to. He wasn't as skeptical as most and even if he was, Courtney could shred doubt. It sure answered his questions that had plagued the back of his mind. Those blue eyes saw right through him the other night. That mouth told him things she couldn't possibly know. And then there was the strange tie to Austin, the way he'd dreamed about her for years. A higher power was at work here.

Serena's voice broke through his thoughts. "I'm sick, Jake."

He met her golden gaze, caught between past and present. "We can go back to the house so you rest." He'd almost forgotten how tired she could get sometimes because of her condition.

"No." She shook her head, frustrated. "I mean, I'm real sick."

He watched her for a split second, fighting panic. Dread was beginning to pound his temples. His gaze darted to the scar on her chest. It barely showed above the neckline of her mint green dress.

He remembered the last time someone said those words to him. *Serena's sick.* Austin had bounded across this very garden, tears

101

streaming down his face. Jake had known before Austin had gotten the words out, and they'd both raced to the hospital.

They'd spent forever in the waiting room for someone to come tell them any little bit of information. He'd realized then his love for Serena. The true, deep, tragic kind one never gets over. When the doctor had come in after surgery to tell them it had gone well, Jake had rushed outside, picked a handful of stupidly cheerful tulips from the courtyard of the hospital, and dodged back into her room in critical care. It was hours before she'd woken up from the anesthesia so he could tell her how he felt.

Ten years and he still hadn't let go of her.

He hadn't liked the vulnerable feeling then, and he didn't care for it now. "What are you saying, Serena?"

She rose and walked to stand in front of him. Her eyes welled. He knew that face, knew the fear and helplessness behind her bravado expression. The lush mouth he'd dreamed about, he'd kissed so many times, pressed together into a thin line.

And the holy shit ache in his head morphed into something so ugly it gave fear a new name.

"Jake. I only have a few months--"

"No!" Was that ragged voice his?

Her lower lip quivered. "Jake..."

Not. Happening.

He sank onto the bench when his legs threatened to give out. Scrubbing his hands over his face, he leaned forward until the wave of nausea passed. The tears in her eyes rushed down her cheeks and he violently shook his head again.

Screw that. She was fine. She'd had a pacemaker surgically installed. Her heart was fine now. Yeah, she still had limitations, but not like when they'd been kids. "There's something they can do, like last time."

She lowered her gaze in answer. And he remembered what the medical staff had said way back when. That the device would only work so long.

Unable to sit, he shot to his feet again. "There's something. Another doctor."

Serena's face, her beautiful face, gave him the answer he didn't want without her saying a word. Every fear they had all these years rested in her bottomless eyes, wrecked by naked vulnerability, and he knew.

No. *God, no.*

He sat back down and struggled to bring in air.

She knelt in front of him and tried to take his hands, but he snatched his away with a violent jerk. Guilt shoved its way to the surface, but he forced it down again. Anger was good. Anger was better than his organs being clawed out one by one by one.

She sniffed and stood.

"So this is what you came back for?" The tremor in his limbs became violent. "To die?"

Resigned, she turned toward the house. Her steps were small but unfaltering, her head held high. That was his Serena, forever brave, always strong.

But her body wasn't. Her body was giving out. In months, she'd be...

Hurts so bad. "You won't do this to me again. Do you hear me?"

She kept going, the very same way she did three years ago, and didn't look back.

Later that night, after she'd helped Grams clean up dinner, when Serena hadn't come out of her room and Austin had locked himself away in the library, Courtney found herself walking across the yard toward Jake's house.

The fireflies were emerging, blinking across the expanse of grass, and crickets chirped as dusk neared end. Humidity clung to the air, dampening her skin.

His porch light was off, as if a beacon to stay away. The back door was open, but no sounds emerged from inside. She knocked twice on the screen and received no answer.

She stood for a moment in the heat, debating whether to turn around and go back. But the alarm and pain she felt radiating from him bombarded her. Jake was not doing well with the news about Serena. Pressing her hand against the door, his mood shoved its way into her mind, wrapping around it, and breaking her heart. She sighed and tucked the hair behind her ears when the breeze blew.

She pulled open the screen door and called for him. No answer. Calling again, she got the same lack of response.

The kitchen was dark. Three empty beer bottles were on the table. Pursing her lips, she ambled through the doorway and into the living room. A coffee table was knocked over and pictures littered the floor. Otherwise the room was dark and empty.

She sighed, putting the photos into a neat pile. Memories swam in her head as she touched the pictures, like a movie flipping through an old reel. Jake and Serena at prom. Jake playing baseball. Austin and Serena with Grams at graduation. The memories hurt, because to Jake, they were no longer happy ones.

She turned the table upright and glanced around for other clues to what he'd been doing. The carpet was dark blue, accent pillows matched the printed curtains. Two end tables were positioned on either side of a recliner, facing a blue and cream plaid printed couch. The fireplace mantle held small trinkets and knick-knacks that looked like they were centuries old. Above them, a large clock with a stone face ticked its lonely miserable sound. She dropped the pictures on the table and folded an afghan that was thrown on the floor.

The hallway was dark also as she made her way down, bearing the same dark blue carpet. She passed a bathroom of gray tones, quickly assessing he wasn't inside. His truck was in the gravel driveway by the barn. She knew he was there, could feel him in the house. There were three bedrooms and the last door on the right was slightly ajar.

She rapped on the frame. "Jake? It's Courtney. Can I come in?"

Silence.

She nudged the door open. More pictures were strewn over the unmade bed. She went to the nightstand and switched on the lamp.

The floor in here was hardwood and polished. Under the bed was a large area rug in forest green, shades deeper than Jake's eyes. A hope chest, as wide as the queen-sized bed, was placed at the footboard.

With some light to guide her, she turned to find him at the window, his back to her and his arms folded over his chest.

"Jake?"

He didn't seem to notice her until she was right beside him. He looked down at her, most of his face hidden by shadows. His eyes weren't playful and bright like they'd been earlier. Distant and sad, all hope having fled hours before, she didn't think he even knew where he was. She wasn't sure what to do, so she remained at his side, waiting.

He turned back to the window. Time stretched before he finally broke the silence. "I thought you were an angel or a ghost when I first saw you out there, walking in the moonlight." He jerked his chin toward the glass, keeping his gaze on the yard.

She knew that, of course, and knew that he did too, but he needed to work some things out. She'd let him talk.

"Your nightgown flowed around your ankles and your golden hair blew in the breeze. An angelic image. Or spectral, depending on how you look at it. Those blue eyes of yours locked on me and I figured I must've died." He made a sound somewhere between a laugh and a groan and rubbed the back of his head. His hand fisted in his hair. "She's...dying," he whispered, as if finally coming to terms with it.

"Yes." Like him, it felt like the word had been ripped from her chest. His emotions warred with hers, making her dizzy.

"I yelled at her for it too, like it was her damn fault she was dying." He turned to her, arms crossed over his chest.

"Anger is normal." Conversations with Serena filtered through her mind. "She said she was mad when she first found out too."

She took his arms, finding them rigid and hesitant, and urged him toward the bed. Jake was dead on his feet and needed sleep. She quickly had the photos piled on the trunk by the foot of the bed so she could encourage him to sit.

"Do you sleep with your shirt on or off?"

He tilted his head curiously. "Off."

Taking the hem of his T-shirt, she yanked it over his head, tossing it aside, wanting him to be as comfortable as possible. It was hot inside his room. She'd have to check the air conditioner before she left.

He leaned against the headboard, watching while she removed his boots. He didn't even seem aware of what she was doing. Sleep helped ease the heart to face another day. So she decided to stay until he was asleep. Maybe he'd talk a little more while dozing off. Some things you could only tell a stranger.

He adjusted the pillow and laid back.

She walked around the bed and sat on the other side, by his hip. "How are you feeling?"

"Numb." He tilted his head to look at her, his eyes suddenly growing round. He gripped her arm. "I'm sorry we scared you earlier."

She smiled to reassure him. "It's okay, just old ghosts." She lay down on her side, propping her head in her hand. "It was hard for her to come back here, you know. Telling Austin was difficult, but you? She fretted over that the entire way. She's not scared of death, not really. She was worried what would happen to you after she was gone."

His gaze darted to hers and he swallowed hard. "I've loved her my whole life. When she went away, at least I knew she was safe, she was okay. Doing something she loved, though not with me. I don't think I can do this. Seeing her today did me in, and now we all have to watch her get sicker and sicker."

"It's not about us." That might not have been what Jake was expecting her to say, but it nonetheless was what he needed to hear. "We may hurt long after she's gone and miss her like crazy, but right now, it's about her. About what she needs. And she does want you, still loves you, regardless of what she says or why she left then." She set her head down on the pillow next to his, suddenly tired now that Jake was decompressing.

He exhaled heavily and briefly closed his eyes. He slanted that green gaze at her. "She said she didn't want me."

Courtney looked straight through the pain in his eyes, ignored what his emotions were telling her, and leveled with him. "What do you think?"

"You're right," he said after a moment. "She wants my forgiveness. She needs us."

She nodded and squeezed his hand gently in reassurance. "You need to sleep. I'll stay until you do."

He searched her face for several long seconds with an unreadable expression. "How can someone from an ugly background like yours turn out the way you have? So affectionate and kind and considerate."

She swallowed hard, her throat too tight. He meant it, what he said. She could feel it radiating from him and hear the compliments in his tone. "People like you, that's how." She smiled and let go of

106

his hand before she could read any more. Her system had been overloaded enough today. She reached behind her and switched off the light. "Go to sleep. Tomorrow's another day."

After leaving Jake's house, comforted slightly by the thought that he was resting, Courtney headed back across the field. The porch light on the main house had been left on, and for a fleeting moment she hoped Austin was up waiting for her.

Not at all disappointed to find Grams on the porch swing instead, she climbed the steps and smiled. "What are you up to?"

"Oh," Grams looked up, startled. She floated a hand over the book in her lap. "Just remembering days past." She patted the bench next to her for Courtney to join her. When she did, Grams smiled. "This is one of my scrapbooks. I have so many and each one tells a story."

Interested, Courtney leaned over. "Tell me about this one."

Opening the cover she pointed to the first page. "This was the first picture taken of the twins when they were born. Notice that Serena is smiling and Austin is screaming?"

Courtney breathed out a laugh and shook her head. She watched and listened eagerly as Grams relayed story after story about them and their parents. Grams had even put the death notices from the paper in her book of memories, claiming all things good and bad should be remembered equally.

"This was the first Christmas after their parents died. It was still a good day despite them being gone."

Courtney made a sound of agreement and leaned against the swing, setting it in motion when Grams closed the book.

"You haven't had many nice Christmases, have you, my dear?"

Courtney pursed her lips in thought, not over the question, but how to answer. "No, I haven't." Grams' eyes grew sad, making Courtney feel bad for her honesty. "It's okay, I never really cared for the holiday anyway."

"How can you not want to celebrate the day Christ was born?"

"That's just it, Grams. Do people even realize what they're celebrating? Everything is commercialized now with lights and presents and greed." She continued to rock the swing gently, looking out over the estate. "Besides, I never really had Christ in my life until I came here."

"Christ was always in your life. You just didn't know until now. He is always there, watching and protecting. He sheltered you, even when you didn't know He was there."

Courtney believed her, had no reason not to. And that gave her consolation.

"I think all this commercialization you were talking about helps us rejoice more. You will have nice holidays from now on. You will change your mind about it then." Grams nodded as if confirming her statement.

She wanted to believe that too. She wished desperately to have that sense of family, of belonging somewhere, even for just a brief moment. But her doubts held her back because eventually, she would go back to Arizona with mere memories and be alone like she always had been. Some people were destined to be outside looking in and wondering.

After gazing out at the clear night she breathed deep. "Grams, did you ever see that Charlie Brown Christmas special they show every year on TV?"

"Ah, I see." Grams smiled in understanding. "You think like the young Charlie Brown did, that you don't understand Christmas and all the excitement."

"No," she said quietly, and laid her head back. "I feel like the tree."

Grams looked puzzled before her hazel eyes cleared. "But, my dear, in the end everyone accepted the tree and helped to make it beautiful."

"It was still pretty much a nothing underneath."

"You're believing what that man wants you to believe." Grams slid her hand over and patted her leg. "He wins when you do that. Where is there room for change when his lies and your doubts take up all the empty space?"

Jake sat on the floor at Edward's End, Austin's shop, and helped him alphabetize the books so they could place them back on the shelves. They'd said very little in the three hours they'd been there, but he couldn't get his encounter with Courtney off his mind. He slid a sideways glance to his friend. "That's quite a woman you have."

Austin brought his head up with confusion. "Huh?"

"Courtney." Irritation grew over Austin's face, so Jake smiled. "She came by my place last night."

Austin whipped his gaze back to the stack of books in front of him, biting down the urge to punch his best friend until that arrogant smile left his face. He had knocked on Courtney's bedroom door once late last night, after standing outside in the hallway for twenty minutes debating whether or not he should. He'd been thinking about her most of the night, wondering if she was okay after they'd all bailed on her after supper.

Of course he'd gotten no answer. She was with Jake. "Why was she with you?" Had they made her feel unwanted? Lonely?

Jake shrugged. "Must've known I was upset."

Austin sighed. Right. Duh. "I'm sorry. I wanted to tell you what was going on, but Serena made me promise. She wanted you to hear it from her--"

"Hey," Jake interrupted, "it's okay. Really, I understand." He put a stack of books to his left for the beginning of the "S" column and grabbed more out of a box behind him. "I went into self-destruction mode for awhile there. Almost lost my shit. Courtney cleaned up all the pictures I threw around the house. And righted the tables."

Austin nodded, figuring Jake would rather talk about Courtney than Serena. He was curious himself. "What did you talk about?"

His gaze grew reflective. "Saturday night, I saw Courtney walking by Grams' garden." He chuckled. "I thought she was a ghost or something. You know, white nightgown, blonde hair, blue eyes. Moonlight."

Austin nodded again, getting the gist.

"Well, anyway. Last night, I rambled for I don't know how long and she just stood there listening, like she knew me and gave a good goddamn. She tucked me in bed and basically told me to get over myself." He shook his head. "I was a mess, and all I know is she helped me out of it." He looked at Austin, heart in his eyes. "She stayed with me until I fell asleep, and when I woke up in the morning, there was a basket of muffins on my kitchen table where the beer bottles used to be. My house was clean."

109

Austin raised his eyebrows. "You trying to steal her away?" A joke. Jake could use it about now. "I got news for you then, she's not mine to steal."

Jake laughed. "Oh, she's yours all right."

The front door opened and two giggling females strolled in, one with endless shopping bags in her hands, and the other with paint cans.

"Oh, Austin, the renovations are lovely." Serena placed her sunglasses on top of her mass of curls. "I can't believe how different it looks in here."

Austin took the paint cans from his sister. "These for the mural?"

"Yeah," she sighed. "Wow. Show me my wall and I'll start this afternoon."

Jake grinned at Courtney when she set the bags by her feet. "You buy out the whole town?"

Courtney shrugged. "Almost. Serena said I didn't have enough clothes." She turned to Serena, as if accusing. "Of course, then I needed shoes to go with all the new outfits. She even made me buy a swimming suit and some lingerie."

Austin groaned, pinching the bridge of his nose.

Serena tipped her head back and laughed. "Well, we'll save that for later, shall we? Otherwise we'll give Austin an aneurism."

Courtney blushed.

Jake, looking leveled, stared at Serena. "It's good to see you laugh again, princess."

Serena sobered, but kept her smile warm. "It feels good to laugh again."

An uncomfortable silence filled the room.

Austin crossed his arms. "Well, I'll get the awkwardness out in the open then." Groans followed. He shrugged. "Serena, Jake is sorry for how he responded yesterday. Courtney, Jake is appreciative for the muffins and kind words. And me, well I'm not going to think about bathing suits right now. So, anyone for lunch?"

The four of them sat encircling a round iron table in the coffee shop section of the store and ate croissant sandwiches while laughing. Courtney smiled at Jake when he told a hilarious tale about Austin's date for prom and a disaster story about dancing. She thought it a nice reprieve that, for a moment, they could laugh and share without the world weighing in.

Courtney got an idea while they'd reminisced, several actually. When Austin got up to throw out his wrapper, she turned to Jake. "Can I talk with you about something back at the house later?"

"Sure." He grinned at Austin's warning glare, then back to her. He wondered if Austin knew how deeply he was already sunk. "But we'll have to stay out of bed this time."

Courtney raised her brows with understanding, seeing the jest for what it was.

Austin mumbled under his breath and leaned over to check out the paint cans on the floor.

Serena rose and shook her head. "Oh no, dear brother. You are to stay out of this coffee shop until I am done. The mural is a surprise."

Austin eyed the wall. It was ten feet tall, and that section was eight feet wide. "A few days, huh? I don't think so."

"I already have the scene mapped out in my head and I have all week to work on it."

He glanced across the room to the opposite wall where the coffee counter took up the length of that wall, then over to the large decorative window behind where Courtney and Jake sat. "Take it easy though, okay? Open the windows so the fumes aren't overpowering."

Serena didn't argue, or tell him she was planning on it anyway. "Its acrylic paint, but I will." She reached up on her toes and pecked his cheek. "Leave now."

Austin grumbled about needing to put books away anyway and circled the divider wall to the bookstore.

Courtney turned to Jake. "Wanna drive me back to Grams' and we can talk?"

"Sure." He poked his head around the wall. "I'm going to drive Courtney back to the house to drop this stuff off. We'll be back in an hour so we can help you."

"Whatever," came in response.

111

Jake sat in a chair next to her closet while Courtney cut tags off her new outfits and hung them up. It was amusing listening to her give a dialog on why Serena said she'd needed each item of clothing and her own take on it. *This one's too short. This one's too tight.* He chuckled and rubbed the back of his head when she decided to put the undergarments away later and left them in the bag.

She strolled over to the bed and plopped down on her stomach, bare feet in the air, done with her task.

Jake walked to her dresser where stacks and stacks of photos sat piled in envelopes. "You take all these?"

"Oh, yeah." She sat quickly and crossed her legs under her. "That reminds me. Do you think Austin would like a picture for his birthday? I already have the one I'm giving Serena framed."

"I think he'd like anything you gave him." He picked up an envelope. "Can I look at these?" When she nodded, he took two stacks and sat on the bed across from her. He shuffled through them and lifted his brows at the detail and mood expressed through her photography. She had an eye, that was for sure. Great lighting, excellent angles. "These are quite good. Where were these taken?"

Courtney looked over into his lap. "That one is from New Mexico when we stopped in the cave." She got up and rummaged through a bag under her bed and then sat back down. "This is the one I'm giving Serena." She handed him an eight by ten photo. "I had it enlarged and framed today when we went out."

Jake stared in amazement at a view from underneath a ray of sunlight. Color danced through stream and behind were layers of rock. Almost like peeking into a window to heaven. It not only was different from anything he'd ever seen, but just looking at it gave him a sense of peace.

"When I first saw that spot in the cave," she said, "it seemed like a higher power was talking to me, pointing me somewhere. Then I glanced at Serena and it was as if she knew what I was feeling, like she sensed it too."

"This is amazing," he said and cleared his throat. "She'll love it. You should show these to Austin. You could sell them in the gift shop or something. You have tons of talent."

"Really?"

Hope resonated through her voice, making Jake's heart swell. "Yeah, really. You're very good." He sorted through some more photos and stopped short.

Courtney searched his face with concern as his eyebrows lowered and his green eyes lost their shine. In the photo he held, Serena stood by a knotted oak tree during a stop in Texas, with her dark curls blown away from her face and her skirt flowing behind her. Serena hadn't known Courtney had taken a picture in her moment of solitude.

"You got her, didn't you?" Jake rubbed his fingers over his jaw. "That's the look she used to get when she thought no one was watching. A wisp of a smile, some muse playing out in her head."

"She was thinking about you." His head jerked up. "She didn't know I took the picture until I had it developed. But even before she told me about you, I saw what was in her head. I felt it."

Jake glanced down at the picture one more time, as if trying to draw out which memory Serena was thinking about at the time, and then set it back in the envelope with the others. He rubbed his face vigorously with his hands to shake off the mood. "So, what did you want to talk about?"

She smiled at him reassuringly and then mentioned the idea she had for Saturday night for their friends' birthday.

He laughed heartily. "Oh, they'll love it!"

"You think so?"

"Yes, most definitely."

Her smile widened. "Good. I'll tell Grams and we can get going on the details."

Courtney had just finished putting little trinkets into the enclosed glass counter by the register when she realized she didn't approve of how she'd arranged them. Getting back onto the floor, she turned all the cherub faces around so the customers could see them and spaced the crystal figurines. Nodding, she rose.

She poked her head around the wall. "Austin, this case is ready to be locked up."

Both he and Jake looked up in unison from where they were restocking the bookshelves. Austin smiled. "That was quick. I'm glad you'll be working for me." He reached into his pocket for the keys. "I'll show you how to lock it up, so you can do it from now on."

He bent down and inserted a small key into its spot in the glass case. "Just make sure it turns all the way or it doesn't lock."

"Okay." But her smile froze in place when she turned toward him.

There he went again. Watching her with a look that said he wasn't even in the same room anymore. His gaze roamed her face, as if taking in the details, before finally settling on her mouth. The black of his pupils nearly swallowed the golden brown irises.

Heat flushed her cheeks and her stomach dipped. The need to retreat crept up as much as the desire to touch him. They were close enough for his warmth to surround her, pull her in. "I'm gonna...check out how Serena is doing before I get to the next box."

He blinked twice, but said nothing.

Courtney grabbed her camera off the counter and wove around the divider wall like her feet were on fire. To calm her heart rate, she took a few cleansing breaths.

Serena was on the second step of a ladder, a determined look on her face. Courtney stepped back to look at the mural and snapped a couple pictures. It was an amazing assortment of greens and blues, and was just starting to take form. Courtney knew what the finished product would look like, not from Serena telling her, but by what was already developing and the sentiment emanating from Serena.

"It looks good," Courtney said.

Serena smiled down at her. "Thanks." She climbed down the ladder and sighed. "You know what it's going to be, don't you?"

"Yeah, he'll love it." Courtney assessed the large space. She already had the background up. "It was a good choice."

"I somehow know you're right." She gazed back up at the wall and pursed her lips. "You really like it?"

Courtney looked at the wall again, knowing she didn't have to, and then back to her friend. "Yes, I do. It will be a wonderful thing to leave behind."

Serena tilted her head. "That's exactly what I was going for."

114

Courtney headed back into the gift shop just as Jake came over with a black iron rotating stand with little slots to hold cards. "Where do you want this?"

She looked at him questioningly. "You should ask Austin."

"He said you were doing just fine without him."

"Oh." She surveyed the space, searching for a spot to put the rack. There was a small area to the right of the register where people would wait in line if the store got busy. It would be a good spot to put the little name cards. "Right there." She pointed. "That way when customers stand in line, they'll see them and might be inclined to grab one."

"That's my girl. Good thinking." He set the rack down, spinning the stand to make sure it worked and was loose enough. He walked up to her with the smile still on his face and cupped her shoulders.

There was an overwhelming sense of protection when he touched her. Brotherly. It wasn't warm where his hands lingered on her arms, like when Austin's skin met hers, and her heart didn't race at the contact. But she felt reassured and important. He was an easy man to be around.

He frowned at the boxes by his feet. "Let me help you unpack these." He flipped out a pocket knife to cut into the tape.

She eased down on the thin office carpet and crossed her legs. The name cards were all a light green color and each had a different name on them with their meaning. "They should be put in alphabetical order before they go up."

Austin strolled in. "I need a break from books for a minute." He plopped down next to them. "Are these the name cards?"

Jake let out a startled laugh, causing both their heads to turn toward him. "Austin, your name is Latin and means "worthy of respect," he read from the card. "It says, "Oh God, make me chaste, but not yet.""

"Yeah, that's you." Serena sat with them, completing a circle on the floor. She dug in a box and brought out a stack of cards still in cellophane. "Courtney, yours is Old English and means "persecuted." It also says "court dweller" and you're "feminine.""

Austin grunted, appearing to agree and not approve of what his sister said. "Jake is from the "Old Testament," meaning "he who supplants.""

115

Courtney dug in the box for her friend's name and stilled. "Serena, also Latin, and means "tranquil and serene.""

That night, Courtney found herself unable to sleep and wandered down the stairs to seek something to help. If it wasn't the nightmares, it was her brain unwilling to shut itself off and let her rest. Figuring Austin wouldn't mind if she borrowed a book, she closed her hand around the knob to the library and gasped when the door opened on her.

Austin blinked in surprise. "Hey."

"Hi," she breathed.

Every time she was near Austin he brought up strange and unusual sensations in her she wasn't so sure she liked. A trip of her heart rate. A flip-flop in her belly. Heat flaming her cheeks.

It always took her awhile to get orientated with new people, even the ones her emotions said meant no harm. Austin was different. Her hesitation wasn't from uneasiness or fear. She didn't know what it was from exactly. On the road, she'd been apprehensive as to whether she would be able to talk with him in person as openly as they had on the phone. He could be short of temper, yet never made her afraid. His anger, when displayed, was always directed at something he viewed as unjust. He was also a man of few words, but when a topic interested him, or he was nervous, he could ramble like a child.

Despite those circumstances, they'd had some nice discussions and conversations. Yet the hesitation remained. He just...he drown out the other voices. Shut down the emotions she sensed from others. And then, in the process, amplified her own. She'd gone her whole life not acknowledging her own feelings.

Austin was striking. There was no other word for him. High cheekbones, wide jaw with a perpetual shadow, full lips. His nose crooked slightly to the left, nature's way of proving even the most handsome of people had their flaws.

He transferred his weight, as if wanting to step closer, but refraining. His jeans rode low on his hips and she stared at a hard wall of bare flesh. His abdomen had slight ridges of muscle, his pecs lightly dusted with dark hair. Wide shoulders and a narrow waist. His biceps had definition when he made the barest flex with his hands.

Biting her lip, she slowly raised her gaze past his Adam's apple to his face. The heat from his gaze scorched a trail through her veins. The breath caught in her throat. Her brain simply stopped functioning.

"I...I'm sorry. I couldn't sleep and was looking for a book."

Why couldn't she sense what he was thinking? With everyone else, their every whim bombarded her. With Austin, it was just her own desires. There was nothing radiating from him, had been that way almost from the beginning. She wanted some way to gauge him, some hint of instinct to guide her.

"Okay." His brows drew together in contemplation.

Maybe she'd interrupted him while working. And now she was in his way. "I'll go back upstairs. I didn't mean to disturb you."

"You weren't," he said, catching her hand before she could walk away.

She stopped her retreat. Waited.

He didn't let go, touch lingering, until he slowly trailed his long fingers up her arm, causing a shiver. His gaze followed the movement, as if delighted and shocked by what his hand was doing. Over her collarbone. Up her neck. His thumb held her jaw, his fingers curving around her neck.

"I've been thinking about you all day." His drawl was deeper, coarse like sandpaper. His gaze slid up from her mouth to meet hers. Held.

"We...were together most of...the day. At the store."

"Not what I meant." He stepped closer, until his chest brushed her nightgown and slid warm sensations down her middle. "I keep thinking about when I kissed you upstairs a few days ago and how much I want to do it again. I know I shouldn't, but I can't help it."

She barely got the "oh" out when he brought his mouth down to crush hers. And any thoughts she had left in her brain were now mush. His mouth was firm and gentle all at once as it danced over hers. Vibrations overtook her, to where she had no idea where or even who she was.

Austin lingered on the sugary taste of her lips, the way she went fluid under him and surrendered. Lost, he trailed his kisses across her cheek, over her jaw, and down to the pulse in her throat, beating wildly at his attention. Pride surged. Lust consumed. When she grabbed the waistband of his jeans and let out a shaky breath, he opened his eyes, suddenly aware of what he was doing.

He had just been thinking about her in the library, and all the ways he'd like to touch her, when he opened the door and found her there. Her innocence, laced with a sexy undercurrent she obviously never explored, was tearing him apart. He wanted her now. She needed time. He was a coiled not of tension as her barely there nightgown teased his nipples. She was so damn soft, even though it seemed her life had been nothing but hard. Which only served to remind him that slowing down was in order.

Damn. Space, needs space.

"I-I'm sorry," she stammered, and tried to step away.

He hadn't realized he'd spoken aloud. "No." He reached for her again. "I was talking to myself." With her at arm's length, his hands curved around her slender shoulders, he waited as those blue eyes of hers began to refocus.

Courtney wasn't like everyone else, and he had to be much more careful with her. It was just so damn hard when she looked and tasted the way she did. And he hadn't been with a woman in awhile. She needed romancing, and caring, and teaching. Needed the patience and understanding she'd never been given.

Like a blow to the solar-plexus, he realized he never wanted so badly to give everything to one person.

He cleared his throat. "Go out with me tomorrow night."

"Where?"

He couldn't resist a smile. She was so damn cute. "Out. To a movie, or dinner, or anywhere. Just... out."

She drew her brows together in confusion. "Like... a date?"

He rested forehead against hers. She was definitely going to be the end of him. "Yes, exactly like a date."

"You want to go out with me?"

"I think that's blatantly obvious, but if you need reassurance, then yes, I do." He tipped his head back and looked at her. "So will you?"

"Okay." Her tone indicated she had no idea why she agreed. Then her gaze met his and the trust there was gutting.

He sighed. In relief? "Great." He pressed a kiss to her temple and stepped back. "I think you'd better go upstairs now. Or I should."

Her pink mouth grinned fully, making his hard-on...harder. "I'll just grab a book real quick. See you tomorrow then?"

"Yeah." He raked a hand through his hair and quickly turned to retreat upstairs.

Chapter Seven

"So where is Austin taking you?" Serena slipped a plain gold chain around Courtney's neck.

"I'm not sure." Nervously, she placed her fingers to her throat and glancing at herself in the vanity mirror in Serena's bedroom. "Are you sure I look okay?"

Serena looked down the length of her and nodded in approval. The black fitted sundress accented her curves perfectly, showing just enough cleavage to tease. "Trust me."

"I do." She frowned and sat on the edge of the bed. "I've just... I mean, I've never been on a date before. I don't know what to do."

"Austin is very traditional." Serena sat next to her, patting her hand. "He'll probably take you to dinner and then somewhere afterward. The night will most likely end with him kissing you on the front porch."

"What if I do something wrong? Or he doesn't like me?"

Serena took Courtney's hand gently in hers. "If he didn't like you, he wouldn't have asked. I know my brother, he doesn't play games. Besides, I've never seen him look at anyone the way he's been looking at you. I think he's more concerned you won't like him."

"That's ridiculous, of course--" A knock sounded on the door. "Oh, God."

They both stood. Serena turned to her, running her hands up and down her arms in the same gesture her brother had used before. "Just a minute," she called, and then smiled warmly at her. "Just relax. It's only Austin."

Courtney laughed, some of the tension draining as Serena opened her door. It was going to be fine. It was going to be fine.

Austin stood in the doorway holding a handful of daisies, looking too good in a pair of light khaki pants and white polo shirt. "Hi," he said in a low hoarse voice, eyes only on Courtney. After clearing his throat, he smiled wickedly. "You look nice."

"Thanks. I'm ready." Courtney looked at Serena. "Right?"

Serena and Austin exchanged a brief glance she couldn't interpret before Serena nodded. "Yes, you are more than ready."

Courtney gave her a brief hug and left the room catching Serena's double meaning. She was ready and she could do this. It was about time she started doing things like a normal person. Mrs. Meyers would be proud, she thought with a smile, as she headed down the hall.

When Courtney was out of earshot, Serena grabbed Austin's arm before he made it to the stairs. "You may be my brother," she said in an even tone, "but if you mess with her, I'll kill you." She released his arm, straightened, and sniffed. "Have a great time."

Austin had taken her just outside of Willowsby into Athens for dinner. Once they'd sat down, face to face at a small intimate table with candles, all the nervousness fled. She'd laughed at stories from his childhood and enjoyed the small Italian restaurant pocketed in the corner of town.

It had never been this easy for her to be around a man before. She had moments with Jake, but nothing like with Austin. There were times she'd been nervous--a giddy kind of nervous that had her heart pumping--but she didn't have to pretend she was someone else to get through the conversation. She could be herself. And without reading anything from him at all.

He made her feel special in so many small ways. Holding her hand while walking into the restaurant. Resting his palm at the small of her back while they were being seated. He didn't laugh at her when she thought she said something stupid or wrong. He listened intently when she spoke about Arizona and some of the people back there. There was an intelligence about him, without the typical conceit, and sexuality without vanity. A great sense of humor and a good moral compass.

"Where are we?" she asked when he pulled alongside a curb and cut the engine.

Twisting in his seat, he reached down and snatched her camera from the floor by her feet. His arm brushed her bare leg, sending shivers and heat on a pursuit to her core. Placing the camera on her lap, he grinned. "At a festival."

Not knowing what to do, she got out when he did, and slipped her hand in his when he held it out for her. "Look up." He pointed to their left.

Confused, she did so and gawked in amazement.

Oh. Oh wow. A Ferris wheel turned measured circles behind a copse of elm trees, colors glowing against the night. People crowded the grounds, eating popcorn, cotton candy, and slow roasted nuts. Booths were set up in a row holding life-sized stuffed animals if one could win a game. Laughter and conversations floated to her, mingling with music. The barely there scent of beer and sweat was muted by roasting corn and humid air.

"I've never been to a fair before." She lifted the camera to her face automatically.

"I had a feeling." But he didn't think she'd heard him. She was clicking away, watching the world through her lens.

She took his breath away. Time after time, in the short while he'd known her, she continued to surprise him. Not only beautiful and talented, she was modest and sincere. He wondered how on earth, with a past as deluded as hers, she could turn out so polite and gracious. She never once put herself or her own needs ahead of anyone. Everything was new to her. It was like seeing the world for the first time through a fresh set of eyes just by stepping out the door. That endearing smile would cross her face until all her features lit up. Blinding, really.

She also had no idea what she could do to a man. To him. What she was doing. Her lips were a wet dream, her legs too damn long, and every shameful curve of her swayed when she walked. And he had no idea what to do about it.

Except to follow. So that's what he did. Followed. Wherever she wanted to go, whatever caught her eye, that's what they did. The camera never left her hands. After exhausting themselves strolling around the fair grounds, riding every amusement, and playing just about every game in the park, Austin assisted her into the car and closed the door.

Rounding the hood, he got in and looked at her. "Ready to head home?"

She smiled sleepily in response.

They sat in a companionable silence on the drive back, him holding her hand. A few miles from home, while stopped at a red light, her hand clenched around his. Hard. Her gaze was intently out the side window, on the cemetery.

"What's wrong?" He tried to swallow around the sudden wedge in his throat and couldn't.

"Can you pull over?" she whispered, tightening her grasp.

"Sure." Checking the other lane, he pulled the car off to the side and parked. "What's wrong?"

Not answering, she exited the car and was at the cemetery gate before he could even cut the engine. Something niggled in his brain, something familiar, but he tossed it aside as she started walking through the entrance. Veering to her right, she followed the narrow path until it forked, then turned left.

His parents were buried in this cemetery, along with his grandfather and the entire Edwards family. Soon, so would Serena. His gut twisted, wondering what Courtney was doing, why she wanted to come.

Abruptly, she stopped and stared at the grave marker in front of her. His father's grave. She'd walked right to it with no direction from him. Her...ability still rocked him back on his heels when her intuition was spot on. Hell, it was rarely wrong.

She slowly walked to the headstone and knelt down in front of it. Oxygen trapped painfully in his lungs. Chills raked his spine.

A woman in a black dress.

Long, blonde hair.

Kneeling in front of the grave next to his mother's.

He'd seen this before. Seen her before. Austin's reoccurring dream since childhood slammed into his mind, causing his chest to constrict and the air in his lungs to whoosh out. Last time he'd had the dream, the mystery woman had finally spoken. *I'm coming.*

And...she had. She was right damn here in front of him.

"Courtney? Has Serena brought you here before?"

"No."

Okay, no. Well, it was one of only two cemeteries in town. Lucky guess? Sensing emotions from other people was a far cry from walking directly through a massive cemetery at night and directly to his parent's grave without having been here before. Perhaps, maybe when his brain worked again, he'd take this psychic thing of hers more seriously.

"It was raining," she whispered, her back still to him.

Every single hair on his body stood at attention.

"Your father was driving." Her voice drifted through the warm, humid night and caressed his skin. More potent than any touch. "The car swerved to avoid a dog. Metal crunched. Your mother gasped. It was instant, their death. No pain." She paused, then repeated herself. "No pain."

Frozen in horror--no, not horror, shock--he battled tears. He'd wondered. Wondered if they'd known they were going to die. If they'd felt pain. And here was Courtney, telling him as if she knew all along he'd needed answers.

"You look like him." She rose to her feet and moved to stand in front of him.

A strangled sound left his lips. "Courtney..."

"I'm sorry." Something between regret and pain passed over her face, but she quickly blinked the expression away.

He swallowed, trying to figure out what to say. Before he could, she rounded him and headed out of the cemetery the way they'd come in. When he could move, he followed and got in the car behind the wheel.

"How...?" He swallowed. "How...?" Damn it, there were just no words.

"I made a mess of tonight, didn't I?" The tremor in her voice gutted him. "I'm sorry. Sometimes I can ignore the visions, sometimes I can't. Some emotions and voices are louder than others. I'm so, so sorry."

Running a shaking hand down his face, he turned to her. "Christ, Courtney. I'm not mad." She didn't look like she believed him. "Honest, I'm not. They died...a long time ago. Serena and I don't remember much about them. Aside from Grams, there's no real family left."

Austin suddenly remembered something his sister said in reference to these visions of Courtney's. Something about how that good for nothing shit of a father beat her for having them.

He was bumbling this big time if her face was any indication. "Look at me," he urged. It took her several moments, but finally she turned to him. "Don't ever be sorry, okay? Not ever again. Never again."

In the course of several minutes, the fear in her eyes was replaced by weariness, and then resolve. She looked at him like she was looking right through him and stripping his soul bare. Eventually, she broke the contact and nodded.

He took a cleansing breath and started for home. In silence, he pulled into the driveway, wondering how to save tonight from becoming yet another bad memory to her.

She went to exit the car, but he touched her arm to stop her. "Smile." A plea. "Could you smile at me, please? Let me know I'm not a complete jackass."

Shifting in her seat to face him, she brushed a kiss on his cheek. "Thank you for everything. I had fun." Twisting her head to the backseat, she admired her prizes from the fair. A rather oversized brown teddy bear with a red bowtie and a giant purple hippopotamus stared back at her. "I don't know where I'll put these, but I can't help but love them."

Then...she smiled.

Unicorns frolicked and rainbows emerged. Or he was just relieved. Nonetheless, she was really something.

He got caught up in watching her, unable to move, to breathe. She'd been in town little over a week, but he was pretty certain he'd already fallen for her. He brought his fingers up to tuck a stray strand of hair behind her ear, and left it there. It ached, everywhere, it ached--this wanting her.

"I'm going to kiss you now." The raspy, desperate voice didn't sound like his, even to his own ears.

In that split second before his eyes closed, before her breath mingled with his, before his mouth captured hers, before his world spun upside down, he vowed to give her everything he had inside him to give. Never before had anyone made him want, not like this. Not anyone before her and, he feared, not anyone after. Worse, it went way beyond a physical reaction. She was in his head, his heart, playing a wicked game of chess with his life.

At her soft moan, he delved deeper, losing his hands in her hair and tugging her closer. Soft. Sweet. She answered his demand beat for beat, no longer tentative like their first kiss, making him lose himself further into this world she created for him.

Her scent--lemongrass and rain?--drove madness into him and blood pumping to organs he better not test just now. So with great will, and even greater restraint, he pulled away. With closed eyes he rested his cheek to hers, panting into her hair and struggling for

126

the calm he had before she'd entered his life. "I think we better call it a night."

She skimmed those perfect pink lips against his jaw, where his muscles tensed. He kept his eyes tightly closed when she tenderly kissed him there, knowing if he looked at her again he'd take her right here in the front seat of his car.

"Goodnight, Austin."

He waited until she closed the car door before he moaned. He waited until he heard the front door shut before he opened his eyes again.

Jake sat with Courtney and Grams at the dining table sipping sweet tea and half-listening Courtney relay her idea for Austin and Serena's birthday party.

The week was almost up. He got through five days in relatively close quarters with Serena at Austin's store. She'd been covered in paint, while he'd been drenched in her laugh. In the past. Next week would be a welcomed change, as he would be able to go back to his carpentry projects when Austin reopened on Monday.

It was killing him being so close to her again. Those golden eyes of hers still had an edge to them when he called her "princess," a nickname she despised, and one he couldn't help but use. She was a princess. Not regal or uptight, but worthy of status. She was every bit the maiden from fairy tales. His, to be exact. She still smelled like vanilla too. Even covered in paint.

Friends.

That's all she wanted was her friend back. She didn't want the soft caresses and moonlight kisses and ecstasy they'd once shared. Didn't want the short tantrum arguments they'd been prone to have before blessedly making up. Making up had been the best part. Granted, she was sick, but he needed her touch, to be touched as if the end wasn't coming. It had been too long.

Serena wanted nothing of it. Pushed their past away like an old dinner plate.

And, man, how it burned him she wanted to forget and move on. He didn't. He remembered the flush on her cheeks after a night of love-making. How her musky scent of vanilla drifted into his senses and clung. He recalled just where she liked to be teased.

127

What her kisses felt like. How soft her skin was on that area below her ear, her breath quickening when he grazed his mouth there.

Oh yes, he remembered everything. And she felt nothing. She'd stopped desiring him three years ago, and he was dying to know what had caused the rift back then. The whys had kept him from a decent night's rest. For years. Sleep was no longer a virtue when the haunt of what-ifs burned in the quiet hours.

"That's a wonderful idea!"

At Grams' exclamation, Jake jerked his head up and forced himself to concentrate on why he was here. On anything but Serena. "That's what I said," he told Grams.

Serena's sudden squeal of joy from the other room had the three of them on their feet and down the long hallway quicker than a blink. Austin had Serena in his arms and was twirling her around the library. He set her down when he saw them and ushered them inside.

"I have wonderful news." Austin grabbed Courtney's hand. "Sit down," he urged when she looked at him expectantly.

"Tell her, tell her, tell her!" Serena clapped her hands like a child.

Courtney glanced at Grams and Jake, who stood just inside the doorway looking just as confused, and then back to Austin who was bent over in front of her. "What's going on?" Her mind was blank. No feelings, no thoughts, just... blank. No intuition to rely on for help.

Austin blew out a breath and snatched a piece of paper off his desk. He held it in front of him. "October twenty-first."

Courtney eyed Grams and Jake again as if she missed something, and then at Serena with a question through her smile. "I don't get it."

Austin laughed and knelt down in front of her. "October twenty-first is your birthday." He handed her the piece of paper. "I did some research and hired an investigator. Your social security number is there also. I couldn't get a copy of your birth certificate without your authorization, but the info is there for you if you want to get a copy."

Her jaw dropped as she stared at him with those unyielding blue eyes rounded in shock. They got bigger, bit by bit, until they almost popped out of her skull. She stared at the piece of paper he'd handed her and then back at him. "I…" She swallowed hard. "I have a birthday?" She drew out every word slowly and looking at him in disbelief.

"Yes." He took her face in his hands and gave her a smacking kiss on her mouth. That made her jaw drop again and he hooted wildly at her expression. "You have a birthday," he assured softly, smoothing her golden hair.

Her shock became something else all together. She searched the paper and then him. Her lower lip quivered and tears caught on her lashes before she lunged forward and wrapped her arms around his neck. He rose, taking her with him and held on tight.

God, yes. She fit so perfectly there.

It was a start. A new beginning for her to end the madness with which she'd existed. A way to make her understand she was somebody, that she mattered. He was hoping the sadness would slowly dissipate, instead of her just pretending it had. Maybe, just maybe, he could help her move on.

"Thank you," she whispered into his ear, shuddering from the rack of tears.

He set her down on her feet and leveled her with a grin. "You're welcome."

Courtney pulled Serena into a fierce embrace, Jake right behind them. Austin eyed Grams over their heads.

"You did well, Austin." Grams smiled and looked over at the rejoicing. "Real well."

He nodded his head in approval. "I did, didn't I?"

Serena turned suddenly. "It's a great day all around. I finished the mural. We should all go over to the shop and admire my handiwork. After Courtney and I meet with Father Jerry, we can go out to dinner to celebrate."

Jake nodded and draped an arm around Courtney. "I think that's a great idea."

Serena stood in the doorway by the separation wall of her brother's shop and toyed with her family a bit. She noticed Courtney's smile in recognition at stalling the mural reveal and grinned wider.

"Come on, sis. Let's just see the damn thing!"

Austin was grumbling again and Courtney was beginning to enjoy his little frustrated sounds. He was quite adorable when irritated and impatient.

"Language, Austin." Grams pursed her lips in that scolding way she used very seldom. Austin beamed a grin at her to diffuse it.

"Go ahead then." Serena stepped away from the doorway. "Go see my masterpiece."

"Oh my," were the only words muttered for a long time, coming from Grams, as everyone stood wide-eyed in amazement. They only had to wait a week for her to finish the mural, but she knew in her heart that it felt so much longer to them.

"Damn, Serena," Jake said, but there was no heat in his words. He rubbed his chest, shaking his head as if unable to wrap his mind around the image. Heartbreak and hope filled his eyes. After clearing his throat, he stepped out of the room, head bowed.

Courtney thought about going after him, to make sure he was all right, but Austin followed him out the door.

In the mural, the long green grass Serena painted held such detail it was as if Courtney could feel the blades between her toes. A night sky was full of stars and, off to the left, there was just a trace of illumination indicating Jake's porch light. To the right was a corner of Grams' garden. In the center, near the top of the painting, was the hill just beyond Jake's barn. The weeping willow that grew there was encased in shadows and hung its branches low to shield the three children running. She could almost hear them laughing.

But the most amazing and astounding part of all were the long stretched shadows of four adults, walking side by side, at the very bottom center of her mural. No actual bodies, just their shadows, deep meaning implied.

Courtney looked at Serena and swallowed hard. "You put my shadow there, with the three of you."

Serena had that far off look in her eyes. Not taking her gaze away from the mural, a slow, conceited smiled peaked at the corners of her mouth. "You belong here." She tilted her head, as if to see the painting from a different angle. "If there is a Heaven, this would be mine."

Father Jerry Mercer replaced the phone to its cradle on his rather large desk in the church office that was littered with papers and smiled at the two ladies waiting patiently in the chairs on the other side. He patted his chest, as if searching for his glasses, and then realized they were in front of him. After putting them on, his rather robust voice asked, "So, Serena dear, what would you like to talk about?"

"I'm afraid I'm ill again, Father," she said without missing a beat. She was prepared for this conversation and the sympathy that always followed. Part of her just wanted it over with.

"Oh no." He edged forward in his seat. A dark red curl fell onto his wrinkled forehead and he absently brushed it away.

Courtney wondered how such a deep voice could come from a man so small when he lowered his tone.

"Is it serious?"

"Yes, it is." She looked into her lap where her hands were neatly folded. "I won't be getting better this time." Serena abruptly remembered him walking into her hospital room, Bible in hand, when she'd been sixteen years old. His face hadn't been as full as it was now, his hair not quite as short. He'd sat by her bedside talking to her, listening. Each Sunday, until she was well, he'd stood before the congregation and said a prayer for her.

No prayers would save her this time. And she had a feeling it hurt him more than it ever would her.

Some things a person could grow to depend on in their lifetime, and he was one of them. He had kept in touch with her when she'd moved to California. Every Friday she looked forward to his letters and blessings.

Father Jerry took off his glasses and rubbed at his eyes, then replaced them on his nose. His gaze searched both Serena's and Courtney's before sighing heavily. "How is your grandmother doing with all of this?"

Serena didn't glance up from her lap, and answered his question without any trace of emotion. "She's well. Everyone who knows has handled it quite well."

"I see." He stared at her in concentration. "And how are *you* doing with it?"

"There's nothing I can do to change the outcome." She shrugged, meeting his gaze. "I'm at peace with it. It's in God's hands now."

"I'm so sorry, Serena."

Courtney knew he meant it, empathy radiated from him. She tore her gaze away from him when his eyes briefly skimmed her.

"Is there anything I can do?"

She nodded. "I'd like to make arrangements, so my family and friends don't have to worry about the funeral."

He shook his head in a mournful way and dug into one of the desk drawers. He pulled out a dark green booklet and handed it to her. "This will have all the songs listed you may use. It also has suggestions on prayers and changes to be made to the mass if anyone should want to speak, give a eulogy."

She sighed. "Thank you, Father. Austin will most likely want to say something, as I'm almost sure Grams and Jake will too." She briefly looked at Courtney in the seat next to her and then back to him. "I don't want a big fuss, just something small. Bury me next to Mom and Dad."

Reality crept into the room, stealing all air and solace.

Father Jerry folded his arms over his chest. "I understand." He glanced at Courtney again and leaned forward. "Serena, why don't you take that booklet into the living room and look it over while I get to know our new friend here. By no means do you have to make a decision today. Take your time."

Serena smiled at him. "Thanks." She turned in her chair to face her friend. "Courtney, I want you to tell Father Jerry everything. You may not get it all out today, but I trust him. He can help you. Okay?"

"Okay." Anxiety filled her chest when Serena left the room. She stared at the dark red office carpet and wondered where to begin. Her father had attempted to beat the visions out of her, and here sat a holy man. Would he feel the same way? She trusted Serena, and Serena trusted him. Still, words wedged in her throat. Father Jerry, thankfully, started for her.

"Austin said you've never been to church before. Is your family not religious?"

She tucked her hair behind her ears. "I, uh…never knew my mother. My father said she didn't want me so that's why she left

132

us. He was very religious. He carried his Bible around with him and would yell passages to me when I misbehaved."

Father Jerry sat back and seemed to be absorbing what she told him with experienced patience. "But you've never been to church?"

"No. I wasn't ready for God, he said. I would embarrass him."

He rubbed his mouth and stared at her blankly. "Doesn't sound like a religious man to me." He waited for her reaction. She gave him none. "He abused you?"

She tilted her head to the side and debated how to answer that. "That's what Serena called it. Abuse. But I was...bad. I think he was just trying to raise me right."

He dropped his gaze to the scar on her arm. "That's no way to discipline. He still has you making excuses for him, doesn't he?"

"Oh no," she piped quickly in defense. "I haven't seen him in ten years--"

"That's not what I meant." His voice was erringly calm. "I mean, he still has you believing it was your fault."

She looked away, unable to withstand his scrutiny.

"It wasn't your fault," he said. Oh, how many times had she heard that? "Your father used God as a weapon, and that was wrong."

She frowned and looked at him again. "Do you think...?" She paused, not knowing how to ask her question. He was a priest and would know the answer. Her ability and the truth behind it would get straightened out once and for all. The subject was always in the back of her mind, not allowing her to move on. "Do you think God curses people? I mean, my father called me a witch because of my visions and said they were a sin."

A crease formed between his brows. "God accepts everyone, even those who don't accept Him. He doesn't curse people, or condemn them."

Father Jerry watched her closely and she could hear his thoughts. He wished desperately he had known her as a child so he could have stopped this then. He could have given her a safe haven. Courtney sighed. There was no such place. Not even in dreams. Not even by wishing for them.

"What do you mean by visions?"

133

She swallowed, sensing there would be no ridicule or blame in this room. "When I meet people, I feel things. Sometimes I see things before my eyes that aren't there." Great, he was going to think she was crazy. "I see pieces of their life, or I sense what they are feeling at the time. And I can't stop it."

"Do you want it to stop?" he asked her calmly.

"I've tried. I've tried so hard to make it stop because he said it was the devil doing it to me."

"It sounds like you're a psychic, not the devil." He smiled at his humorous ploy, but her stomach twisted. "Does the devil speak to you and tell you to do things?" He kept grinning when she shook her head. "Well, okay then. We've ruled out the devil. Courtney," he said, a little more serious, "I'm not much one to believe in this sort of thing. But I have an open mind and there sure are a lot of unexplained mysteries to this world." His mouth went into a thin line. "But this sounds as if it's something to treasure, not fear."

Serena had told her that very thing, in not so much the same words. She wanted to believe him, but sensed that Father Jerry was holding back. "Can I take your hand for a minute?"

His grin faded in confusion. "Sure." He stretched his hand across the desk when she crept forward in her chair.

She took his hand and closed her eyes. After a few seconds, she opened them and focused on him. "Your mother used to sing "You Are My Sunshine" before you went to bed every night as a child." The color drained from his face. "Your father had a heart attack the year Serena left for California and every Sunday after mass you go to the cemetery to see him." She paused when his jaw dropped. "She has a beautiful singing voice, your mother." Courtney probed deeper, hoping she wasn't going too far. "You loved a woman named Emily when you were young, but when she died, you joined the church, thinking you'd never love again." A strangled sound left his throat. "She loved you too. Still does from where she is."

He stared at her in disbelief as his hand grew cold. He opened his mouth to speak, but no words came out. Slowly, he took his hand from her grasp and puffed his cheeks, expelling a breath. "Okay, I believe you."

She smiled hesitantly. "I didn't do it to make you believe. I did it so you can understand what it's like. All the time, there's voices, images, emotions. It never stops. It's easier for me to believe what my father said than what you do for that reason."

He nodded slowly and, after a few minutes in silence, he stood and rounded his desk to sit in the chair next to her. "I think you need to talk with someone about these issues. Before long, they will eat away at you and you won't be able to move forward. Sometimes talking helps." He reached over and fumbled for his calendar off the pile on his desk. "Would you be willing to meet with me on Fridays? We can discuss whatever you like. I do have a psychology degree too."

She smiled in return, meaning it completely. He would help. "That would be fine. You're easy to talk to, Father." He looked up at her after writing down her name on his calendar. "Serena said you could help me. I didn't know I needed help until I got here."

He breathed out a laugh and patted her arm. "My dear, you are one of a kind."

"What time do your parents get in?" Courtney asked Jake as she placed a white table cloth over a small round glass table by Grams' garden. The two of them had been at it all morning, preparing for their friends' birthday party.

Jake stood from where he was setting up a platform and wiped his sweaty brow with his forearm. He checked his watch. "Their plane should be coming in at Ben Epps in Athens in a couple hours." He knelt back down and used his power drill to put the last screw in place for the makeshift stage. He flopped down on the grass and stretched his long legs out in front of him.

She decided she needed a break from the humidity as well and lay down on her side next to where he sat, propping her head in her hand. "It was nice of them to come in for the party."

"I called them last night to tell them about Serena being sick. And the party. My mom didn't say anything except that they were hopping a plane in the morning." He sighed and wiped his brow again. "They always thought of Austin and Serena as their own."

"That's nice." She rolled to her back. The grass at least cooled her bare legs somewhat. "Especially since they lost their parents so young."

Jake didn't respond at first, so she glanced up at him. His collar-length brown hair was drenched in sweat, as was his face. He was flushed red from working so hard.

At length, he asked, "Did you see the look on Austin's face when we told them it was black tie tonight?"

"Yeah, probably brought back old prom memories you were telling me about."

He chuckled and rubbed the back of his head. "You sure those two will keep away from here until tonight?"

"I told them they had to stay at the shop until six forty-five, so they'd get here by seven." She shrugged against the grass at her back. "They're getting dressed there too, and Austin said he had a couple things to set up before he opened on Monday anyway."

"What is she wearing tonight?"

She knew he couldn't help it. Jake thought about Serena so much, missed her to the point of pain. "I'm sworn to secrecy." She snickered when he slapped her arm playfully. "Sorry."

Grams came out of the back door with a tray of lemonade. She had been working hard in the kitchen making a feast that Serena could actually eat. She set down the tray on one of the nearby tables and lowered herself to a chair.

"You're a heaven sent, Grams." Jake reached for a glass and downed it in one gulp.

"Oh, shush up," she shooed with one of her many smiles. She looked around and apparently liked what she saw. "You two work well together." Courtney looked at her, too tired to move to grab a glass herself. "Father Jerry tells me you two had a nice talk."

"We did, yes." Courtney smiled. "He's a nice man."

"That he is." Her eyes grew serious for such a brief minute Courtney wondered if she imagined it. "You talk with him, dear. It will be good for you."

"Okay--" A cold sensation shot down her leg. A squeal erupted from her mouth. She removed the ice cube from where Jake set it on her thigh and stood. But before she could reencounter, he shot up and she chased him through the yard.

"Got you up, didn't I?" He hooted and dodged her grasp. Expression solemn, he stopped short. "Seriously, we should get back to work."

She bowed forward, hands on her knees, panting. "You're right." She squealed again when he slipped another ice cube down the back of her tank top. This time she caught him and jumped on his back before he could run away. "Just wait, I'll get you back."

Grams watched the excitement from her chair before she rose to go back to baking. Jake had that little darling on his back and was spinning her around. He had her laughing.

Grams nodded her head in satisfaction. "It's about time," she whispered to herself. "It's about time."

Chapter Eight

Austin pulled into the driveway to their plantation house behind the wheel of his sister's yellow Mustang just at sunset and cut the engine. "I still don't see why I have to wear this monkey suit," he grumbled, referring to the stupid tux Jake insisted he wear.

From the passenger's seat, Serena shook her head with fondness. "My dear brother, you'll be happy when you see what Courtney's wearing." She stepped out and adjusted the ankle-length formal sage-colored dress she was wearing. A slit went all the way up her left leg. It had a high neckline, was sleeveless, and swooped down low in the back to expose her smooth olive skin. Her shoes, the same color as the dress and very high-heeled with complicated straps, made her almost as tall as her brother when he got out to stand next to her.

"She'd better be wearing nothing." He got a roaring laugh in response.

"If you play your cards right, maybe she will later."

He ignored that comment and looked around. "There are no cars here but ours." He smiled wickedly. "That means the party's off. We can go."

She slipped her arm through his and marched him to the front door. The lights inside were on, but there was not a sound. They walked down the hallway, past the stairs and the library. Entering the formal living room they discovered no one there either. The family room was empty as well as the dining room and kitchen.

"Where are they?" he questioned just as he noticed a flicker of light through the kitchen window. He led his sister through the doorway to the backyard and stopped short.

The trees that lined the back of the estate twinkled with thousands of tiny white lights among their leaves. There was a platform to the right of the garden where a small orchestra of six was set up and waiting. To their left were two tables, with white cloths and candles glowing against the fading sunset.

"Mary Mother of God," his sister said. But before he could respond, she took a step forward with a dropped jaw. "Is that…?"

She took off running, well, as much as one could run in a dress, and wrapped her arms around...Jake's parents. Wow. They came.

"Mom." She kissed the woman's cheek. "Dad." Another kiss to his cheek. "Oh my God! I can't believe you're here!" She stood back to look at them. "When did you get in?"

Jack and Irene Warner smiled warmly back at her. Her hair was wrapped in a formal twist, the same shade of brown as her son's. Jake had inherited his mother's small nose and mouth, but his father's green eyes. His hair was salt and pepper. But instead of making him look aged, it made him distinguished.

"We just got in a few hours ago," he answered her question.

"You look wonderful, dear," Irene told her.

Serena looked down at the woman's simple black dress that her slim figure fit so well into and sighed. "You look better. How have you been?"

"Ah." She waved her hand. "The same. You are stunning in that dress."

"That's my line." Jake slid next to her. He placed a kiss on her cheek and damned whatever company made vanilla scented anything. "You are beautiful, princess."

"Thanks." She tried to graciously step away, only to be held firm to his side. It had been so long since he'd held her, but her body remembered and reacted. "I can't believe you had your parents come. Thank you so much." She turned to them. "Oh, you haven't seen Austin yet." She spun and found him standing in the exact same spot she left him in by the back door.

Austin couldn't move. There had to be a medical explanation for it, but his brain couldn't think of one as he stood like an idiot ogling Courtney.

Her golden hair was pinned up in a maze of curls and showed off her long neck. The dress--oh, the dress--came down to her ankles and was pale pink. It had no sleeves, no straps, just fitted perfectly around her breasts. Her skin in comparison was like strawberries and cream. When she started coming his way, every glorious curve swayed with the movement. Time slowed. His heart pounded. His lungs emptied.

"Hi."

His gaze dropped to that mouth in the same shade as her dress and stayed there until he cleared his throat. He needed a drink. "Hi."

"Happy birthday."

"Thank you." He cleared his throat again and swiped a hand through his hair. "You make it real hard to stay mad for dressing me up like this when you look like that."

Her blue eyes danced as a smile crossed her lips. "Jake's parents are here too. They'd like to see you."

"If you say so." He followed her over to the tables, groaning because the back of her was just as heart-stopping as the front.

"There's my other boy." Jack rapped a hand on his shoulder, bringing him back to earth. He'd have to thank him for that later. "How have you been?"

"Good, and you?"

"Jake tells me the shop's ready to be reopened. That's good news."

"Yes." Austin grinned, pride swelling his chest. "You should stop by and see it before you go."

"Afraid we're heading back tomorrow." Jack shrugged. "Next trip."

Grams clapped her hands to get everyone's attention. "Get over here and eat, everyone, before it gets cold."

They feasted on lemon-peppered chicken with steamed asparagus, laughing, as they shared stories of years past. Though the night was warm and sultry, the food was great and the company better. Serena couldn't ask for a better birthday.

When the orchestra began playing after dinner, Jake took Serena's hand and led her to the platform. "I haven't danced with you in ages." His other hand slid around her back. He bit back a groan at the discovery of just how low the dip of her dress crept. His skin charged at the meeting of flesh.

"You guys did a wonderful job." She leveled those golden eyes on him. "This is the best birthday I've ever had. Thank you."

"It was Courtney's planning, but you're very welcome." He set them in motion, humming the tune into her curls and tried to fight the longing. Useless endeavor. "You still fit." He lifted his head, forcing her to look at him. "With me like this, you still fit."

Serena gripped the lapel of his jacket, strain in her eyes. "Don't, Jake. Just...don't."

"Don't pretend? Like you think I don't know that look on your face, haven't seen it a thousand times?"

She tore her gaze away without missing a beat.

"I know you still have feelings for me, Serena. A love like ours doesn't ever stop." He leaned close, and had some satisfaction at her shiver when he whispered into her ear. "Your pulse is racing."

"I don't need to remind you that I haven't much time left, Jake."

He stiffened against her. As if he needed a reminder that there was no "ever after" for them. No matter how much they wanted it. No matter how much they desired one another. She was going to leave him in the permanent sense. Soon. Allowing himself the chance to be with her again would only leave more hurt in the wake.

And he wouldn't regret one second of it.

"How long will you use that excuse, Serena? If you haven't much time, why waste it? Why deny us?"

"You know why." She sighed, resting her head on his shoulder despite her cold tone. "It hurts, Jake."

His eyes slammed closed. "I know, princess. Don't I know it."

At their table, Irene glanced away from Jake and Serena and grasped her husband's hand. "She doesn't even look sick."

Austin's gut dropped. No, his sister didn't look sick, but the telltale signs of her decline were peeking through. She used oxygen masks at night and napped often during the day.

Grams pursed her lips. "She hides it very well."

Jack's brows furrowed in concern. "There isn't anything they can do? All this technology and all her surgeries, and they can't do anything?"

"No." Grams folded her hands.

"It's so unfair." A haze of tears shone in Irene's eyes. "She's too young. I remember them just yesterday, playing in that field, chasing each other. They haven't had enough time."

"There never is." Grams began stacking her china with seemingly detached interest. She would let go later in her room, Austin knew, where no one could see her hurting.

Austin rose and held his hand out for Courtney. "Dance with me?"

She took it without question and followed him to the platform. She avoided looking into his eyes and stared at his chest instead as he set them in motion. She was nervous, he realized. It always seemed as if it was him feeling the butterflies when they were close, and it gave him a miniscule amount of satisfaction to know she didn't hold all the cards. That he affected her too.

"You all right, Courtney?"

She smiled, as if coming out of a trance, and met his gaze. "I'm fine. It's just that…when I touch most people, or I'm near them, I sense things. What they're thinking or feeling, even if they don't know they are thinking something. But with you, I haven't sensed anything since that first day when I touched your hand. There was some intuition, but not like it usually is." She cast a gaze heavenward, as if drawing a reserve of courage. "My mind is quiet with you. Everything is still. It's never like that for me."

He studied her, trying to make sense of her declaration. "Does that scare you? Not knowing what I'm feeling?" She nodded and glanced away. "Look at me, Courtney." He stilled their dance and waited for her to meet his eyes. "I feel that I'm damn lucky to have met you, and so is everyone else. I think it's disgusting what that man did to you all those years and I'm amazed at how thoughtful you are because of it. Most of all, I think about what it felt like to kiss you and how I can't get out of my mind that I want to do it again." He chuckled rather oddly, resuming their dance. "The craziest thing is you don't even know how badly you affect me. You're going to be the death of me."

She stiffened, drawing them short.

"What's the matter?" he asked, suddenly concerned he said too much too soon.

"My father used to say that to me when he was mad," she whispered. "You're going to be the death of me."

Christ. She gutted him. He stared at her a long time, fighting anger and grief. Austin could kill that bastard with his bare hands for ever laying a finger on her. And probably get away with it.

"I'm not him." For emphasis, he repeated himself. He expelled a breath he didn't realize he was holding when she regained color, and he made a decision on the spot. Actions spoke louder than words. "Come upstairs with me tonight, to my room." When she didn't respond, just measured him through thick pale lashes framing storm cloud eyes, he quickly added, "Let me show you what it's like. What caring is supposed to feel like. Be with me tonight."

He nearly wept in relief when after an achingly long pause, she nodded her agreement.

Austin thought they'd never leave. He'd danced with Grams and Irene and his sister, and God help him, Courtney too. Hours that seemingly stretched into days. They'd had just as many hours of small talk, catching up with the Warners. Then there were the long goodbyes and good nights until he thought he would implode.

He strode down the long hallway upstairs with his hand firmly in Courtney's, and prayed this wouldn't be over in five minutes from the want of her. The anticipation was blinding.

"I really should help Grams clean up--"

"Tomorrow." He marched to his bedroom door. She hesitated only a moment before stepping into his room. He closed the door at her back and eased her against it.

"But tomorrow we have church and..."

There were times--many, many times--he could listen to her talk for an eternity, but this was not one of them. His mouth swallowed her words as he dove himself into the kiss. God, it was like coming home. The scent of lemongrass mingled with the familiar taste of her as he lavished her glorious mouth.

Finally.

He wanted to see her, all of her, to take this slowly being her first time, so he regretfully tore his mouth away and peered into her eyes. And saw fear. Those eyes---all that blue--grew immense as she searched his face. Dear God, look at all that blue.

You could hurt her and never even know you did.

Serena's words from earlier filled his head and he winced. "Christ. I'm sorry, Courtney. I'm going too fast, aren't I?" She just stared back at him, expression unreadable, so he dropped his brow to hers. Guilt panged. Swiftly, he backed away and paced to the balcony, his back to her.

Cold seeped through Courtney's skin, bone deep. She was petrified. Completely freaked out of her mind that he would realize she wasn't worth the effort and order her to leave.

She hugged herself instead of walking to him, like she wanted. She glanced around his room, speculating what to do next. The layout was the same as hers except the coloring. His carpet and bedspread were a grayish blue where hers was cream. The bed didn't have a canopy like hers, but the headboard went halfway up the wall.

"I wouldn't blame you if you didn't want to do this," he said, drawing her attention back to him from across the room. It may as well have been miles. Taking his time, he walked back to her and grazed his hands up and down hers arms. It left a trail of heat where he touched. "I want you, but I won't force this on you. Make sure you're ready. It's your choice."

She didn't know what to say. Doubts stopped her from responding. After a long silence, she decided to be honest. "I don't want to disappoint you, Austin."

"That's what worries you? Disappointing me?" Sadness etched his eyes, the curve of his mouth. In a blink, heat replaced it. "You could never disappoint me. If you're scared--"

"I am, but..." She looked away.

"I won't hurt you." His words were spoken quietly, imploring her to believe him, as he inched closer. "I wouldn't hurt you for anything."

"I know," she whispered. "But I've never..." She sighed harshly at her inability to communicate her feelings. "I'm not unaware. I mean, I've read books and I've seen movies, but I've never been this close to being intimate with someone. My father kept me on a pretty tight leash at home, and in Arizona, there just weren't any possibilities. You've had more experience at this. What if I'm not any good?"

"I've never told a woman to shut up before, but I'm inclined to now." His eyes were molten pools of lava. "There will be no doubts in this room. It's just you and me here, Courtney. I'm the lucky one. I'm the one worried about being good enough."

Could that be true? Austin certainly looked like he was telling the truth. How could he, magnificent and beautiful and experienced as he was, be worried about measuring up? She raised her hands to his shoulders, and that was all the answer he apparently needed.

Austin captured her lips, more tenderly this time, and mated his tongue with hers in a slow dance meant to ease her fears. Remind her that it was just him and he'd never hurt her. She softened against him, giving her all like she'd done from day one, and nearly brought him to his knees. How was it remotely possible to go his whole life without knowing her? He didn't seem to exist without her next to him.

He slipped the tuxedo jacket from his shoulders, letting it fall to the floor, and tugged off the tie he'd loosened hours ago. Bringing his hands back to her face, he deepened the embrace, urging his body to slow down. She moaned into his kiss and trembled.

Courtney's fingers inched upward into his hair and to the back of his head, letting those short dark strands play through her fingers. He was so warm and inviting she forgot where she was. Who she was. There was suddenly nothing and no one else but them. His mouth moved down over her collarbone and up to her jaw with heated torment until she didn't think she could withstand the pleasure much longer.

Austin removed his hands from her face to unbutton his shirt, keeping his mouth locked on hers. Clothes were suddenly too tight, too binding. He needed her skin against his. No barriers. Carelessly, he tossed his shirt on a pile and grabbed her hips to spin her around. She complied, her back to him, nerves dancing. He slid the zipper of her dress down, inch by excruciating inch, skimming his knuckles down the length of her back. He stepped out of his pants. She leaned back against his chest.

His hands were suddenly everywhere, torturing her and pleasing her all at once. Kisses and fiery breaths on her neck sent waves of delight up her spine, and she arched her back to urge his hands to continue the exploration. Her dress slid to bunch at her waist. He gave each breast equal attention until their tiny buds pressed against his palm and her breath caught.

She tried to turn in his arms, but his fingers fell on her hips and held her still. When the last barrier between them--her dress--fell to the floor, she stiffened. His gaze landed on why. A long protruding scar, harshly put on her back years before, marred her perfect pink skin. An angry white, jagged slash slicing half her back.

Biting down the curse on his lips, Austin enveloped her in his arms from behind, and held her close, pressing her against him. He wanted to take it all away. To banish every painful memory and mark that had been left. All he could do now was show her, love her. Teach this miraculous creature how it should have been. How it could be.

When he was sure she was ready to continue, he steadily turned her to face him and backed her toward the bed slowly, never taking his arms from around her, nor his eyes from hers. Never wanting to let her go again.

He couldn't determine how much more he could withstand, but if it killed him, he'd take all night. He wanted to be inside her, feeling her surround him in every way possible. Needed it like he needed his next breath. Though his body was screaming, he knew this ache went way beyond physical.

Laying her down, he knelt between her knees and looked down at her. Golden hair spilled over the pillow and blue eyes looked at him expectantly. Knowing he couldn't take her mouth again or this would be over all too quick, he focused solely on her needs. For the next he didn't know how long, he touched and tasted until she was pliant under him and not a trace of tension coiled her muscles. He encouraged her to touch him, explore his body, so that her doubts were reassured. She would not be afraid of him. He would make sure she was never afraid of anything again.

When he thought she was ready, he sheathed himself, pressed her gently into the pillow with a kiss, and nudged her knees a little further apart. Aligning their bodies, he laced his fingers with hers and entered her slowly. Sweat broke out on his forehead. Her eyes flew open and a gasp escaped. Her muscles clenched around him.

He stilled. "The pain will only last a moment," he whispered against her lips. "I promise, only a moment." He remained motionless, an eternity, muscles straining, until her eyes slipped closed again and she let out a quiet exhale. With great care, he let go of her fingers and slid his arms underneath her, cradling her to him. So precious. Her arms wrapped around his shoulders, telling him she was ready, saying without words what she wanted.

Drugging himself in her kiss, he moved inside her, and the world fell away. In time, they came together, pleasure drenching them both, and he didn't think he'd been a part of anything more beautiful.

A sleepy grin curved her lips as she ran her hand down his back. "Thank you."

It had never been like that for him before. Never had he given and taken and received so much. Never before had he...loved like this, like he loved Courtney. His chest filled to capacity. "I think I should be thanking you."

He lifted his head, the only part of him able to move at the minute, and looked down at the top of her head. Her hair was a tangled mop and had pins of some sort still stuck inside. "I didn't hurt you, did I?"

"No." She smiled as if satisfied with herself. "I feel wonderful."

"Yes, you do." He grinned, fingers playing with the ends of her hair. Though he'd been gentle, she'd be sore in the morning since this had been her first time. The need to take care of her rose. "Want to take a bath? My tub is more than big enough for two." He wiggled his brows and relished her laugh in response. "I love your laugh."

She squinted her eyes, playfully. Endearing. "I do need to wash my hair."

"Bath it is." He lifted her off the bed and carried her into his adjoining bathroom. He set her down on the blue and white checkered tile and leaned over to start running water. When he turned back, she was facing the vanity mirror, naked in all her glory, and pulling pins out of her hair. She was flushed from their round of love making and had a hint of smile on those small pink lips.

"You're really beautiful."

Her eyes met his in the mirror and her hands faltered where she removed pins. She dropped them and crossed her arms over her chest as if ashamed.

"What's wrong?" He took her arms from where she covered herself and wrapped his around them. They looked so right together, fit so perfectly, he wanted to weep at the sight of them.

"You said I was beautiful."

"Yeah, I did. And I'm right. You are so very damn beautiful, Courtney."

She pivoted in his arms and wrapped hers around his neck. Sinking her forehead to his bare chest, she muttered, "My father was wrong about so many things, but compliments are still so hard to hear. They feel like a lie, you know?"

He clutched her tighter, and knew in that moment he would never let go. Right then and there, he knew there'd be no one else. She was wrapped around his heart so completely he feared he'd never be whole without her again. He wanted to shout it. He wanted hide from it. "Then I'll just have to keep telling you until you get tired of hearing it." Drawing her away from him, he held her at arms length. "You're beautiful, Courtney."

They both climbed into the massive tub, her between his legs and his arms still wrapped as a shield around her. The calming fragrance from the beads soothed as the bubbles surrounded them. He traced the scar on her forearm with his finger. "How did that happen? Serena told me about your back, but I don't know what happened here."

Laying her head against his chest, she sighed heavily. "My father got hurt at work one day and needed a cane for his foot if he walked other than around the house. Well, I had this head cold or something, so I wasn't feeling well and fell asleep. I left the biscuits in the oven five minutes too long and they burned." She shrugged against him and stretched her legs out. "He took one look at the dinner I ruined and started swinging his cane. I grew to hate that cane. I tried handing him his bottle of gin to calm him down and told him I would make more biscuits, but I was so sluggish from being sick. He broke the bottle over my arm." She lifted her leg out of the water and brushed the suds away. "That's how I got this one too." She pointed to yet another scar on her thigh.

He wished he hadn't asked. When Serena told him about the scar on her back, he wasn't given details, didn't know her like he did now. Her calm placid voice wasn't reliving what must have been a horrendous experience. It was too much. The pain and anger, along with aching sadness, was too much.

He held her tighter, wanting to draw her inside him, as if she still needed protecting. He buried his face in her neck. "How did you survive that man, honey?"

She tilted her head, resting her cheek against his. "I learned how to hide. I knew his routine and what he liked. I could read his moods and never looked at him directly because that made it worse."

That's not what he meant, but with her new information, his misery deepened. As if she sensed his mood, she turned and wrapped her legs around his waist. It was hard to think of much else when she kissed him like that. He figured she'd found a new defense mechanism and tried used it--him--willingly. That nearly broke his damn heart.

He gave into her for now, knowing her walls wouldn't hold out for long. Eventually she would have to look at him, she would have to face her past and see he was here. The shields would come down if he had tear them down himself. Running his hand down the slippery skin of her back, ignoring the scar, he grabbed her bottom and lifted her onto his lap.

Courtney tiptoed into Serena's room sometime early the next morning and sat down on the side of her bed. "I slept with your brother last night," she whispered.

"What?" Serena mumbled and rubbed her sleepy eyes. She propped herself up onto her elbows, her eyes suddenly more clear. "What?"

Courtney giggled and bit her lip. "I slept with your brother last night."

Serena waved her hand back and forth, sitting up. "No, I heard you. How was it? Are you okay?"

She pressed her lips together, unable to hide a grin. "It was great. He was so gentle the first time, but then later, in the tub--"

"Whoa." Serena shook her head. "More than once?" She slapped her arm, playfully. "That's all the details I need, seeing as he's my brother and all." She shook her head again and beamed a grin. "So why aren't you there in bed with him at this hour of the morning?"

"I forgot to give you your birthday present last night." She tucked her hair behind her ear. "And I just had to tell you about last night. Sorry."

"You look positively happy." Serena searched for Courtney's hand in the dusky light and took it. "I'm so glad. So, give me my present."

Courtney handed her the box and watched her rip through the paper like a child.

Serena paused and glanced down at the photo. "I knew, that moment in the cave, you were different from everyone else." Serena looked up at her, golden brown eyes swimming with tears. She peered back at the picture and sniffled. "You felt it too. You sent peace to me. I knew everything would be okay when I was there, looking in your eyes." Serena made sure she voiced her thoughts this time. "There is a Heaven, Courtney, and you showed it to me."

Courtney didn't respond, just sat with her savior, because that's what Serena was--her savior. She would have nothing if Serena hadn't taken the chance and brought her here. She would never have known what it felt like to have family, what it was like to be touched and respected. The understanding of friendship she passed to her, never having a friend before. If Serena only knew it was all her doing. It was all part of a wonderful package Courtney would be able to take back to Arizona with her.

"What happened with Jake last night?"

Serena set the picture down on the bed in front of her. "Nothing. Nothing can happen."

Courtney didn't understand. "Why?"

She sighed, irritated. "I can't do anything with Jake when I have no idea how long I have left. I'm dying. It's not fair to him."

"It's not fair to ignore what you both feel either. And you still love him." Irritation grew over Serena's face, but Courtney didn't back off despite the trickle of apprehension that ebbed. "You can't go on without telling him. It's more unjust to ignore that kind of love and make him always wonder, than it is to celebrate the time you have left."

Serena drew her curls away from her face with both hands. "He doesn't need any more pain."

"He'll hurt more after you're gone knowing you didn't want him with you."

Serena opened her mouth to respond and quickly shut it again. How could she argue with that? Logic was a tricky thing when hearts were involved. She searched her friend's face and knew she only spoke truth and knowledge. She hadn't been wrong yet, unless it pertained to her own image.

151

Courtney stood and, before she left the bedroom, turned at the door. "You forget, Serena, that you don't need any more pain either."

Chapter Nine

Dear Mrs. Meyers,

Willowsby is so beautiful, though sometimes I get strange looks from people who don't understand what blurts out of my mouth before I forget to think. See, they're encouraging me to be more open, so I'm trying. Most of the people are great, though, and understanding. Serena calls them small minds. You would love it here. There are trees everywhere and Grams has this amazing garden with so many kinds of flowers I can't even spell half of their names.

Austin has his own business, which is a bookstore, coffee shop, and gift shop all in one. There's a woman who works with us there that reminds me of you sometimes.

Serena is well, so far. She started dialysis two weeks ago to help kidney function. She's looking weaker. And I can't get her to have a real conversation with Jake. They still love each other and I wish they would just talk already.

By the way, Austin and I did more than kiss since I last wrote you. Yeah, yeah. Be quiet. I'm not agreeing and saying you were right.

I've talked with Father Jerry five times now, and I feel better every time I leave. He listens with an unbiased ear and gives good advice. I go to mass every Sunday at the church too. It's not scary like I thought it would be.

The birthday party went well, and both Serena and Austin loved the pictures I gave them. Some people around town have been asking me to take some for them, but we'll see. It's entirely different doing it professionally.

Oh, just one more thing before I go. My birthday is October twenty-first. Isn't that great? I have a birthday now! Austin figured it out somehow on that computer of his.

Tell Dr. Maynard hello and I sent some pictures of everyone. Their names and such are on the back so you know who they are. Share!

Love and miss you,

Edith Meyers did a little happy jiggle behind the counter. Awkward and out of character, but she didn't give a rat's ass.

Richard rubbed at his beard and chuckled. "What's the good news?"

"Here, read for yourself." She slapped the letter down. She continued her bouncing while he skimmed the letter and raised his brows.

"That's good news."

She grabbed the counter and leaned forward. "That's right. Who was right all along? Me! She's thriving there."

"Okay, oh great one, you were right."

Courtney shook her head and giggled at the story the woman before her was telling.

Annabelle Gish was a forty-year-old woman who Courtney had grown very fond of in the six weeks since Austin reopened the shop. She had worked for him before he remodeled and enjoyed manning the coffee counter. Her hair was unnaturally red and kept so short it spiked in odd places. She was round in her torso and waddled slightly when she walked, reminding Courtney of a duck.

She was telling Courtney about her youngest daughter, Jessica, and the fun she had getting the bubble gum out of the six-year-old's hair. She'd had to give her daughter a makeshift haircut.

Courtney shook her head. "At least we took her birthday pictures before it happened."

Annabelle lifted a pudgy hand. "And thank the Lord for that too." She wiped at a spot of coffee on the counter with her rag. "You did good work on those photos. I got lots of compliments and more people who want you to do their portrait."

"I hadn't thought about it. It would be nice to have the extra income, and I love doing it." Annabelle had seen the picture she'd given Austin for his birthday--the one of Jake and him in his bookstore with their backs to the camera, loading books on the shelves. It was her first attempt at black and white and it came out wonderful. He loved it so much he hung it above the register where Annabelle laid eyes on it.

"Do what?" Austin asked after coming downstairs from his office.

"I was telling Blue Eyes over here that some people were asking for her number so she can take pictures for them cause they loved mine." Annabelle plopped down on a stool and sipped her water.

Austin pointed to Courtney. "See, I told you. Which is why I'm down here." He tugged Courtney by the hand toward the back of the shop.

"Where are we going?"

"Upstairs."

"Austin," she giggled. "Brett is still on break. We can't be…you know…and leaving Annabelle by herself down here."

He stopped short and whirled around. "What a charming thought, Miss Morgan." He planted a kiss on her lips until she felt all warm and squishy inside. "But I had something else in mind."

She trailed him upstairs, only slightly disappointed. Ever since that first night they'd made love, they'd been attached at the hip. Working together and eating dinner together and sharing his bedroom.

The second level of the shop was split into two sections. To the right, where the door was open, was Austin's office. To the left, behind the closed door, was extra storage space they rarely used. Both sections were exceedingly large and Serena called it a waste of space. Courtney pushed back her hair from her face. "What's going on?"

"Open the door." He raised his eyebrows.

She pursed her lips at him, knowing that look he got in his eye meant he was up to something wicked. She twisted the knob, expecting to find boxes, and found something else all together.

The floor, which had been an old stained rug, had been replaced by new cream-colored carpet. Pastel yellow covered the once white walls, and gold curtains hung open on the two great windows to the right. In front of her was a desk, similar to Austin's, that had a computer and phone. Pictures she'd had taken since she left Arizona hung in various sizes and framed on the walls. A shapely plush couch in the same rich gold as the curtains sat against the partition near the door. In front of it was a coffee table in the same wood as the desk. There were green plants in the corners and a large screen in the far left corner. A couple of floor lamps with different colored bulbs to change the screen's color sat next to it. There were at least two new cameras on a workbench and just as many tripods leaning against it.

Courtney brought a shaking hand to her mouth when Jake and Serena walked over to her from the workbench.

This wasn't possible. They had not spent all this time, and thousands of dollars in equipment, on her. It was so lovely, and thoughtful, that she quaked with emotion. Her stomach threatened to roll over with nerves. She wasn't this good. Not enough to have her own studio anyway. All she'd ever done career-wise was ring a register and pour coffee.

"Oh, God."

Austin draped an arm around her shoulders and squeezed. "We all decided, after seeing your photos, that you were just too talented to waste. Customers who've come into the shop have raved about that picture you gave me. Annabelle has spread the word around town about the ones you did for her, and you already have three messages on the machine right there from people wanting to make appointments."

She glanced at the blinking light on the desk.

Serena sighed. "I know what you're thinking, Courtney." She walked the couple steps to stand in front of her and took both her hands. "People would not be interested if they didn't like your work. Small minds, remember? You are very talented and you have a great eye for detail."

Courtney could only nod her head. Which made her dizzy. "I have to sit down."

Jake walked her to the couch and knelt in front of her. "Remember what I told you before? Don't let the past get in the way of now." He grinned for good measure. "You still have to name your business. We can't do everything, you know."

She laughed at that and rubbed her hands over her face. "Thank you." She rose slowly, unsure of herself, and peered around the room again. "Thank you so much, you guys. I love it."

"Austin's got a head for business." Serena crossed her arms. "He'll handle the paperwork and stuff like that, so don't worry. You just do what you're good at."

Courtney pressed her lips together and searched the gaze of the man she was not only sharing a bed with, but most of her heart as well. Not since she'd arrived in Georgia had she ever had anyone treat her with such respect. All these people were serving to shape her life, and helping her to comprehend the justification in doing so. And here he was, looking at her with those fierce golden eyes trained to see her reaction. His unconditional trust and complete unselfishness had surprised her more times than not.

He deserved so much better.

She didn't know what else to do besides thank him for giving her more than she ever thought possible and try to not disappoint them. She would ride out this phase of her life until it was over, and then go back to Arizona a more complete person for having known them. Leave Austin to find someone who could give him everything she couldn't.

While she slowly closed the distance between her and Austin, she secretly wished, for a split second, that she could go back to when she never knew what this felt like. What the sense of family and love and friendship meant. A part of her thought it was easier not knowing.

She wrapped her arms around Austin's neck and buried her face in his shoulder. "Thank you." For more than he would ever know. "Thank you."

Serena figured it was time. For a more than a month now she'd thought over what Courtney had told her in her bedroom about not needing any more pain either. She was already feeling the fatigue and strain from her heart. Getting out of bed took effort, she was depending on her oxygen tank more at night, and ignoring the man across the way took too much out of her. Her heart, broken as it was, wanted what it wanted.

It was time to be honest with Jake.

She found him in his workshop behind the barn. It was a metal roof held up by four posts and no walls. Brown Eyes was a few feet behind him and stopped chomping on hay long enough to look at her. As if it took the horse a few minutes to recognize her, she glared at the disruption, and then started trotting over to her.

She nuzzled her nose in Serena's neck, a fond old gesture she discovered she'd missed dearly, and whinnied. Serena buried her face in her soft brown hair and murmured to her in a comforting way. She used to ride her every night at sunset. Jake would wait for them to return in the barn, arms crossed and a grin on his face.

She patted the horse one more time, only to find Jake had ceased working and was eyeing her too. She forced a smile. "She always followed you everywhere," she said, referring to the horse.

He rose from where he was squatting over a pile of wood and brushed off his jeans. He seemed distracted and irritated, a look she knew well. And a sign she should just leave. She kept her eyes on his, trying her damnedest not to gawk at his bare chest. Ripples of muscles, tan skin, wide shoulders. If possible, he was even more built.

"She missed you." Those unyielding green eyes met hers.

She gestured to the lumber. "What are you working on?"

He rubbed the back of his head, causing that thick brown hair to dance, and looked at the wood. "It's a hope chest for Courtney's birthday. I thought maybe she could use it to put equipment or photos in." He looked up at her. "I wanted to talk with you about it. I've been meaning to pop over, but…" He laughed tensely and rubbed his head again. "I was hoping you could paint it, some kind of design for her. I think this is the first birthday she's celebrated and I wanted her to have something special."

Serena pressed those lush lips together and his heart flipped, exposing its underside. "That's a very sweet thing, Jake. She'll love it. You two have become incredibly close since we got back." She paused as if weighing her words, and that pissed him off. She'd never had to do that with him before. "You make her laugh and challenge herself. With Austin and me it's not the same. She's attached to you in a different way, like she sees you as family."

He nodded and looked away. If he stared at her too long the yearning would get worse. He couldn't be within a mile and not miss the holy hell out of her, not want her in his arms. "She is like family. She knows when I'm upset and what I need before I do. She puts me in my place." He swallowed when she stepped closer, his nerves frayed.

"Courtney told me something awhile back. We were in my room, and I was giving her a thousand reasons why you and I couldn't be together, and she discarded all of them."

Jake stepped back in retreat when he caught wind of her scent of vanilla over that of freshly cut pine. He called for Brown Eyes with a whistle. He led the horse through the barn to her stall and patted her once before closing the door. Serena didn't want him any longer, had said so herself in no uncertain terms, and he'd be damned if he was going to chat about it.

Hell no.

He turned to tell her just that, only to discover her right at his heels, nearly on top of him, and searching him with those golden brown eyes. That sensation grew in his gut again, pain and longing. His mouth was as dry as sawdust. He had nowhere to go without touching her with the door at his back and her blocking the exit.

Like there was ever anywhere to hide from her anyway.

"Like I was saying." She tilted her head, continuing the I-don't-want-to-talk-about-it conversation.

His gaze dropped to her mouth. Immediately he closed his eyes and memory to any image of what those lips could do.

"Courtney said it was unfair for you to go on thinking I didn't want you, and for us to not be together. I thought about that a long time. Time I don't have. You tried to tell me too, but I was hoping to spare us all more pain." He could feel her inching closer until she was just a whisper away from him, her heat surrounding him, her scent. "I only hurt when you're not around."

He let out a rush of air he didn't realize he was holding and opened his eyes. And sure enough, there she was, right there in front of him where he wished for her all this time. Her sunglasses sat on top of her mass of dark curls, those eyes of hers holding an old familiar song. He wanted to pull the reins in and pretend he didn't hear what she'd said. But a bigger part of him, the part that missed her so damn much, wanted to touch her, to see if this was real. If she was real. Or if he was having another out of control effed up fantasy.

"Please, Jake."

His heart thrust against his ribs for escape. He thought his eardrums would burst from the rush of blood. "Please, what, princess?" He was pretty sure he'd give her anything, so it didn't matter.

"Touch me."

Hell. Her chest rose and fell against her tight yellow tank top, drawing his attention there. He traced a finger down the line of her scar. She was real. She was here with him, in the barn where it

159

began all those years ago. His hand shook when he removed her sunglasses and set them down on the pile of hay next to him.

"Are you sure?"

She nodded and came closer, pressing those breasts to his bare chest.

He swallowed hard and lifted a hand to play with the ends of her curls. "Are you sure?" he demanded again. Annoyance, in himself, with her, edged his voice.

She spread her fingers across his chest and around his back. She tilted her head up, exposing that long neck and smooth olive skin. "I've always been sure."

He drove his hands into her curls and took her damn mouth with blinding fierceness. Home. Serena was home. The world was right again. He remembered what she tasted like, had memorized every angle and curve of her long ago, and his body pulled those things from memory. It was like being found after years of roaming lost.

She gripped the waistband of his jeans and hauled him flush against her.

So it was going to be rough the first time after this long. He could do rough.

Groaning at her need, at his need, he lowered his mouth and traced his tongue along the curve of her neck where he knew she went mad. He seized the back of her thighs and spread them, lifting her until she wrapped those long legs around him. He backed them into the stall and went down onto a pile of loose straw.

Smoothing away the curls from her face, he took her mouth again. They were always good at this, never lacking for passion. Nothing had changed in that regard. Nothing would amend after either, but he didn't care. He had her now.

He tore his mouth away from hers long enough to pull her shirt off. He groaned at the discovery. No bra and her rosy peaks were already hard. She bit her lip when he slid his rough calloused hands up her legs, taking her skirt with them. He fumbled with her panties, bringing his hungry mouth back to hers, while she struggled to unbutton his jeans and free him.

There was no air. Capturing her hands in his, he pinned them above her head and held tight. He looked into her golden eyes a heartbeat too long. His heart stopped mid-beat, a roaring clash from the pounding before. "Say it," he whispered. Her sharp inhale told him she knew what he wanted, that she remembered their routine before making love. "Say it, Serena. I've gone too long without hearing it."

Her eyes glazed with tears. "I love you, Jake."

He plunged into her, relishing her heat enveloping him and that cry of gratification from her lips. She matched his rhythm as if she never forgot, as if it was yesterday. He buried his face in that silky skin below her ear, waiting for her quaking, and joined her.

Courtney turned from her desk upstairs in her office, where she was packing her cameras for the weekend, when a shuffle came from behind. The smile came easily. "Hello."

Austin sat on the corner of the desk Jake built for her and pulled her into his arms. "Hello to you." Laying his head on her shoulder he breathed deep. "How is it you can make the smell of lemongrass seem erotic?"

She grinned down at the top of his dark head. They'd make a picture. If only there were two of her--one to take the shot and one to pose. She toyed with his soft hair, loving the silky strands through her fingers. "Are you still going with me to the Anderson wedding tomorrow?"

He looked up with his one hundred percent male grin still in place. "Yes." He tugged on the neckline of her white blouse, kissing her there. "Are you going to wear that short purple dress I saw hanging on your closet door?"

She laughed. "I was planning on it."

"Good." He nodded in satisfaction. "I can't wait to see you snapping photos and maneuvering around with the hem line riding up…right…about…here." He traced a finger up her outer thigh and paused. "What's wrong?"

Her face had paled several shades as she stumbled backwards. She would have fallen had he not reached out and held her up by the elbows. Her eyes were glazed, her focus not in the room with him any longer. She grasped for his hands and squeezed them hard before plopping to the carpet on her knees.

"Serena…"

No. God, no. "Is she…?"

Her pink mouth trembling open, her eyes round. He was this close to losing his shit when a smirk started at the corners of her mouth and spread out, lighting her whole face right up to her storm cloud eyes. She breathed out a laugh and tugged his hands to pull him down to the carpet with her.

"They're..." She swallowed and the tension drained from her shoulders. "They're together again. Oh." She patted her chest. "Austin, Jake and Serena are together again."

He stilled. "Christ, you can see that?"

Laughing, she looked at him, her eyes lit from within. "No, I can feel it. Well, sort of...never mind. I'm so happy! She's been hiding her feelings for so long."

Austin gazed at her with utter amazement. She had to be the most unselfish person he'd ever met. Here she was, kneeling in front of him, and feeling the joy of two people as if it were herself. She would put them first. She put everyone first. In fact, he didn't think she thought of herself at all in her equations.

The words were on the tip of his tongue. There were times, like now, he'd wanted to tell her how in love with her he was. It was almost as if he knew before they'd met. From his dreams. From their phone conversations. Her voice in his head, her eyes that haunted him, that smile that came easier now, the scars she endured--were all part of a package. All parts of the woman he loved.

He wasn't sure she was ready to hear the words yet. At times she held herself back, no matter how hard he encouraged otherwise. A defense mechanism, no doubt, and one he was working to get past.

"I didn't think I'd be able to return to Arizona after all this was done knowing they didn't get back together in her last months." Relief shone in her eyes.

For him, everything came to a screeching halt.

"They belong together." She carried on, off in la-la land, unaware of his speeding heart.

Silence stretched. Crickets chirped.

"What?" She flinched at his tone, and he felt a little bad about that, but...what? Clearly he'd heard her wrong. "Go back where?"

The smile left her face in varying degrees. That sadness and regret in her eyes he saw less and less of made a comeback.

162

"Arizona." She said the word slowly, as if talking to a child. "I'll, of course, stay until Serena...until it's...over. But then, I have to go back."

"What do you mean *go back*? Go back to what?" He rose from the floor, taking her with him, and ground his jaw hard enough to make his molars protest. "You never intended to stay? Here?"

Courtney opened her mouth to speak, but only air came out. She'd hurt him, in spite of trying not to, she'd hurt him. Horribly saddened, guilt swirled in her belly. "I thought you understood. No, I never meant to stay. I don't belong here. I came for Serena, and will take my memories--"

He jerked out of her grasp. Fighting for control, he stalked around her studio like a caged beast. "How could you get involved with me and not tell me you never intended to stay?"

"I wasn't expecting this, Austin. I wasn't expecting you. But that doesn't change--"

"This is your home." He was going to blow an aneurism. Panic collided with fear. Raged inside his skull.

"I left home when I was seventeen."

"That was hell, not home! Home is where they love you, where they care about you. Home is where you go back to when there's nothing left and you want to find peace again." He paced some more. "I know you've never had that, and it's hard for you to understand, but this is your home. We can provide you with everything you've ever needed, all you've ever wanted. We can give you what you never had."

You'd have me, he pleaded in silence, searching her gaze.

"You don't get it. That's exactly why I have to go back, Austin."

Frustrating, maddening woman. He whirled away, then back to her, confused beyond all reason. Sheer, unredeemable pain hit the blue of her eyes. Pain he'd tried so damn hard to erase, but evidently hadn't made a dent. He needed to make her understand. Somehow, she had to grasp what he was saying.

"Austin." He hated the calm in her tone when she was trying to rationalize something and, apparently, when she was attempting tear his heart out. "I have nothing to offer any of you in return. Before Serena brought me here, I didn't exist. The only difference now is you all made me feel like I do. I will go back to what I

163

know. That's as it should be, the way it was meant to be." She sighed and rubbed her temples. "Look, I'm planning on coming back here every summer, or at least I've thought about it, if I'm welcome. Especially with the studio and everything. But I can't stay here, live here."

When she made her way to the door and slowly turned around, he thought he would weep right then and there. The sting was there, edged in her eyes, blurring his. She mumbled so softly it was almost as if she never spoke at all. "You could never love someone like me anyway."

His feet wouldn't move. His voice wouldn't come. He simply stood there and watched her walk out as if that was the end of it.

Serena slumped in Jake's bed and listened to the water down the hall from his shower. She felt damn fine. Tired, her chest achy, but fine.

She threw the sheets aside and wondered if he still had a couple pairs of her panties in his top drawer, along with an extra set of clothes. She rose and fished around in the dresser. Her hand closed around a small hard object. Curious, she took it out and froze. After a beat, she stumbled back to the bed.

The tiny black velvet box shook in her hands at the same time the air rushed out of her lungs. She heard Jake come in the room but she didn't look up. "This was my mother's wedding and engagement band."

He leaned against the doorframe with a towel around his waist and crossed his arms, searching her profile for a reaction. Aside from shock, he couldn't get a read on her. "Yes, it was."

Her lips trembled when she finally looked at him. And there was his Serena, heart in her eyes. "How did you get it?"

Jake sighed and lifted his brows, straightening from the doorway. "Grams gave it to me when I asked her for it three years ago." He strolled over to the dresser and closed the top drawer she'd left open. He opened another and pulled out a white T-shirt, throwing it over his head. He painstakingly took his time stepping into shorts before turning to look at her.

He'd never intended for her to find out. Salt in the wound. Old wounds, new ones, it mattered not. Awareness crept into her eyes when he took the box from her. "In case you're wondering, yes, I was going to ask you to marry me the same day you told me you were leaving."

She pinched her eyes closed, as if doing so would remove the past, and dropped her face into her hands. She hurriedly picked her head back up and ran both hands through her mop of curls. He almost forgot what she looked like after a round of lovemaking. Her skin was still flushed, her hair wild, and the sheets wrapped tightly around her midsection. More beautiful than anything he'd ever laid his eyes on.

"Why didn't you say something?" A violent, unmistakable tremor tinged her voice.

Jake didn't care for the anger that grew inside him, and for three years it had been building. He shoved it down as best he could and dialed his tone to flat. "When, Serena? After you said 'I'm leaving' or before you walked out? You didn't want me, and didn't want to be here, so what was the point?" His voice rose a painful octave. "What was the damn point in telling you that I loved you more than my next breath and I wanted to spend the rest of my life with you?"

Recognition swamped her eyes as she shot up off the bed and began dressing. Skirt. Shirt. She fished around behind him in the top drawer and grabbed another pair of underwear. With clipped movements, she stepped into the panties and yanked them up.

"You haven't forgiven me. That's all I wanted from you. Even now, after making love again, you hold this over me."

He hit his breaking point. "It would help to know why the woman I loved for more than half my life decided I wasn't good enough and suddenly quit loving me!"

That stopped her. She went deathly white and abruptly the shadows under her eyes seemed like caves. It took the fight right out of him. She sank on the bed shakily when he reached out for her.

"Is that what you think?"

He knelt between her thighs and ran his palms over his face. He could go the rest of his life without seeing that look again. "What else was I supposed to think?"

Serena took his jaw in her hands. "Oh, Jake. I never stopped loving you. There's never been anyone else. I didn't leave because of you. I tried to tell you that. I had to go where no one knew me, away from people who lifted a hand and gasped every time I got so much as a headache. I needed to try my art on my own. I wanted to come back before I even knew I was ill. I wanted to come back to you. I never..." She closed her eyes. "It wasn't your fault."

He vaguely remembered her trying to say something similar when she'd left. At the time, he'd been too shocked and too wrecked to listen. He rose and backed into the dresser. "I lied to you."

She lifted her head, a question in her gaze.

"I lied to you in your grandmother's living room, when I said I didn't wait for you." Repressed tears threatened, blurring her form before him. "Every night, every day I waited for you to come back to me. Since you were sixteen and I brought you tulips in the hospital to the day that big heart of yours finally gives out, I will wait for you. Will you wait in Heaven for me? For me to come to you?"

Her throat burned and her chest ached. Her tears were hot and heavy where they traced a path down her cheeks. He understood. He forgave her. And it was real. She was going to die and he knew it. She could read the gutting realization in his eyes. Denial fled, and it had finally sunk into him that this was all they could have. These few broken, scattered fragments.

"Yes." She cleared her throat and spoke louder. "Yes, I'll wait for you."

He jerked to attention. "Marry me."

"What?"

"Marry me, Serena." He closed the distance and knelt down in front of her, gripping her hands. "I know there's not much time, but we can't waste any more. We fit. There has never been anyone else and I don't want there to be. We've waited long enough. Stay with me. Stay with me until it's your time to go and wait for me to come to you again."

The sobs racked her body until she couldn't breathe. She nodded when he slipped her mother's band on her finger. She doubled over into his lap as he held her until the quaking stopped. Pressing kisses to her hair and wrapping her tight, he rocked her.

"I love you, Serena. Damn it, I love you. I don't know what I'll do without you, but I couldn't stop if I wanted to."

166

Chapter Ten

"I really don't think this is a good idea."

Jake looked over from the passenger seat of his truck and smiled at the beautiful blonde next to him. "Courtney, everyone needs to learn how to drive sometime."

"What if I crash, though?"

He rubbed the back of his head and grinned. "Well, then I guess I can finally buy a new truck. Austin's been after me to do it for awhile now."

"Not funny, Jake."

He thought it was pretty funny. Figuring she would start in her own time, he waited patiently for her to be ready while the truck idled. After a few minutes she sighed her resignation.

"Okay, darlin'." He shifted closer in the bucket seat. "Now put your foot on the left pedal. That's the brake." He pointed to the gear shift. She shifted the truck into drive and let out an amusing squeal when the truck rolled forward. He couldn't hide the humor in his voice. "Good. Now lightly touch the gas pedal and steer straight."

She glanced around briefly at the house and the gravel road before her, and then did what he instructed. When the car lunged forward she panicked and slammed the brakes, throwing Jake into the dashboard.

He cleared his throat, still grinning, and scooted back next to her.

"See, I told you." Her shoulders sagged.

Shaking his head, he laughed heartily. "You're doing fine. Now try it again."

After several attempts, she maneuvered the car onto the street, appearing to get the hang of it. Jake stretched his legs out in front of him and draped his arm over the back of the seat.

"Wonderful. You said you had to go to the shop today, so drive there."

"What?" She side-glanced him with a look of pure DEFCON and then reverted back to the road. She slowed her already crawling speed. "No way! I'd have to turn and park to do that."

"And I'll teach you that too." He hooted. "Courtney, you are a gem." When he caught her worried brow and pouting mouth he grabbed his abdomen and bent over, tears welling up from the laughter. No wonder Austin was whipped. "Oh, man."

"I'm glad I amuse you so much, Jake. It's good to hear you laugh, but how am I supposed to drive and you teach me, when you can't breathe?"

Rubbing his hands over his face briskly, he sat up. "Just keep going and we'll learn as we go along."

After a half hour, on what should've been a ten minute drive, Jake climbed out of the truck. He peered down at the curb and grinned. She had managed to pull over and park. However, the entire passenger side of the pick-up was on the sidewalk and at a very odd angle. He looked up at sparkling blue eyes as she squealed and clapped her hands. After a few beats, she dragged him by the arm into the shop.

They found Annabelle and Brett sitting at one of the tables in the coffee section, obviously at a down time. The place was completely empty.

Courtney let go of his arm and jumped up and down. "I drove here today! Jake taught me how to drive!"

Annabelle was on her feet immediately and waddling over. "That's wonderful." She wrapped Courtney in a brief hug.

Brett looked out the window and lifted his brows.

Jake put up his hand to silence the smart remark coming. He leaned close and whispered, "We're still working on parking."

Brett smirked. "I guess so."

When a customer strolled into the bookstore, Brett went back to work in his section while Jake said his goodbyes. When it was quiet again, Courtney plopped down across from Annabelle and beamed a smile.

Annabelle shook her head and grinned back. "You could have stayed home today and practiced driving some more. It's quiet here today."

Courtney waved her hand. "I can't. I have three appointments upstairs later."

Annabelle tilted her head. "You've had good business since you opened."

"Yeah." Courtney sighed. "I was surprised myself. A lot of people were disappointed that I would only be here in the summer."

"Hmm," she muttered. "I heard that somewhere."

Courtney shrugged her shoulders. "I'll return next summer and reopen then. I can't imagine spending the season anywhere else. I'd have to come back for the photo shop now, and to see everyone again."

"Yeah." Annabelle's eyes narrowed. "Austin won't be happy about that."

Courtney waved the comment off, not wanting to think about it right now. Annabelle's thoughts were loud enough. Nobody understood, had come from the place she had. It was better to ignore and deny her desires than to have them taken away when she'd least expected. She rose and reached in her pocket for a band.

After tying up her hair, she looked around. "Everyone must be out enjoying the weather. It certainly is sad in here today."

Annabelle stood and wiped down the table. "Yes. Yes, it is."

Austin rubbed his eyes and pushed away from the computer. Since Courtney had opened her shop upstairs, his business had doubled in the last few weeks. Content with that, and not anything else, he strode out of the library.

Courtney had started sleeping in her own bed again. He didn't have the faintest idea what to do about that, or about her.

It was as if a breath of fresh air had swept through the whole house when she'd arrived. She brought laughter, and innocence, and comfort. Life. She brought life. That tiny blonde, with those big sad eyes and smiling mouth, opened feelings inside him he never thought to explore, never figured he was missing. It was much more than his basic need to protect. She had awaked him from a long sleep and he never knew he was dreaming. He loved her. And that killed him.

When Serena had returned home from California, weak and pale, he noticed even the change Courtney had brought out in her. A peace and understanding for what was to come, tethered to a friendship his sister had not experienced before. Jake saw Courtney

169

as the little sister he always wanted. She kept him smiling and focused when he would otherwise be brooding. She'd brought Serena and Jake back together, and Grams another grandchild.

She'd told him she had nothing to offer them. Austin may have given her the studio, but she had the talent, he'd just handed her the opportunity. She didn't see how happy she'd made them. Or didn't want to. She wanted to go back and…what? What was there for her to go back to?

And what was left for him when she did?

He found Grams on the front porch swing, one of her many scrapbooks in her lap. He couldn't fight the melancholy hitch to his chest. Some things never changed.

"I love how predictable you are, Grams."

"How so, my dear?" Her hazel eyes warmed at the sight of him.

He sat next to her. "I can always find you remembering out here, or in your garden." Leaning back, he breathed deep and closed his eyes. The scent of damp grass and freesia clung to the breeze.

"I noticed Courtney is sleeping back in her own bed."

Mortified, he opened his eyes and lifted his head. "You aren't supposed to notice things like that."

Her warm smile had a teasing note. "I suppose it's hard for you to think of me as anything but your Grams. But I wasn't always, you know. Your grandfather and I had many wonderful years together too. Not as many as I would like, but we had them just the same."

Looking away, he sighed into the night. "I don't know how Jake does it. It's like driving for hours with nowhere to go, then suddenly there's a dead end in front of you."

Grams nodded. "That's the way of it sometimes. But it's the things you see while having nowhere to go that matter. It may not seem this way now, but he's better for loving for a short time, than not at all. I don't think he could help loving Serena if he tried."

He peered over at the wisest woman he knew. "You sound like a proverb. Has anyone ever thanked you for being you? You make it look easy."

"Nothing worthwhile is easy, child. Especially love. But if you're lucky, you have a lot of it before you go." Drawing out a heavy sigh, she set the swing in motion. "That little darling Serena brought home hasn't had a lot of love. It's not as easy for her to accept it as it is for you. She's learning, but you must be persistent and patient."

Persistence he could do. Patience was never his strong suit. "She wants to go back to Arizona."

"Hmm." She tilted her head, mulling that over. "Going back to what she knows and what's safe."

"She told me she has nothing to offer us, that I could never love someone like her."

Grams laughed, and despite her age, it didn't sound rusty. "But you do love her."

Austin leaned forward and placed his face in his hands. He dragged his hands through his dark hair helplessly, pressing his lips together in a frown. "God help me, but yes, I do."

The Anderson wedding, which resembled a circus more than nuptials in Courtney's opinion, was set at the edge of town on one of the old plantations and teaming with family she was pretty sure the bride was trying to avoid. The woman had no idea how lucky she was. Regardless, the wedding had been lovely. This was the second time she'd been asked to photograph an event, and though it wasn't her favorite aspect of art, she enjoyed doing it.

Courtney brought the camera to her face and snapped shots of a few young troublemakers eying the cake. Before she could put the camera down, an uneasy sensation crept up her neck and spread to her head, crushing. Turning slowly, she found a group of teenagers giggling and pointing at her. She froze.

Suddenly, it all came back. Every harsh word, every drunken slur washed up and held her locked in place, awaiting a blow.

The blonde girl, with a lilac dress and shoes too old for her, strutted up to Courtney with a wry twist to her lips. She placed a hand on her protruding hip. "I hear you're a witch. You read people's fortunes." She twisted around when the other girls giggled and then whipped her head back around to Courtney. "We don't like your kind in our town."

Witch. That's all Courtney heard. Ice crawled over her skin, sank bone deep. Her heart beat an erratic rhythm inside her chest.

Her throat closed. With her lips trembling, tears welled before she could stop them.

Dropping the camera from her limp hands, she raced against the panic and terror toward the gazebo on the other side of the vast yard. The teenagers' giggles followed her until she neared the white trellis and climbed the stairs. Away. Just get away. Sitting on a bench, placing her head between her knees, she waited for the attack to pass. Breathe. In and out. Had she made of fool of herself?

Footsteps echoed on the steps and she jerked before she remembered she was safe. And the man walking toward her was about as safe as she could get. Relief washed over her. "Father Jerry." She sniffed and wiped her cheeks. "Nice day for a wedding."

He sat casually next to her and gazed out at the people. "Yes, it is." Without another word he handed her a tissue and leaned back, giving her time to collect herself.

"Thanks." She blew out a cleansing breath and tilted her face toward the sun. "I'm glad you're here. I needed you today."

"No, you didn't. You only have to believe in yourself. That will come." He brushed a strand of red hair from his forehead. "Why did you let those girls bother you?"

"Knee-jerk reaction, I guess." She glanced away. "I feel like an idiot."

He turned to face her fully and placed a firm hand on hers. "You are many things, but an idiot is not one of them. Nor are you a witch." She stiffened against him. He studied her another beat. "Look at me, Courtney. Witch. Witch." She covered her ears. "It's just a word, Courtney. It has no power unless you give it. Witch. Witch."

Her backbone straightened until finally, she rose. "Stop it! I am not a witch." Eyes wide, she threw her hand over her mouth and plopped back down. "I'm sorry. I yelled. I'm sorry."

With a satisfied smirk, he nodded. "No need to apologize. Now say it a few more times and you just might believe it. Besides, I don't associate with witches, generally."

Her laugh started hesitantly, eventually became erratic, and she hunched over, holding her abdomen. So ridiculous, so silly, so right. She needed that today. Straightening, she pulled him to her in a brief hug. "You're such a nice man."

Patting her shoulder, he released her. "Now that that's done, let's talk about weddings. You've done photography for a couple now. Any plans to have one of your own?"

"What? No. Father, I'm not the kind of woman men want to…"

"Want to what? Want to marry?" He leaned closer. "I beg to differ. Still some of Daddy's junk in your head. How's it going with Austin?"

Her head spinning, she tried to put words to her thoughts. "It's been going okay. We had a fight last week."

"About what?" He sat back again on the bench, his pose casual.

"I told him I was leaving when everything was done with Serena. He got mad. I mean, I never intended to stay."

He pondered that a moment. "Well, if the woman I spent my whole life looking for decided to leave I think I might get upset too." He watched her, but she didn't react. "I'm not taking sides, but if he loves you, like I assume he does, he has a right to be upset. And to fight. Talk to him. Work it out."

She rose and smoothed a wrinkle from her dress. "I have to get back to work. Thanks, Father."

"One step forward, two steps back," he mumbled.

She pretended not to hear that too.

Serena set the front porch swing in motion and studied her brother in the dark. He had a good brood going on. "You're either getting too close to Courtney or not close enough."

"Who made you Yoda?"

"Very funny." It was a rare sight to see Austin worked up over a woman. "How long have you been in love with her?"

He slapped a hand on his thigh. "That's it. I'm tired of you and Grams ganging up on me."

She smiled and tossed up her hands in surrender. "Just trying to help."

He crossed his arms. "So I'm in love with her. So what? I can't do a damn thing about it. She wants to leave. A man has pride, you know."

"Okay, enough. I've let you brood all week. You've never backed down from a fight in your entire life. This is just a different sort. Use different gloves."

He cleared his throat and narrowed eyes on her. "Suddenly the bride gets what she wants and is wise to everyone else's problems."

"Be as smug as you want. You'll lose her then. Fight and you won't. I know her better than most, better than she lets most know her. This isn't about love or losing. It isn't a game. Life isn't a game. It's about her."

He sighed, turning his face toward the yard. Ignored the sharp stab in his chest that never went away. "Yeah, okay. Go to bed. I'll work on it."

She smacked a kiss on his cheek. "About time you listened to your wise older sister."

"That whole five minutes older made such a difference."

Throwing her head back, she laughed in that irritating, rhetorical way of hers, the one that could spread through a room, and went inside.

"I still can't believe you knew the exact moment we were making love."

Courtney smiled at Serena's reflection in the mirror from where she stood behind her. Today she would help her friend become a wife to the man she always wanted. Pulling a pin from her mouth she stuck it in Serena's mass of curls to hold her veil in place. Her mother's veil, her mother's dress. What a sight she made.

"I think it's secure. A hurricane couldn't blow this thing off your head."

Serena laughed and stood. "I'm not even nervous. I should be nervous."

"No, you shouldn't." Grams walked up behind them. "You climbed trees with the boy, you fell in love with the man. It's about time, if you ask me."

Courtney sat in a chair and strapped on her shoes while Grams began fastening the start of many tiny buttons on Serena's dress. The design was so simple it was stunning. The dark ivory satin formed to her figure and flowed out at the knees in a forties style fashion. She'd had to have it taken in twice in the three weeks it took them to prepare for this day because of Serena's weight loss.

Her friend had been using the oxygen tank almost all the time, not just when she slept. She napped at least four hours during the day and crashed for ten at night, woken only by coughing fits. Her blood tests weren't optimistic. She was eating less and less as the days went on, and the circles under her eyes were almost hidden by the makeup she'd painstakingly applied. Her once olive skin had a wan, yellowish tint.

Courtney watched Grams' steady hands close the back of Serena's dress. It had a series of thirty delicate buttons, bore no sleeves, and was altered to have a high neckline to hide her scar.

Grams wore an elegant peach-colored dress with a matching jacket. Her long gray hair was swept up, as it usual, in a knot behind her head. Those hazel eyes held as much sadness as they did delight.

Quietly, Courtney reached for the camera on the vanity next to her. She'd print the shots from this room in black and white, give a timeless quality to them. The color arrangement from the stained glass in the bridal room at the church had low light filtering through. It would set off a soft tone on film.

Courtney waited patiently until Serena turned her head just enough to get a full profile of them both. Serena's hand was clasping her gold cross around her neck and Grams' would forever be paused on a button from behind her granddaughter. She set the camera down in her lap and smiled. How she wished they could stay like that forever. At least in a photograph, they would.

Austin knocked and strolled in, closing the door behind him. He glanced down the length of Courtney's light blue bridesmaids' dress, which mirrored Serena's except for the buttons in back. A muscle ticked in his jaw.

They hadn't spoken much more than pleasantries since their argument three weeks earlier and she didn't know what to do to bridge the gap, or even if she should. It would be easier to leave with things this way, but she missed the kind words he would whisper into her ear at odd moments, yearned for his arms to hold her again. She feared she would never stop missing him, no matter how far away they were.

Regret tore at her. She understood why they wanted her stay. She wanted to also. For the first time in her life, she desired something just for herself. But did she deserve it? It seemed selfish on her part. She'd escaped her father's wrath, skated death as a teenager, throwing off what she'd thought was her fate-designed timeline. Ever since, she'd felt...off. Like she'd been doing something wrong just by being here, by breathing. By inserting herself into the Edwards' lives any more than she already had, would they be punished for her actions?

Truth was, people like her weren't meant to be more than a passing glance. What did she know about family or relationships? Her own father couldn't love her, so how could she expect to make anyone else happy?

Austin took his sister's hands, snapping Courtney's attention back. "Aren't you a vision."

When he wrapped Serena in his arms, Courtney lifted her camera and tried to forget how it felt to have those arms around her. She took the shot of their embrace, Grams standing beside them and, completely unnoticed, slipped out of the room.

It figured if Serena wanted a small event, the world would find out. When news she was finally marrying "the Warner boy" spread, the entire town had come, fanning the humidity from themselves in the pews. Most knew the reason why the wedding was being rushed. This community had watched her grow, helped her heal, and formed who she became. They'd be here for her on her special day.

Courtney decided she had enough time to climb the stairs to the balcony and capture the patrons seated below before the procession began. It brought tears to her eyes to think some of the older townsfolk below had sat right there for Serena and Austin's parents' wedding thirty years before. Full circle.

Jake stepped out of a side room with Father Jerry and made his way to the altar. She quickly snapped a picture of them and rushed down the stairs to take her position.

Chapter Eleven

"**O**kay." Serena grinned, gesturing wildly with her hands. "So there are a few more people than expected. While Courtney is taking some photos, can Mom and Dad Warner go help Annabelle back at Grams'?"

"Sure, we can do that, baby." Irene patted her arm. "You look so lovely today."

Courtney stood back a ways and had already taken dozens of shots of them quickly brainstorming after the service. They were all glowing from their day, a day they waited too long to have. "I just need a picture of Serena and Jake with Mom and Dad and then I'm finished."

Austin's eyes searched her face with an unreadable expression. "Someone should get a picture of you and Serena too."

"Oh, yes." Serena's eyes widened. "We don't have any of us together."

"I've used a camera or two in my day." Jack lifted the camera strap over Courtney's neck. "I can manage."

Courtney, not knowing what else to do but go along, handed Mr. Warner the other camera. "That one's got black and white film, use this one. It's digital." She leaned in and showed him how to focus and what button to push. "You won't need flash. Hold this down half-way to focus. It's automatic. Then it will take itself."

"Got it. Let's see," he said and glanced around. "How about you stand over by the fence there."

Serena stepped over to the black wrought iron fence, climbing with jasmine vines, and wrapped her arms around Courtney in a fierce hug. "Thank you for everything. I love you."

Serena's love, her affectionate warmth, flowed from her into Courtney. "I love you too."

"Smile!"

Courtney rode back to the house with Austin to give Jake and Serena some quiet time alone. He hadn't said anything of substance in so long she thought he'd lost his ability. Or will. She'd always known when to keep her mouth shut and stay in the background. It had been ingrained in her since birth. But if it was anything this family had taught her, it was that she could be comfortable with them. Be herself, whoever that was. And she needed to fix this thing between her and Austin.

"I'm sorry, Austin."

The only response she got was his jaw muscle clenching and a sheer determined glint in his eyes as he pulled into the driveway. His features didn't soften in the least when he cut the engine and...banged his forehead to the wheel.

"I can't do this." He sighed and twisted in the seat to face her. His golden eyes were riddled with pain as he searched hers. "I can't do this anymore. I shouldn't have reacted that way back in your studio, getting angry with you, and I'm sorry. It was my fault. You did nothing wrong." He quickly glanced to the house in front of them and then back to her.

The *thud, thud* of her heart was deafening as she sensed where this conversation was going. She grabbed for the handle and raced from of the car, but he was faster. He pinned her against the vehicle with his hard, tense body.

"Don't, Austin." Desperation clawed at her. She tried to move around him, but it was futile.

Austin snapped his hands around her hips to hold her still. "I love you."

Slacking from the weight of his words, she grabbed his arms as if he'd delivered a death knell. "I told you not to say it." Tears slipped past her pale lashes and onto her cheeks.

She averted her gaze when he cupped her cheeks. She struggled against his patience when he kissed her lips. A sob tore at her chest when she finally gave in and opened to him. There was no fight left. Gripping his shoulders, she forced herself to draw in air as he rested his brow to hers.

"I love you and you're just going to have to get used to hearing it." He pressed warm caresses to her cheeks as if they could stop the tears. Drawing her close, he buried his face in her hair. "I just wasn't expecting you, Courtney. Being without you these past weeks has been torture. I tried to give you space. I tried to show you how good we can be, how good we are. You think you have to go back to Arizona, but you don't." He pulled her away at arms length, forcing those blue eyes to look at him. "What more can I do? Why can't you let me love you?"

"Because it's wrong." There. Honesty. Finally. She wiped her eyes and cheeks. "I'm here with you for a little while longer, so let's not waste the time we have left."

As he watched her struggle for calm, he discovered something. Like a slap upside the head. In all his scenarios, her *wanting* to stay never factored in. He thought with words and actions he could change her mind, make her desire a life together. But that was never the problem. She *did* want everything he offered, but through her years of experience she thought she didn't deserve it. Pain, unlike anything he'd ever seen before, infused her eyes every time they'd discussed her return to Arizona. He'd been too pissed off, too desperate to notice. Too selfish of his own needs to see what she needed.

As of right now, that was about to change.

"All right, Courtney. I give up. We won't discuss you leaving anymore. You think whatever you need to think. But understand this. I'm not letting you go. I love you. And you love me. It's not wrong. At some point, you're going to have to let someone love you. Because you deserve it." That was the crux of her issues. Her past had hammered home that screwed up belief system in her head. He kissed her, closing his eyes as the tension drained from him when she relented. "You deserve everything."

And he'd give it to her.

Austin and Courtney were a tangled mass of limbs, but he didn't care. The time had been too lengthy since he last had her in his bed beside him. Satisfied, he drew her tighter to his side.

In the quiet between them, he wondered what it was about Arizona that made her feel so safe. "Tell me about Mrs. Meyers." He kissed her temple.

She pushed her hair from her face and smiled up at him. "She's a heavy woman with gray hair. I don't think I've ever seen it out of its bun. When I need it, she'll offer comfort, but most often times she's real blunt. The direct approach is more her style. She doesn't like to coddle." She burrowed into his chest.

He wondered if she regretted her decision to get in the car with his sister, a virtual stranger. What had possessed her to in the first place? Before he could ask, she was talking again.

"When Serena first walked into the diner, I sensed her right away. Mrs. Meyers and Dr. Maynard had just tried their latest tactic to get me to travel or move on from that town. It seemed too perfect that she walked in at that exact moment." She let out a wistful sigh. "You would like Mrs. Meyers. She tells you exactly what she thinks, whether you want to hear it or not."

He grunted and kissed the top of her head. She spoke of no one else but this Mrs. Meyers and doctor somebody. Who would be there when she returned? Who would hold her and tell her they'd missed her? Running his hand down the silky skin of her back, he frowned. There was no one in Arizona who loved her like they did here, people who kept her out of her shell and challenged her. No attachments. It must be easier for her to have that, a lack of connection, than it was for her to accept happiness.

Fall had crept in prematurely for the south, bringing a slight chill to the air and an assortment of colors. Green leaves were struggling for life, a losing battle against the beauty their death portrayed.

Austin listened from his position against Courtney's office window while she patiently struggled with a screaming three-year-old who flat out did not want her picture taken. He turned only when, after twenty minutes, the blaring had stopped.

Courtney had pulled away the carpeted block the girl had been sitting on and was cooing to her in a soothing voice while changing the backdrop. A park path was behind the girl now, making it seem as if she was strolling down a trail.

He smiled as Courtney went from posed photography to journalistic style. That was her element, what she was best at.

Courtney unwrapped a rather large lollipop and handed it to the girl with a smile. When the brat was engaged with her sucker, Courtney dabbed at the girl's eyes while the mom stood by in obvious admiration. Courtney moved behind her tripod and asked what the girl thought of the latest Disney movie.

Austin was dumbfounded when the girl began twirling around on the makeshift garden path and describing scenes from the movie. The camera clicked several times, catching the girl with a large grin and dress flowing with the movement, lollipop in hand. After a few moments, the child sat on a fake rock and contentedly licked her sugar high, unaware that Courtney took a few more shots and called it a successful day.

"The pictures should be ready in a few days," she told the mom.

The mother turned to her, perplexed. "How in God's name did you do that?"

Courtney laughed and wrapped the cords around her hand and elbow so they wouldn't tangle, causing her dress to dip at the chest and Austin's mouth to water.

"Distraction is a wonderful tool. The pictures might not be a traditional sitting pose, but they should come out great. You have a lovely daughter."

"Oh, she's something all right. Do you babysit too? I'll pay a million an hour."

Laughing, Courtney shook her head and crouched down by the little girl. "All right, sweetie, you are all done. That wasn't so bad, was it?" When the girl shook her head, still distracted by the treat in her hand, Courtney showed them out and then slumped on the gold-patterned couch.

Austin sat next to her and smacked a kiss on her cheek. "Woman, you are amazing. You'd make a great mom."

Courtney looked at him through slanted eyes.

He laughed and took her hand in his. She'd changed so much from when she'd first arrived in Georgia. She had confidence and verve now, so much more than even she realized. A woman he grew more and more in love with as the days went on.

He looked forward to their evenings alone, when he asked about her day, wanting to know what she thought about everything. While he worked in his shop, he actually had withdrawals away from her. He wanted her in a white dress meeting him at the altar. He wanted their kids running around the yard like he used to with Jake and Serena. He wanted her to be completely his, in every way.

He wanted, and she drew away.

He peered down at their joined hands. Her skin was pale in comparison to his olive tone. So small and delicate, but he knew she was far from that. The woman had escaped unspeakable torture to live the life she thought she could never have. She still thought that. He was doing everything in his power to change her mind about leaving, and though they didn't speak about it, he knew it was always in the back of her mind.

When she sighed next to him, he cut his thoughts short and looked at her pretty face. "What should we do for your birthday? It's only a month away."

His grin spread when she pursed those pink lips in thought. If he had to move a mountain, he would make her first birthday a memorable one.

Abruptly, she stood, spine erect and muscles tense. She grabbed her chest, wide-eyed, and wheezed out an unsteady breath.

He shot to his feet. "Are you all right? What's going on?"

"We have to go home. Now."

It was too soon, Serena thought in a panic.

She was barely a bride. Courtney wasn't settled yet. Jake wasn't ready. Austin, there wasn't enough time with him and Grams yet.

Gripping the edge of the kitchen counter, she fought to bring in oxygen. She'd left her tank in the bedroom. A mistake. It was as if a thousand knives penetrated her lungs. Cold sweat laced her face. Reaching for her chest, she looked desperately around for Jake.

Recalling he was working in the barn, she attempted to round the counter. Another stab knocked her to her knees and had her wheezing out what little air was left in her lungs.

She had seen the signs coming. The lab work results showed a rapid decline in liver and kidney function. Her skin had been insipidly pale this morning. She'd been sleeping too much. It was harder to breathe walking from one room to the next. She'd lost so much weight. The littlest things required so much effort.

But she wasn't ready.

Crawling for the door, the edges of her vision grayed. Dots swam before her eyes..

The door was so far. Too far.

Laying down, she gave in for the moment, but was not giving up. There were things to be done yet.

I'll just close my eyes for a minute.

Just for a minute.

Austin and Courtney found Jake and Grams in a waiting room of Athens Regional Medical Center, huddled together holding hands.

Courtney sat on the chair next to Grams and rubbed her hand over her back. She glanced around the cold room, decorated in an attempt to mask visitors true whereabouts. Large artificial plants were propped in the corners as magazines lay scattered across the tables. Cheap prints of neutral colors in abstract art were hung on the peach-colored walls.

It was enough to make anyone go crazy.

Jake jerked his chin up when Austin sat next to him. "I was working on the cabinets for the Murphy's kitchen. I found her face down on the floor when I came in for a bottle of water. She was barely breathing." He ran a shaking hand down his face.

"It's all right." Austin squeezed his shoulder. "Have they told you anything yet?"

"No. It's been two hours."

Courtney rose, needing something to do. Guilt spread in her belly, fast and heavy. She hadn't sensed Serena's collapse right away, couldn't feel Serena now. It was after the attack she'd felt pressure in forewarning. She had no idea why these visions hadn't warned her sooner. She might've been able to get there faster.

Austin had distracted her. Perhaps that was why. And now, now her mind was blank. She dreaded the worst--that Serena had already gone before goodbyes could be said. Panicked, she paced, pressing a hand to her stomach to quell the nausea.

"I'll go find a nurse's station."

Before she could take a step, an older man in teal-colored scrubs walked in and hunkered down in the chair across from Jake. He nodded to each of them and rubbed his solemn brown eyes. Salt and pepper hair was neatly combed and parted to the left.

"I'm Dr. Grant. You may remember me from Serena's past hospitalizations."

Jake and Grams nodded, then proceeded to introduce Courtney. As discretely as possible, Courtney gestured for Dr. Grant to just get on with the news.

"Serena's kidneys are almost completely shut down. With the dialysis, we were hoping to buy more time than this. Because of them failing, she's retaining too much fluid and not putting out enough. Nothing is being filtered like it should be." The doctor rubbed his jaw. "Be prepared. She's swollen all over and her color's not good. Her heart function is extremely weak. Her congestion has improved, but her lungs can fill again at any time. You're aware there's nothing we can do but make her comfortable now. She has a living will stating no feeding tubes or machines. We can only give her oxygen at this time."

Courtney choked back a sob.

"How long does she have?" Jake's voice was flat, resigned.

"It's hard to say. A few days, maybe." The doctor shrugged and stood. "I'm really very sorry. She exceeded her life expectancy with this kind of diagnosis, which truly has been a miracle."

"I'm taking her home," Jake said and rose. "I don't want advice or arguments." Flint in his gaze, he stared down the doctor before he could protest. "She's not taking her last breaths in a hospital. Give me everything I'll need and get the ball rolling. I'm taking her home."

Dr. Grant nodded and exited the room.

Serena didn't even look like the same person. Her face looked like a punching bag and her once beautiful olive skin was yellow. Her dark curls lay limp against the pillow while tubes brought oxygen up her nose. The IV in her arm left bruises around the tape.

Serena had been home for a couple days and she rarely stayed awake longer than five minutes at a time. It was such a burden on Courtney's own heart to see this once active and agile friend of hers fight to hang on in a hospital bed by the fireplace in Jake's house. She was holding on longer than she needed to and Courtney suspected the reason.

Placing her hand to Serena's forehead, Courtney's vision flashed again. Serena dreamed of the white light and her parents calling, but yet she held back. The pain was immense, so overpowering Courtney had to let go of her hand because she couldn't take it.

Months ago, while they'd traveled to Georgia, she'd told Serena that when the leaves stopped falling was when she would go. Eyeing the window, she took in the sunlight filtering through the mostly green leaves. Some trees, like the younger oaks, had colorful arrangements blooming and dropping, but the mature trees were just beginning the change.

Serena would die before they were done falling. Before autumn was complete. These visions and feelings had never been wrong before, so questions built in her mind why the leaves played such an important part in timing.

Serena moaned and opened her eyes. Courtney whirled back to the bed. The bright golden light was gone from Serena's eyes and was replaced by clouded confusion.

"It's all right, Serena. I'm here."

They took shifts staying with her in case she awakened and needed anything. Neighbors brought over casseroles and called constantly to give their support. It was almost as if Serena was already gone.

"When I first saw you--" Serena coughed and struggled for breath. After several long moments, she continued in a raspy voice. Gone was the sexy drawl and smoky laugh. "I saw you and felt relief. You healed me. I wish you could heal yourself."

Courtney couldn't heal Serena. Nothing could. But she suspected her friend wasn't referring to her body, but her spirit. She searched Serena's face, delved into her mind, and found a love so genuine it brought tears to her eyes. "You healed me by bringing me here. I owe everything to you."

Serena weakly shook her head. In the instant before she gave in to sleep, Serena muttered, "Everyone's angel, you are."

Courtney pressed her face into her friend's palm and wept. So much hurt, so many memories. Why wouldn't she let go? "Give in to the light, Serena. There's no pain there, I promise." She sniffed and laid her head down on the bed beside her. "We'll be okay. We have each other now. It's okay to go."

After Austin came in to stay with Serena, Courtney wandered over to the barn. Jake was slumped against an interior wall, straw coating his jeans. He gestured her over to sit with him and patted the floor between his knees.

Obliging, she nestled in between his legs and leaned against his chest. He wrapped his arms around her and squeezed gently. "How is she?"

"Sleeping. She's holding on too long, Jake. I know she's ready, but I think she needs us to say it's okay to go." She rested her cheek over his heart. "I told her it was okay."

Pressing a kiss to her hair, Jake sighed. He had no idea how different things would've been had Courtney not come home with Serena, but he suspected the outcome would've been very different. Would he and Serena have gotten married? Forgave each other, even? "I've never had a sister before. It's odd, isn't it? Some families you're born into, while others you form along the way."

"I never realized how little I had, what I was missing by not having family. Until she showed me." The tears were heavy in her throat, scorched her cheeks. Sobs shook her to the core and racked her system. "Jake, it hurts so bad."

"I know," he whispered and drew her closer, rocking, figuring the situation was much harder on her. Physically, she could feel Serena's pain, think her thoughts. They all had to stand back and watch, but Courtney? She had to live it. "I know."

It was a long time before she calmed and he shifted her in his arms. Pushing her hair away from her face, he kissed both her cheeks. "With everything going on, I think I should give you your birthday gift early. It's actually from both of us."

"You got me a present?" She smiled and stood with him, walking to the back of the barn.

"We *made* you a present." He watched her stoic profile and prayed she liked it. When she didn't say anything for a long time, he got nervous. "I can make you something else--"

"It's the loveliest thing I've ever seen. You made this for me?"

"All for you," he replied, letting out a relieved breath.

Bending down next to the large hope chest, she ran her hand along the top where Serena had painted their moment in the cave. It looked just like the photo Courtney had taken. The sunlight filtered in and the dimensions of the rock seemed as if they were real, not painted. Jake had built it out of pine, the scent filling her nose, the wood smooth.

Love. So much love went into this.

What a difference a moment can make. A blink of an eye and a decision to get in a yellow Mustang made all the difference in her life. A single moment. A bleep in time. And all the pain...it was worth it. Life was nothing without both the hurt and the joy.

Lifting the lid, she pressed a hand to her heart when she read the inscription underneath.

May you always remember the day God spoke to you, and when you brought Heaven to our door. Jake and Serena

Jake waited patiently for Serena to wake, the process slow as the hours pressed on. He squeezed her hand gently to let her know he was there. It was no easy task, watching the friend he grew up with and the woman he fell in love with at the end of a life cut too short. But there could be no regret in being with her, in giving her his all.

"I gave Courtney the hope chest today. She loved it."

She smiled weakly in response. "Take me out to the garden, Jake."

He shook his head. "It's too chilly for you tonight, darlin'."

"Please," she pleaded. "Take me out to our spot."

Concern and grief shredded his gut when it hit him why she was asking. She was ready. He couldn't deny her anything, not when they'd been kids, and not now. So he rose and turned off her heart monitor with a click. Time stood still when he removed the oxygen tube from her face and hung it on the green tank beside the bed. He pulled out the IV the way the nurse showed him and removed the tape with shaking hands.

It was not so long ago her skin was smooth and beautifully tinted. Her full lush mouth could argue him into a corner. Her golden brown eyes would light up a fraction of a second before the smile reached the rest of her face. Images of her throwing that head back to laugh swam before his memory.

No more.

He fetched the softest blanket from the bedroom and placed her thin frame inside it. Lifting her, he carried her out the back door and across the field, her lax in his arms. Sitting in the cool grass with her in his lap, he cradled her to his chest and rocked.

There was a faint scent of lavender that wafted on the breeze and it reminded him of long ago summer days. Leaves crackled in the trees as the air shifted. Grams' water fountains trickled in the distance. The estate's lone weeping willow's branches drooped at the top of the hill behind the barn, as if it felt the bittersweet withdrawal.

It was there, in the cool fall evening, in her lover's arms, surrounded by memories she held dear, that Serena left this world behind. From her bedroom balcony, Courtney nodded through her tears, because that was exactly what her friend had wanted the end to be like.

When it was over, and the raw pressure in her chest subsided, Courtney tucked herself into bed beside Austin and held him. Only when the children's laughter ceased to echo over the field did she close her eyes and join him in sleep.

Chapter Twelve

Austin sat in a not so comfortable chair at Ben Epps airport with the only real parents he knew--Jake's. The frigid rain poured down in sheets outside, soundless against the glass behind him.

"I think it's too soon to leave," Irene fretted for the umpteenth time.

Austin said nothing as Jack took her hand. "It's been long enough. Jake needs time alone to mourn."

"He hardly leaves his room. He hasn't eaten since the funeral."

Jack sighed and looked at Austin. "How are you holding up?"

"I'm all right." A lie.

He hadn't spoken to his best friend in two weeks, his grandmother sat on the porch every day and night crying over her scrapbooks, his sister was lying in the ground, and Courtney was going away tomorrow. He was just perfect.

He couldn't believe she was leaving. After everything, she was going back to Arizona.

It didn't matter to her that they all wanted her here. Serena had wished with her last breath that Courtney would find the right path. He had no idea how Jake would react, since he never left his house, nor let anyone inside. But Austin was certain that it was not what Jake wanted either.

"That's us," Irene said when the boarding call sounded over the speakers. "You take care." She encased him in her arms. Drawing back, she patted his cheek and attempted a smile. "I love you."

Swallowing hard, he nodded at the constant goodbyes. "I love you too."

Jack squeezed his shoulder in a familiar and once encouraging gesture. "I know you're worried about a certain blonde back at home. But don't. She'll come around." He heaved a hearty sigh and adjusted the strap of his bag over his wide shoulder. "Watch out for my son, Austin. He needs his friend right about now."

Austin planned on breaking down Jake's back door if he didn't let him in soon.

"I will. Take care." He drew the older man to him for a brief hug and released him. "Have a safe trip back."

Courtney watched the night sky through the front window. Grams had been out on the porch all day, and it was looking like she'd be out there all evening. There was such sadness in her hazel eyes and Courtney had a hard time not sensing it even through the glass. She drew her sweater tighter to her chest and stepped out onto the porch.

The days were getting shorter and the air smelled like burning incense. But the nights had a nip to the air as fall settled in for its stay. The wind kicked up, scattering leaves across the yard in a scraping echo against the walk.

She sat gingerly on the swing as a strand of hair came loose from Grams' knot. Thoughts drifted to her mind, emotions swirled. She reeled when she realized Grams wasn't thinking about Serena. "What troubles you about me, Grams?"

Grams passed the book in her lap to Courtney. "I was going to give you this tomorrow."

Courtney opened the scrapbook. Grams had scrolled her name on the cover and filled its contents with pictures. Tears stung her eyes when she saw some of her snapshots from the time she'd left Arizona to present. All the places Serena had taken her to on their way here stood out on the pages. Photos from the wedding and the invitation were placed inside. A clipping from the funeral and a picture of Jake, Serena, Austin, and her in front of the mural at the shop adorned the last page.

"I thought you should have one of your own, for your memories." Grams' voice was so soft Courtney had to strain to hear. "But I fear there won't be anymore memories after tomorrow."

Courtney closed the book, shut down the regret. "I'll be back next summer."

She sighed and set the swing rocking. "But it's not quite the same, is it?" Grams craned her head and looked at her for the first time since she'd sat down. "Do you know what joy you brought to our lives? No, I suppose you don't." She nodded understandingly.

"I wonder why you must return to contentment, when a lifetime of happiness is right here."

Courtney didn't know what to say. It was her deep-seeded desire to remain here. To wake every morning next to Austin and laugh with Jake. To keep her shop year round and not just the summer months. To sit right here every night with Grams. But her head had kept her safe all these years, no matter what her heart alleged.

Grams gazed out over her yard. "Do you remember what you said to Serena about the leaves?"

"Yes." The visions and feelings had never deceived her before. So why that one in particular was mistaken haunted her mind. Serena was supposed to go then. When the leaves stopped falling.

Grams folded her hands in her lap and pinned her with a no nonsense gaze. "When the leaves stop falling was not the time for Serena to die. It was your time to live."

Her breath caught. The words pierced straight through Courtney, couldn't be ignored. The past collided with the present, images and emotions pressing inside her skull. The conclusion shoved doubt away. There was the answer she'd been seeking.

Grams rose and smoothed her nightgown. "The only problem now is, will you?"

Courtney's bags were packed. They sat on the bed behind her, taunting her to pick them up and just go. The giant teddy bear and hippopotamus Austin had won smiled at her. The hope chest lay at the foot of the bed with all her cameras and photos.

So why was it she couldn't contract her feet to move?

Breathing deep, she peered next door where Jake's house could be seen from her balcony. He hadn't left the house once in the two weeks since they'd buried Serena. Grams would pop over now and then, but she never stayed longer than five minutes. He didn't even let Austin into the house. Too much of her in him.

Giving a fleeting look at her watch, she noted there was three more hours until her flight. After her talk with Grams late last night, Courtney had changed her plane reservation from Arizona to Utah. It was time for her to face her worst fear. Only in doing that could she truly move on. Austin deserved all of her, not the empty

191

shell she sometimes still felt she was. Whatever happened in Utah with her father would determine if her flight out of there was bound for Arizona or Georgia.

The ache and longing were fierce inside her. She would miss Grams' garden, her thoughtful words, and calming presence. She would miss Jake's childlike teasing and half-cocked grin. And she couldn't deny how she would miss Austin's arms, and scent, and love. It was these things that cemented her decision to return to that hell of a house and face her father.

But Courtney had to patch things up for Serena before she left, in case she didn't come back here. Time would do the rest, but Jake needed Austin right now, and she could help with that. Then she could go, with her memories. And possibly, hope.

Sometimes, when she was feeling particularly weak, she wished with all her heart she had never gotten in that little yellow Mustang and come here. The emptiness inside grew each day for the loss the world suffered when Serena died. It was easier not knowing what it was like to be loved, what it was like to have family.

What it was to be truly happy.

But it couldn't be taken back, and she knew deep down it shouldn't. That wonderful woman, with a heart too big for her body, brought Courtney more than all these miles to her home.

For the past couple weeks, Austin had made demands, claiming she didn't have to leave. That he didn't want her to go. He loved her. She imagined it wasn't fair to tell him that she loved him too. So much it hurt and left her hollow inside.

In the end, she couldn't make him happy. Not until she reclaimed her life, her past, and her memories. She may have started out as nothing, as a nobody, but she was somebody now. Best to remember that when the future scared her.

Knowing Jake wouldn't answer the door, she stepped right into his house, finding him in his bedroom the very same way she had all those months ago. His back was to her, where he gazed out the window, seemingly lost.

"I came to say goodbye."

Slowly, he turned to face her, confusion in his emerald eyes. "What do you mean goodbye?"

"My flight leaves in a couple hours."

He took two steps toward her. "Why? I mean, why are you leaving?"

Lowering her head, she sunk to the bed, gliding her hand fondly over the quilt. "I have to." He didn't need to know what she had planned or why.

"After everything that's happened, you still think that?" He offered a grunt of frustration and sat next to her. "Do you think it was some random coincidence you two found each other that day in the diner? A dying woman and a lost soul?"

"She has her peace now, that's what she needed and wanted. I stayed until then."

Taking her hand, Jake struggled for patience. "Oh, honey, your visions didn't show you anything tangible? Everything your life lacked before she gave to you. This was what she wanted for you." He stormed to the window and pointed. "That man over there, he loves you more than I've ever seen him love anything. You're what he wants. You're all he wants."

"He deserves better." And she was going to make herself worthy.

"Next to my wife, there is no better." Taking hold of her hand again, he sat next to her. "Don't deny my wife what she truly wanted or what her brother loves. Most of all, don't deny yourself. You've had enough. Be happy, Courtney."

She was going to try, but she couldn't tell him that, not until she was sure. "I want this so badly, Jake, I just don't know how. I keep telling myself just take the damn chance…"

He yanked her up off the bed and dragged her from the room. "We're going next door and you're telling Austin you love him."

She stopped him dead before they hit the door. He whirled around impatiently and all irritation subsided when he found tears and a smile. A grin such as he hadn't seen from her, and it was about time. She was genuinely remarkable. He kissed her offset nose and enveloped her tight. "It's about time you listened to me."

"Thank you, Jake. I will go with you, and I will tell him I love him, and then I will get on that plane. You don't need to understand, but you do need to trust me, trust that I have to do this."

Neither Grams nor Austin could be found anywhere. Courtney's heart began to sink. They'd searched the entire house and were about to give up when they walked into her room. On the bed, a small box sat on top of her bag that she was certain had not there before when she'd been packing.

"Pick it up," Austin demanded. He stood in the corner of the room next to where Grams was sitting in the chair.

Confused, she did just what he asked, and gasped. The ring was small and gold, with two leaves joined to the band and a diamond in the center. It was the most beautiful thing she'd ever seen.

"I refuse to take you to the airport, because you are not leaving." He paced to the foot of the bed where she stood, gaping at the box. "Jake gave Serena our mother's wedding band. This was my grandmother's. I love you and I--"

"Austin..."

Austin held up a hand, impatience winning. "Stay out of this, Jake."

Jake shook his head and chuckled under his breath. His friend could be quite dense and blind when angry. "Um, maybe you should let her talk."

Austin lifted his brows and eyed the woman who'd changed everything with her arrival. Her storm cloud eyes flooded with sentiment when she finally looked up at him. He stopped breathing, he was sure of it. Her ivory skin glowed and that adorable pink mouth was just dying to be kissed. Golden hair flowed around her oval face when she...

Smiled.

If she didn't say something soon he was going to shake a response out of her.

"I love you." She said the words so calmly he thought he imagined it.

"What? What did you say?"

Jake hooted at the two of them and stood next to Grams when she rose from her chair. "She said she loved you, you idiot."

Austin waved him off while still gawking wide-eyed at her. He never took his eyes from all that blue. "Say it again." He grabbed her arms.

"I love you." She hesitantly searched his features. "But, I--"

"Uh huh." Austin shook his head. "No buts."

The beautiful smile from just seconds before evaporated. She swallowed hard. Twice. His gut dropped. "Austin, I have to go back home," she said, too calmly. "If I don't, I can't ever know for sure if this is the right thing. You deserve more than half a woman." Her voice broke.

When Austin looked down, she was pressing the ring into his palm. His heart went into cardiac arrest. "Courtney..."

"I understand if you can't wait for me. But do know, whatever happens, that I loved you as much as a woman like me could."

She turned to a solemn Grams and walked across the room. "Thank you for everything." Courtney gave her a hug, squeezing gently, then looked at Jake. "Please, can you take me to the airport?"

With a silent nod, Jake removed her suitcase from the bed and left the room.

When Courtney tried to follow, Austin grabbed her wrist. "Don't do this, Courtney. Don't go."

"I have to. Goodbye, Austin."

After ten years, the old neighborhood still looked the same, but worn down from time and seemingly too tired to care. The bungalow-style homes rested in neat rows, like little cookie-cutters, but the yards were overgrown, the paint peeling from their exteriors, and rotting garbage strewn the street.

Courtney's taxi pulled up to the curb of 258 Brackwood Lane and parked. She made no attempt to exit the car. All it took was one look at her old house to bring every painful slap, kick, and stitch from the recesses of her mind. Ten years couldn't erase pain that ran that deep.

"Miss?" the driver said in a thick Indian accent. "This is not so good area. You want me to stay?"

Courtney turned from the window to him. "Yes, please. I'll pay you extra. Keep the meter running."

Leaving her bags in the car, she swallowed her reservation and exited the taxi. She didn't even know if her father still lived here. If he was even alive. And there was only one way to find out. Sucking in a much needed breath of air, she rang the bell. She envisioned the door flying open, a fist landing on her jaw, and screaming. There was always screaming. But none of that came. Just silence.

With shaking hands, she tested the knob. It turned easily in her grasp. Deciding to just take a quick peek inside, to see if he was home, or if she even still had the house correct, she stepped over the threshold.

The stench hit her first. Stale urine. Gin. Rotting food. Her stomach reeled as her hand flew over her nose. Memories threatened to paralyze her. But she called out for him anyway.

Taking two more steps inside, she looked around. The living room was smaller than she remembered, but the same ugly recliner was in the corner, an old TV not far from it against the wall. There were no pictures, but there weren't ten years ago either. He still lived here. In filth. "Dad?"

Again, no response. No way was she going deeper into the house, so she turned on her heel, thinking she'd come back, and ran solidly into a woman. "Oh, God. I'm sorry. I didn't see you."

"Who are you?" A cigarette dangled from a mouth full of rotting teeth. Her hair was unnaturally black, spiking in knots, and she reeked of alcohol too. Beer, to be precise.

Instead of answering her, Courtney said, "I'm looking for Clint Morgan. Have you seen him?"

The woman narrowed her eyes. "You a bill collector?" Courtney shook her head, and the woman eyed the cab on the street, then turned back to her. "What you want with Clint?"

"I'm..." What, exactly? "A distant relative."

The woman didn't look like she believed her, but inside her head Courtney could hear her thoughts. None of them were pleasant.

"He's up at McKay Dee Hospital. Has been for a few weeks. I'm watching the place for him. So don't you steal nothin'."

Duly warned, as if there was anything to steal. If the woman was so worried, she should've locked the doors. Instead of voicing her logic though, Courtney thanked her and hurried for the cab. After directing the driver to her new location, Courtney sat back, thinking. What was her father doing in a hospital? Had he gotten drunk and fallen down the stairs? Re-injured his leg?

It turned out to be none of those things.

196

Clint Morgan was in ICU with liver failure, a result of alcoholism. His organs were shutting down. Courtney returned the chart to the rack by the foot of the bed and examined her father's sleeping form. He didn't look so menacing now. His nose was enlarged, so much so his pores seemed like craters. His cheeks were ruddy, but the rest of him was a gross shade of yellow. Her gaze dropped to his cane against the wall, remembering all the damage it had once done to her youthful body.

He stirred. Though his hair was still dark and greasy, it had strands of gray woven now. Her father was an old man. Too young to be this old, but nonetheless old.

After watching him fight for consciousness, Courtney dragged a chair to the side of the bed, wondering where all her fear had gone. It felt like a light switch had been turned off inside her. She felt nothing. Not for him, nor herself.

"What's a pretty girl doing at my bedside?" he rasped, his black eyes sweeping over her.

Courtney sighed. "You never used to think I was pretty. In fact, you called me ugly. You called me a lot of things."

His hand fisted in the sheets as recognition dawned. The fear in his eyes was as unmistakable as it was surprising. Though it seemed to take an unimaginable amount of energy, he shook his head against the pillow. "Court...Courtney?"

"That, you never called me. But yes, it's me."

"Shit." His voice was just as bitter as always. "Where have you been?"

She stared at him. "I didn't think you cared. I've been here and there." No way was she giving him any more than that. "I read in your chart that you're dying. I assume you never quit drinking." He had no answer as he looked away. "Did you ever look for me?"

"Why would I? Good riddance, I say."

That should have stung. Instead, anger pounded inside her skull. Years and years of rage. "What did I ever do? What could a five year old little girl have done to upset you so much she needed ten stitches in her foot? Or an eight year old with a broken arm? Or black eyes nightly? Cigarette burns? Hair yanked out?" Courtney rose. "Huh, Dad? What did I ever do to you?"

"You were born," he ground out through clenched teeth, then wheezed in a coughing fit. Courtney sat down, appalled. "You

197

killed your mother being born, you stupid little shit. Took her from me. Murdered her."

And suddenly, it all became so very clear. The air whooshed out of her lungs with the realization. Her mother had died in childbirth. Her father blamed her and drank to cope. In another life, Courtney may have taken pleasure in knowing that even a man like her father could love once. But Clint Morgan wasn't one bit sorry for what he'd done. He never would be. He'd blame her until the day he died, which looked to be very soon.

And she refused to blame herself anymore. She may have been a scared, helpless kid then, but he was the helpless one now. Wasn't the sorry excuse for a human.

She stood, anger draining, relief flooding. It was over. It was finally over. She bent over his bed and he shrank back against the pillows, expecting a blow. Though sad, because she'd never hurt another they way he had, she couldn't deny the satisfaction she'd scared him.

Courtney kissed his cheek. "You're done hurting me. I will live and thrive and love, no thanks to you. But I forgive you."

By the look on his face, he would've been less surprised if she'd hit him.

Straightening, she raised her chin. She took the cane from beside the bed, tossed it in the trash can, and left all her ghosts behind.

Austin paced the floor in front of the fireplace in the great room. Courtney had never returned to Arizona. No one had any damn idea where she was. When Austin had called the diner, the only number he had for her, Edith Meyers was as shocked as he was. Edith hadn't even known Courtney had purchased a plane ticket to return.

Jake stood from the couch and crossed his arms. "Could her flight have been delayed?" he asked stupidly, out of suggestions.

"For two days?" Austin barked. He fisted his hands in his hair. "Did you actually see her get on a plane?"

Jake sighed. "No."

Austin's worst fears were playing before his eyes, like a warped movie reel. "What if she was taken? Hurt somewhere?" Or what if she just hopped a plane bound for somewhere else and disappeared. His stomach revolted.

Grams pursed her lips. "Let's go over what she said before she left."

Austin stopped pacing. "You were all here. She gave the ring back and said she had to go back to Arizona. Said she'd never know if this was right until she did. But she's not there."

Jake closed his eyes, trying to recall what he and Courtney had discussed at his place that day, before they'd gone next door.

I will go with you, Jake, and I will tell Austin I love him, and then I will get on that plane. You don't need to understand, but you do need to trust me, trust that I have to do this.

"No." Jake sucked in a breath. "She didn't say she had to go back to *Arizona*. She said she had to go back *home*."

Austin froze. "Oh, man. No. No, no, no." He looked at Grams. "She wouldn't go back to Utah, would she?"

"I don't know, dear." Grams shrugged, genuine fear flicking in her eyes.

"She told me I had to trust her to do this," Jake said. "I had no idea she meant that. Meant to go back..."

Austin shuddered, every memory Courtney told about her father filling his head. The panic seizing his chest nearly brought him to his knees. "Christ. If he touches one hair on her head..." He turned for the door. He had no damn clue where in Utah she'd grown up, but he'd figure it out at the airport. "What was she thinking?"

"I'm thinking a lot of things." Courtney walked into the entryway. "First being why the front door was unlocked. Anyone could get in."

"Courtney," Austin breathed, her name a prayer on his lips. "Mary Mother of God, where have you been?"

He didn't give her a chance to respond. He flew across the room, wrapped his arms around her, and fisted his hands in her hair. Pulling her head back, he kissed her soundly, and then hugged her to him again, shaking in relief.

Without hesitation, her arms encased his back. Over his shoulder, she smiled at surprised-looking Jake and Grams. "He never lets me get a word in." Releasing Austin, she went to Jake and hugged him, then Grams. After that kind of welcome home, how could she doubt her decision now?

199

Stepping away from them, Courtney looked at each one. "To answer your first question, I was thinking that I wasted too much time being afraid of my father. I let him hurt me way too long. I had to go to Utah so I could leave the pain there." She swallowed and looked Grams in the eye. "I was thinking that the leaves stopped falling."

Grams grinned. "So they have, my dear."

Courtney met Austin's gaze, her heart pumping fast. Not out of fear, or worry, or embarrassment, but because she loved him with all of her being. She was whole now. "And I was thinking," she lowered her tone, keeping her gaze locked on him, "if you still had that ring, I'd like nothing more than to wear it. Forever."

"Are you kidding?" A rush of air left his lungs and, in a flash, he was across the room and seizing her mouth. All heat and heart, his kiss consumed. He snaked an arm behind her back and hauled her flush to him, thigh to thigh, chest to chest.

Missed her so damn much.

He savored her, just like he had all the other times he'd lost himself to her, but without the weight of the past. She was his, finally without doubt to hold them back, she was his. He may never fully know what happened to her in Utah, may never want to know, but none of that mattered. Because she came back. She was here.

She was home.

"I hear an Amen approaching." Grams swiped a stray tear from her cheek.

Jake let out a roar of laughter and draped his arm around her shoulders. "Your eyes are leaking, Grams." He eyed the two friends in front of them, his own eyes misty. If only Serena could be here to see this. Then again, maybe she was. "I always said you were a wise woman."

Edith Meyers dropped the letter from Courtney on the counter in front of her, scattering pictures everywhere. She pressed chubby fingers to her eyes and gave in to a short bout of tears, not giving a damn who saw this time. Let them talk and tease. It was damn worth it.

Richard Maynard looked at her, seemingly confused and a bit concerned that she not only could cry, but that she did it with witnesses. He rubbed at his graying beard. "What's going on?"

Edith sniffed and straightened, not bothering to wipe her red, swollen eyes. She sighed profoundly and slapped a hard hand on the counter in satisfaction. "Close up shop, boys," she bellowed. "We're going to Georgia for a wedding!"

www.AuthorKellyMoran.com
Enchanting ever-afters...

Sign up for Kelly Moran's newsletter and get a FREE eBook!

 **About the Author:**

Kelly Moran is a best-selling & award-winning romance author of enchanting ever-afters. She is a Catherine Award-Winner, Readers' Choice Finalist, Holt Medallion Finalist, and a 2014 Award of Excellence Finalist through RWA. She's also landed on the 10 Best Reads and Must Read lists from USA TODAY's HEA. Kelly's been known to say she gets her ideas from everyone and everything around her and there's always a book playing out in her head. No one who knows her bats an eyelash when she talks to herself. Her interests include: sappy movies, MLB, NFL, driving others insane, and sleeping when she can. She is a closet caffeine junkie and chocoholic, but don't tell anyone. She resides in Wisconsin with her husband, three sons, and her two dogs. Most of her family lives in the Carolinas, so she spends a lot of time there as well.

She loves connecting with her readers.